ILLUSION OF FREEDOM

BOOK FIVE OF THE CLOVIS ACADEMY LEGACY

Ross Harringway

Omega Press
El Paso, TX

CLOVIS ACADEMY LEGACY:

ILLUSION OF FREEDOM

OMEGA PRESS

An imprint of Omega Communications Group, Inc.

For information contact:

Omega Press
5823 N. Mesa, #839
El Paso, Texas 79912

FIRST EDITION

Printed in the United States of America

PROLOGUE
THREE YEARS EARLIER

General Leta Tan ruled the Lynott's Land Province with an iron fist and cold heart. Although the land area was as large as the nation of France on Old Earth, her population was only one fourth that of Clovis City. People were afraid of living there, especially men. Tan hated men and frequently searched for excuses to execute men in public. Tan avoided confrontation with the wealthy Lynott family and the politically connected Ward clan. Anyone else was at risk, especially those out after her mandated midnight curfew.

But Lynott's Land had what was perhaps the loveliest mountain range on planet New Edinburgh. The location was filled with lovely light blue snowcapped ranges and large trees of orange, yellow and green. One couple from Clovis City decided to give their vows at the base of that mountain range and they invited their closest friends.

The portion of the mountain range selected by the couple was at the southern border of Lynott's Land. It was a spectacular sight. As the sun set behind the towering snow covered mountains the red orange light reflected off of the light blue snow and the purple sand and rocks. The attendees at the base camp of the largest mountain in the range were in awe of the view. The cool wind bathed the humans below. Most of the gathered at the base of the large mountain were present to attempt climbing to the top. The mountain had been named Knox Peak after the first human that had successfully ascended to the summit.

It had been the perfect location for the wedding of two young lovers. The priest was dressed in his normal suit but was covered in a neck to ankle brown fur to keep the cold air from his body. The priest was an elderly man in is eighties and was proud to preside over this specific wedding as one of the two women exchanging vows was his great granddaughter. As Felix Essex read from the Bible he smiled at the two women and the witnesses before him. He watched the look of love in the eyes of the soon to be joined in matrimony and the joy of those that were their closest friends.

Felicia Essex was a senior cadet at the Clovis Academy. Her childhood dream had been to serve in the Space Command as her mother had done. She was twenty-two years old and stood just under six feet tall. Her long dark hair filled with multi-colored flowers flowed in the wind. There were some light blue snowflakes in her hair and on her lovely white wedding gown. Her cheeks were red from the cold and her light blue eyes beamed with love. During her years as a student she made many friends and had gone through three relationships. Her third potential love interest was one that immediately proved to be something special.

Dia Cho had been that woman. Cho was shorter than Essex, had short dark hair and eyes. She looked upon Essex with love filled eyes and a smile that could melt any heart. Their relationship began when the two women were in their second year at the Academy. They were both dual majors in computer science and weapons technology. Cho and Essex gravitated to each other in that stress filled second year when they had to defend each other from the campus bullies led by a cadet named Francois Zerbe.

After two dinner dates and a whirlwind courting period, the two women became inseparable.

Essex was born into a historic family. Her father had been the first Mayor of Clovis City and her mother founded the first major hospital in that same city. Her father had been a lawyer and was now living out his years in retirement and writing children books. Her mother had been a surgeon and had specialized in organ replacements, specifically heart transplants. She was the fourth oldest of eleven siblings and the first to attend a military academy. She was related to other original settler families on the planet New Edinburgh. The influential Kander family was her cousins.

Cho had come from another life. She had been born on a transport space craft that had left old Earth and was en route to planet New Quebec. When she turned seventeen, she applied for acceptance at Clovis Academy due to her affinity for the color purple. She had seen pictures of the surface of the land and the differing shades of purple in the sands and some of the vegetation. She had also seen live broadcasts of the famed Dinosaur Wars on the news reports and the life forms fascinated her.

Essex had chosen four younger women to serve as her best women. To her left were fellow cadets Julia Steiner, Mary Lincoln, Yesenia Guevara and Aura Lynda Glenn. The four women were dressed in dark blue dresses that exposed their arms and shoulders. The dresses were long and flowing in the wind. Steiner, Guevara and Lincoln were in their first year at the Academy and became friends with Essex through Aura Lynda Glenn. At the time of the wedding, Glenn was a cadet junior that was studying computer science and advance weapons design. She was also an accomplished pilot from private lessons and studying the art as a minor at the Academy. She was from one of the first families to settle on planet New Edinburgh.

In fact, her mother and father had been involved in many of the early historical events of the founding of New Edinburgh that were taught to the young children in schools. Her parents had been scientists that were filled with thoughts of finding their fortune mining the precious minerals and stones of this seemingly virgin planet. Although the Glenn family found some success, it was far from the wealth they had envisioned. They lived well on their business income and were able to send many of their children to attend the major universities throughout the eight solar systems. But Aura Lynda Glenn elected to be the first of her siblings to go to a military Academy. Glenn had become friends with Essex and Cho when the two women protected her from the hazing activities of the infamous Francois Zerbe and his minions.

Dia Cho chose four men to stand for her. In their matching dark blue tuxedos the four men stood to Cho's right and watched the ceremony with pride. Cadet Senior Joseph Essex Kander was the closest to Cho. Kander was a cadet senior in the engineering school. He was tall, skinny and had the same dark hair as his cousin, Felicia Essex. Standing next to Kander was his current boyfriend, freshman cadet pilot candidate Michel Darcel Evart. Next to Evart were freshmen twin brothers Marco and Dominic Andolini.

Evart was from France of Old Earth and was struggling to adapt and learn the ways of this new planet. He commented often that the cultural views of the local citizens of New Edinburgh were vastly different than Old Earth. The citizens that had populated planet New Edinburgh referred to Earth as "Old Earth" and they had clear animosity toward what they referred to as "illegal immigrants." That term was a description given to the people such Evart that had travelled from Old Earth to either attend Clovis Academy or a person that arrived to open a business or settle there. Evart never understood the local hostility against them or others from Old Earth by the settlers of New Edinburgh. They were all humans and had come from the same place. But the original settlers of planet New Edinburgh and their offspring thought differently.   Evart had met Joseph Essex Kander shortly after his arrival on the planet. Evart called him Joe as did all those close to him. Kander and Evart became lovers quickly. Through Kander, Evart met the members of a group of cadets that called themselves Gorski's Gang. Two of the members of that gang, Dominic and Marco Andolini, were standing next to Evart as members of the wedding party. Across from Evart were gang members Steiner, Lincoln, Guevara and Glenn.

In the wedding audience were other members of the gang. Each of them was wearing large black or brown overcoats to protect themselves from the cold. Yuri Gorski nodded to Evart and smiled at him. The two men had grown into good friends over the few months they had known one another. Drew Harrison was the tallest member of the gang and stood next to Gorski. After joining the gang, Les Gillis had found that the Andolini's, Gorski and Harrison were together almost all the time. The Andolini family was one of the most well known in Clovis City as they were among the first settlers on the planet. Their parents had been engineering technicians and were responsible for the design and construction of the Great Protective Walls that surrounded Clovis City, Lynott's Land and other settlements on the planet.

Gorski was the son of a famous military commander and high ranking officer that was serving in Clovis City. Harrison was the son of an Admiral and his mother had status in the Space Command as a diplomat. Both were referred to as "military brats" by the local civilians. Gillis understood the term to have some negative meaning among the citizens. Gorski's younger brother, Piotr, was also in attendance. It was rare that their father would allow the younger Gorski to attend events with the gang. But a wedding would be, one would assume, the safest type of evening one could participate in. Piotr Gorski was wearing a long black trench coat that concealed his nice black double breasted suit, white dress shirt and red bow tie.

Les Gillis stood behind the Gorski brothers during the wedding ceremony. Next to Gillis had been Drayton Love-Easter. Gillis and Love-Easter were from Old Earth and joined up with Gorski and his friends for protection at first but the two men grew to consider the other gang members as their clsoest friends. Gillis had been born in Ireland of Old Earth and Love-Easter was the son of a wealthy religious leader. Gillis noticed that Yesenia Guevara blew a kiss in Love-Easter's direction. The relationship between Guevara and Love-Easter was no secret. The two were open and notorious in their affection for one another. Gillis and Love-Easter had grown into close friends and were constantly together. Gillis recalled that Guevara and Love-Easter were constantly trying to introduce him to women that they believed would be a good match for him. Each introduction proved disastrous when the woman would learn that Gillis was a foreigner.

Gorski and Mary Lincoln had also become lovers and were constantly together. The match made sense to Gillis in that both Gorski and Lincoln were military brats, both were cadet pilots and both were excellent hand to hand fighters.

Julia Steiner and Drew Harrison seemingly shared nothing in common. Harrison was a body builder and an expert in weapons. He was studying how to kill people with efficiency. He often displayed an explosive temper. Steiner on the other hand, was a peaceful lady that was learning how to terra form other worlds so that others could live there without fear. She was also the constant conscience of the group in that she was the first that would suggest an alternative to fighting. While Harrison would sometimes intentionally seek out potential opponents and pick a fight to soothe his boredom. Gillis wondered if anyone else saw the conflict in that. He once asked Steiner what it was that kept them together. As she laughed, Steiner told him it was the sex.

Standing next to Love-Easter was cadet pilot Frank Glenn, Aura Lynda's younger sibling. He was in his second year at the Academy and was Evart's cadet Flight Leader. Frank Glenn was married to a local girl named Orellia Li. Glenn and Li were from some of the oldest families on New Edinburgh and had been friends since the age of six and they were in love by the time they were thirteen and married at seventeen. Li's family was huge in that her father had taken several wives and was a believer in producing as many offspring as possible. Her father and his wives all regularly ingested the fertility drugs that were easily acquired so that pregnancy was a foregone conclusion. The only question would be how many children would be born during each cycle. Orellia Li had been born with three sisters. All in all, she had forty-seven siblings and half-siblings. She was attending the Clovis City School of Advanced Computer Sciences while her husband was learning to become an astronaut.

Orellia Li Glenn stood proudly next to her husband and was smiling as the ceremony continued, recalling her joy the day she married her husband. She was always remarking to her family and friends that she felt so lucky that she was able to grow up with him as her friend and watch him develop into the handsome and caring man he was today.

Glenn stood next to five of the youngest that were in attendance, fourteen year olds Venus, Stella, Giola, Paolo and Lucius Andolini. They were younger siblings of Marco and Dominic. Their parents began using the breeding stimulation drugs that were readily available for all citizens, just as the Li family had done. The drugs vastly increased sperm and egg count which caused more twins, triplets and even more children to be born to the consumers of those drugs. The parents of the Andolini's produced a few large sibling groups before they gave up the drugs. At some point they realized they had more than enough children to watch over. These five teenagers had also developed better physical and mental abilities than a child born to parents that did not utilize the fertility drugs. Paolo and Lucius were handsome, well-toned and smart. Giola, Venus and Stella were already beautiful women and caused men to turn their heads when they walked by. The three girls were brilliant as well with their grade point averages competing at the highest levels. The five teens were invited to the wedding due to their closeness to Cho and Essex. The Andolini family was famous for their generous hospitality and warm greetings of others. Stella had especially been friendly to Dia Cho over the past several months and referred to her as Aunt Dia.

Also in attendance were medical students Esther Macinlock and Qiu Chan. Macinlock was the flavor of the week of Marco Andolini while Chan was seen associating with Dominic Andolini on campus. The two women were dressed in beautiful dark gowns and seemed to enjoy being witnesses to the union.

The parents of Felicia Essex and Dia Cho were also in attendance. Their extended family members were also there to share in the joyous moment. Cho's parents had made the long trip from New Quebec to New Edinburgh to stand next to their daughter during her special day. All those present applauded when the priest announced that the bride could kiss the bride.

The reception was to be held at the most popular restaurant bar in Lynott's Land called the Mouse Trap. The entire entourage made their way via several Raumschiff Transport space ships from the base of Knox Peak to the landing ports at the capital of Lynott's Land, Lynott City.

The flight took under thirty minutes.

To the shock of everyone, save Dominic Andolini, Felicia Essex and Dia Cho revealed that they were both pregnant. The women refused to reveal who the father or fathers were. Dominic kept the fact that he was the other parent a secret. Months before the wedding, Cho and Essex had decided that they wanted to have a family. They searched to find the man with the best genetics available to them. Cho and Essex had carefully considered each of their male friends. They mutually determined that one of the two Andolini brothers would be the donor. The choice was difficult but the Andolini's won out due to their athletic prowess as soccer stars and that each man possessed excellent abilities as cadets. Marco was an excellent pilot and Dominic was proving to be the best marksman at the Academy. Essex and Cho discussed the brothers at length and finally agreed to approach Dominic. The reason for his selection was that Marco seemed to be a bit of a playboy. Cho and Essex had watched as Marco would keep the company of several women at the same time. His twin seemed to be more reserved and would normally stick with one woman at a time.

Cho and Essex were pleasantly surprised that Dominic was agreeable to the arrangement. He provided the sperm samples that the women required and they went through the in vitro process. Both women were pregnant with twins.

Gillis marveled over the group of friends and family that were present. Such a diverse group both in culture and background. But yet they were all close friends. Gillis had always believed it was the life on this strange new planet that forced them all together to find protection and companionship.

After landing, the entire party made their way to the Mouse Trap via rapid moving sidewalks that were similar to conveyer belts. The moving sidewalks were ten feet wide, made of transparent metal and moved at a speed of ten miles per hour. Each of the party leaped onto the belts and were held upright by the gravitational mechanisms hidden inside the belts. They walked on the moving walk ways at a rapid pace and ended up in front of the Mouse Trap in less than twenty minutes. Other than the five younger Andolini teens, only Aura Lynda Glenn, Piotr Gorski and Les Gillis seemed to be without a companion. All of the others had someone to hold hands with and cuddle.

Gillis did notice that Piotr Gorski and Stella Andolini seemed to have a close bond between them. They were always laughing together and interacting with a familiarity that long term contact would create. Gillis recalled speculating that there might be a romance in the works for those two. He could see that Stella looked at the younger Gorski with affection and trust. Piotr looked at her in a similar manner. They would flirt openly and joke that if they were unmarried by the time they turned twenty-one that they would marry each other.

The Mouse Trap was a red and pink stone three floor building that had over forty thousand square feet per floor. The roof was made of pink metal and the front had white granite stairs leading to the walkway to the large sliding doors. There were Doric columns that were supporting the overhang under the front facade to the building. The Mouse Trap was a popular destination for space travelers and local citizens for fine dining. The second floor of the building had been converted into a five star restaurant and was managed by chefs imported from Old Earth. As the wedding party approached the large structure they noticed that the parking lot had many hover transports and there was something curious that made each of them frown.

There were fifteen old style motorcycles parked side by side. The motorcycles were varying in size and color.

Yuri Gorski saw the license plate on the rear of one of the black motorcycles. He cursed.

"What's wrong baby?" Mary Lincoln asked as she held his arm tight.

"Bragg. The license plate says Bragg," Gorski muttered to himself. "That bike belongs to Bill Bragg."

Harrison and Steiner were arm in arm just a few steps behind Gorski and Lincoln. They heard Gorski's observation.

"Maybe Bill is here alone," Steiner stated hopefully.

"Don't count on it. If he is here then that means Zerbe and the others are, too," Harrison warned. "That other black bike is the one I saw Reynita Calderon riding around on back at the campus."

"Maybe they won't want a fight tonight," Steiner smiled at Harrison hoping to calm the man down. He had that look in his eyes that would signal to Steiner that a brawl was imminent. "Maybe they will be peaceful and see that there is all this love in the air."

"I doubt it. Calderon put Marco in the ER last month when we tangled." Gorski sighed as they approached the entrance. "She is one tough woman."

"So are we," Lincoln asserted and pointed at Steiner, Guevara, Essex and Cho.

The party entered the lower level and saw no sign of Francois Zerbe, William Bragg or Reynita Calderon. Gorski and Lincoln held hands as the hostess directed the party to the stairs leading to the second floor and the wedding reception. The group moved quickly. There was an ample amount of food and drink waiting for them all. The lower level of the establishment was solid black and the lighting was dim so that the patrons could enjoy a modicum of privacy. Many of the tables in that lower area were hidden behind black curtains and it was rumored that sexual acts were encouraged as the house received a percentage of the fees charged by the prostitutes that worked there.

After ascending the stairs, Gorski and Lincoln stood at the entrance of the large ballroom and took in the lovely view. There were forty large round tables near the windows that looked out over the city. The tables were covered with white table cloths and each chair was the color dark blue. In the middle of each table was a lovely flower arrangement of yellow, blue, red and white roses inside crystal vases. There was a large dance floor next to a stage for the brides and their immediate family to sit and eat. The three level cake was to the right of the stage and there were several ice carvings of doves and swans around the ball room.

While the lower level was dark this upper level was bright and full of color.

Harrison followed Steiner inside as she skipped and hopped to an empty table near the windows. Steiner always had that childlike quality about her to take each moment in life as an adventure.

Gorski kissed Lincoln softly on her lips and led her toward the table where Harrison and Steiner had seats waiting for them.

The evening progressed nicely. Toasts were given, dinner was served to all, and the cake was cut and distributed. Dancing began to old style jazz music which was a favorite genre of Cho and Essex.

The trouble began when Joe Kander and Michel Evart were sitting in each other's laps on a black leather sofa near the rear of the room. Kander had to have what he had considered the most difficult conversation of his life with his young lover.

"Michel, you know that I love you," Kander told him.

"And I love you," Evart responded and kissed Kander on his lips.

"Michel. You know that I finished my assigned

classes early," Kander said with regret in his voice. "I will be among the early graduates this December. I will most likely be leaving New Edinburgh in January. If I do leave, we may never see each other again."

"Joe, I have never known love like this before," Evart held his hand in his. "Together, there is nothing we cannot accomplish. We can hope that one of the local units here will select you in the draft process and we can stay together. We could be married like Dia and Felicia."

"And if I get assigned off planet?" Kander asked. "What then? You are just starting your Academy days. It would be about four years before we would ever see one another again. I love you too much to ask you to be loyal to me during that time."

"What? Joe, what are you saying to me?"

"You have wonderful friends here," Kander pointed out toward Gorski and Lincoln who were on the dance floor. "They all love you. I can see it. Stay with these people over the next few years. You will be a better man because of it. They give you friendship and loyalty which is rare among humans. They do not judge you and me because we have a different sexual preference. These are all good people, Michel. I guess what I am saying is that you need to enjoy your next three and a half years with these wonderful friends. I will go off and begin my career as an officer in the Space Command. If by some miracle we are assigned to the same location when you graduate, then perhaps we can rekindle our love."

Evart bit his lower lip, "Joe, I love you. I don't want to lose you. There has to be another way. This cannot be the beginning of our parting."

"I would give everything for us to be together again," Kander said softly. "But our lives are at a fork in the road. We have separate paths ahead of us. If there are deities out there that have mercy then they will set our paths together again. Nothing would make me happier."

Evart nodded to the words of his lover. He felt as if his heart had been cut out. But his logical side knew that Kander was correct. If he was assigned to a ship or another planet then they would never see one another again.

"I need to be alone for a moment," Evart finally managed to say despite the lump in his throat. "Please excuse me."

Without waiting for an answer, Evart rushed toward the staircase and rand as fast as his feet would allow as he descended the winding stairs. He moved for the first floor men's restroom so that he could locate a stall and shed his tears in private.

Lincoln and Gorski witnessed the display from across the dance floor. The two approached Joe Kander and sat down next to him. Gillis recalled overhearing the conversation.

"Joe, what was that all about?" Lincoln took his hand. She observed that the older cadet was clearly distraught.

"Michel and I will most likely have to split up," Kander said with sadness. "I think I broke his heart."

"You broke up with him?" Lincoln inquired. "But why?"

"Because I may be shipped off soon," Kander explained. "We cannot continue a relationship if I am dozens of AU away. It would be unfair to him."

Lincoln motioned with her head to Gorski, "Yuri, go to Michel."

Gorski nodded and walked toward the stairwell quickly.

"I did not want to hurt him," Kander whispered to Lincoln. "I love him so much."

Lincoln held his hand, "And he loves you. We all love the two of you. You are our friends. Look. No more talk about breaking up, okay? This is a celebration of epic proportions. We have two people that found love and declared that love for all to see. You and Michel enjoy this and each night you have left to share together. Treat each night like it is the last you have so that if you do leave you both have the most wonderful memories of one another. Think you can do that?"

Kander squeezed her hand, "Yes, I can do that and much more."

"When Yuri returns with Michel you two enjoy the rest of the evening," Lincoln instructed him. "Remember that love is a hard thing to find in this universe. There is so much cruelty out there. You and Michel are lucky to have one another."

"Just like you and Yuri?"

Lincoln nodded, "Absolutely. I look into his grey blue eyes and feel his arms around me and I feel so alive. I love everything about him."

Kander sat forward and put his free hand on his chin, "You realize if we were alive say five or six hundred years ago, people would despise us. Two men together would be ridiculed and attacked vehemently. Felicia and Dia, two women marrying, would be equally attacked."

"As would I and Yuri," Lincoln pointed out. "I am as black as can be and Yuri is white. In the past our relationships would have been an anathema. But today, Yuri and I can hold hands in public, cuddle, kiss and make love without fear of persecution. I am so grateful I was not born in those years full of hate. Sometimes after we make love I look at my hand in his when we snuggle together. It is so beautiful. Our hands are so different in color, but the blood under the skin is the same red color. We are all the same, Joe. The color of our skin or our preferences do not separate us at all. We all want to love and be loved and that includes you and Michel. Got it?"

Kander nodded and smiled at the young woman for her words of wisdom. "Got it. I will wait for them to return and make the best of this marvelous event."

Harrison was at the other end of the hall telling the bartenders to pour a round of tequila shots for everyone. Steiner was glaring at him with her disapproval.

"Could be trouble in paradise over there," Yesenia Guevara observed as she sat down in Drayton Love-Easter's lap. Love-Easter and Gillis were sitting at a round table with drinks in front of them. Gillis smiled as he watched the negative interaction between Steiner and Harrison.

"Why does he always drink so much?" Gillis wondered out loud. "I hope it is not some bigger problem for him."

Love-Easter shrugged, "We drink, too."

"Les is right, Dray." Guevara said softly. "Drew does seem to overdo it."

"Julia is not happy about it," Gillis added.

"She told you this?" Love-Easter said as he nibbled on Guevara's neck.

Gillis nodded. He and Steiner had grown to become good friends. She had confided in him about her feelings with Harrison and his issues with alcohol. "We have all seen it. He gets a little out of control if he drinks too much."

Guevara kissed Love-Easter on his nose, "My love, I promise there is nothing wrong with you."

Love-Easter laughed and looked over at his friend. Gillis was staring out the window at the rear of the hall. He was lost in his thoughts. "Les, what is wrong, buddy?"

Gillis shook his head and faced the couple, "Nothing. Just, sometimes I miss home."

Guevara reached out and took Gillis' hand, "Les, you need a woman. How long have you been here? Five months? Six? Since I have been with Dray I have never seen you go out on a date that you picked on your own. You need a woman that will rock your world. I think I know a few willing women that would be able to take care of you. I promise that I will find some girls that are not locals. I think we have all learned how they hate us foreigners."

"Thanks, Yesenia. That would be nice," Gillis said softly. In his homeland, back on Old Earth, he never had any issue dating. But on this new world of different ideas and thinking, Gillis felt like he was an outcast. He felt fortunate that he had found friends like Love-Easter and Guevara.

Even though the women outnumbered the men by eight to one, Gillis could not seem to catch a break in the romance department. He longed for home. He would never have left Earth and Ireland had it not been for the advice given to him by his mother and father. They both prodded him to reject the offer to attend the Dublin Academy and accept admission at an Academy on a different planet. His parents believed that another place would broaden the perspective of the young man.

Yuri Gorski had walked into the first floor restroom area and quickly deduced that Evart found the privacy of a toilet stall. He knocked on the individual doors until Evart responded.

"Yes, Yuri, I am here," Evart answered as he unlocked the bathroom stall he had been hiding in. He walked out slowly and faced his friend. "I apologize for causing any concern for anyone."

Gorski wrapped his right arm around Evart's shoulders, "You are my friend. That means you never have to say you are sorry. Understand?"

"Thank you, Yuri. I was just a little bit emotional. That's all."

"Well we should get back to the party. Joe was worried about you."

Evart and Gorski began walking and made it to the bathroom entrance. Gorski waited as the automatic sliding doors opened for them. Gorski saw two men standing before him. Gorski cursed under his breath. One was

Carletto de Vida Brock and the second was Jeffrey Cobb. Both were devout followers of the group that had taken on the name the Bragg Gang. Both of the men were wearing maroon one piece leather biker suits.

Brock was the first to recognize Gorski and Evart. "Son of a Verburgt!"

Cobb scowled and immediately threw a wild punch at Gorski. Gorski ducked under the fist and rammed Cobb with his left shoulder. Cobb fell backwards onto the stone floor. Brock kicked Gorski in the side and sent the cadet sprawling to the floor. Evart punched Brock in the nose and sent the man staggering backwards. Before Brock could regain his composure, Evart hit him with a flurry of punches to the face and body.

Brock fell and slid a few feet until he collided with an empty table. Many of the patrons in the lower level began to cry out in surprise. To the chagrin of Gorski and Evart there were many friends of Brock and Cobb sitting at the bar just a mere one hundred feet away. Gorski smiled as his eyes made contact with the lovely and formidable Daniella Bragg. She was in a black leather suit and black boots that came up to her knees.

She snarled when she recognized Gorski and Evart, "What the hell are they doing in Lynott's Land?"

Her twin sister, Lisa Bragg, set her beer mug on the bar counter top. "Gorski and Evart? Here? Are they stalking us?"

Both Daniella and Lisa Bragg were the same height, weight and hair color. There was virtually no way to tell them apart. They were two of the infamous members of the Bragg Gang. Both of the women were in their third year at the Academy and both were studying advanced weaponry and astral navigation. They jumped to their feet. The stool that Lisa Bragg had been sitting on crashed to the floor. Next the Bragg sisters was one of their younger brothers, William. He was also in a dark leather suit and had been enjoying a cold ale when Brock smashed into the empty table. He also rose to his feet.

"Gorski!" William Bragg bellowed as he drew a six inch blade knife from his biker boot. "You son of a Poggie! I am going to cut you!"

Evart motioned to the stairwell to his left, "Yuri, it might be a good idea to get back to friendlier company."

Gorski nodded in agreement, "Let's get out of here."

Evart and Gorski began running for the stairs as William, Daniella and Lisa Bragg gave chase. Jeffrey Cobb and Carletto de Vida Brock followed the three Bragg's up the winding staircase. Evart was leaping over some of the steps as he raced upward. Gorski was right on his heels. The two eighteen year old cadets rushed into the second floor ballroom to see many from the wedding party dancing and drinking.

Gorski saw that Mary Lincoln and Joe Kander were still sitting on the couch that he had last seen them.

Lincoln noticed that Evart and Gorski were not smiling, "Yuri, what is it?"

"Trouble," Gorski responded and took her by the left arm. "The Bragg's are here."

Kander was on his feet, "The Bragg Gang is here? In Lynott's Land? Are you sure?"

Evart was standing next to Kander and held his hand in his, "They will be here any second."

Gorski looked over in the direction of the Andolini's. Marco was at a round table with seven lovely futbol groupie women. Two were in his lap and a third was massaging his shoulders and neck. The other four were seated around him. Esther Macinlock was glaring at Marco, clearly not pleased with his decision to surround himself with so many women. Gorski whistled at him. Marco stood up with an inquisitive look on his face.

That was when Daniella Bragg entered the ball

room. She walked about seven steps inside the ballroom when her sister Lisa joined her. The two women realized that even with Cobb and Brock by their sides they were hopelessly outnumbered. Before any violence occurred, Daniella Bragg turned and began to leave. William Bragg ran into her and she grabbed his leather jacket with both hands and began to whisper into his ear. William was breathing heavily and held his knife in his right hand. By the look on his face it was clear he did not like what his older sister was telling him.

The Bragg's departed back down the stairs without incident.

Frank Glenn and his wife, Orellia, had noticed the scene and had stood up just in case they were needed. The Glenn family were no strangers to the brash and aggressive Bragg family. Before Gorski began assembling his group, the Glenn's, Dia Cho, Felicia Essex and Joe Kander had numerous street fights against the Bragg group.

"I am surprised that they had the decency to leave in peace," Orellia Glenn whispered to her husband.

"You and me both. I didn't see Alexis de Vida Brock or Francois Zerbe with them. If those two were here then there would have been a riot." Frank Glenn smiled at his wife. "Shall we join the others on the dance floor?"

Orellia stood and extended her hand, "How kind of you to ask, my dashing and debonair husband."

He took her hand in his and led her to the dance floor.

Gillis learned what happened downstairs from the woman that he would later become involved with. She had shared the story with him after their first night together.

Lisa Bragg landed with both feet on the first floor of the Mouse Trap. She calmly walked over toward a table in the corner of the bar. The lights were off and the area was dark. There were several naked women entertaining two men. One of the men was Azeem Nour, a cadet senior and best friend to Francois Zerbe. Nour was a dark skinned man that stood over seven feet tall and was muscular and handsome. He sported a mustache and a goatee that was neatly trimmed. His piercing dark eyes, chiseled chin and jaw line were enough to make any person take notice of him. He had long dark hair that was permed and hung past his shoulders. Nour was finishing his academic studies in advanced weapons. Nour had killed a man once in a bar fight. The death was not accidental. Nour had become enraged enough to intentionally break the neck of his smaller opponent. Nour was never arrested or charged for the offense due to the fact that none of the Bragg Gang was willing to sell him out to the Criminal Investigation Division officers. Nour had been born on a transport ship that was en route to planet Cootron. His parents were mineral and energy speculators and would go from planet to planet in search of their fortune. After purchasing some mineral rights in the New Edinburgh area called Ferro Province, the Nour family emigrated to pursue their financial interests there. The family struck it rich, finding a diamond mine and other precious metals to rip from the planet, process and sell. Nour had several sisters and brothers as well as countless cousins. He had been the first Nour to seek a career in the military by attending the Academy.

Francois Zerbe was the second man at the table. He had two naked women in his lap, running his hands over their bodies. Zerbe was also a handsome man and muscular. He spent his free time in the gymnasium lifting weights and practicing martial arts. Zerbe was over six feet tall and had dark hair and light colored eyes. He was a womanizer and did not hide that fact. Zerbe had slept with all of the Bragg Gang women. He occasionally would take Lisa or Daniella Bragg to his bed as they practiced a friends with benefits relationship. His sexual conquest of Alexis de Vida Brock took some effort on his part, but even she could not resist his advances for long. Renee Starr had also shared his bed on several nights. The only Bragg Gang member that seemed to be bothered by Zerbe's sexual desires was Reynita Calderon. When Zerbe had seduced her, she believed that they were starting a committed relationship. Zerbe led her on for a few months before breaking off that relationship. He had considered a long term life with Calderon as she was very attractive and head strong. But in the end, Zerbe could not stop his carousing and wanderlust for other women.

Francois Zerbe glared at Lisa Bragg when she approached him. "What is it? Can you not see that I am very busy?"

Lisa Bragg noticed that one of the naked women was performing oral sex on Zerbe. Slightly embarrassed, she looked up at the ceiling. "Francois. Gorski and his friends are here."

Zerbe let out a moan of pleasure. "So what? That's it, girl. Ahhhhh. You are amazing."

"They beat up Jeff and Carletto," Lisa Bragg told him part out of anger at Gorski and Evart and partly due to her jealousy that another woman was pleasuring Zerbe.

Zerbe nodded as his head rolled back and forth, "You should take lessons from this girl. She is really good. Round up the others. Once I am finished, oh man, we, we will go kick their tails. Ahhhhhh. Give me about another ten minutes. Aaaaaahhh."

Lisa Bragg shook her head in disgust and stormed away from the scene. She found her sister waiting for her at the end of the bar. "Francois said to round up everyone. Ten minutes."

"And then what?" Daniella Bragg inquired.

"And then we kick Gorski and his friends into next week."

Daniella Bragg dutifully wandered over to a booth on the backside of the first floor. She found that Reynita

Calderon was showing off her new tattoo. The younger girl had a death skull on the back of her left shoulder. The artist that had done the work was talented. Calderon was wearing black leather pants, a black halter top, black leather jacket and steel reinforced black boots that came up to just below her knees. She had sent Gorski Gang member Marco Andolini to the emergency room in a previous fight when she cracked two of his ribs by kicking him with her boot. Calderon was an attractive eighteen year old that came from a larger Clovis City family. Her parents had been just like the Andolini family and used the state of the art procreation drugs. Reynita would jokingly tell her friends that she could not remember all of her siblings' names. She had light brown skin, brown eyes that changed to a lighter color in the sunlight and straight black hair that fell below her shoulders. She had a very alluring smile and full lips. She kept her body slender and toned by playing basketball and was an excellent three point shooter. She also helped her father build motorcycles when she wasn't studying at the Academy or spending time with the Bragg Gang. Her love life was rife with bad endings. Reynita had recently been dumped by Francois Zerbe and she had not found a new lover to replace him with.

Alexis de Vida Brock and Renee Starr were admiring the younger Calderon's new tattoo. Alexis was the twin sister of Carletto and she shared his hair color and height. She was an investigation major at the Academy and had a fiery temper and would sometimes lose control in fights. Daniella Bragg had to personally drag Alexis off of other combatants as she feared that she might actually kill someone someday.

Renee Starr was a cadet pilot and in her senior year. She had been named the cadet squadron commander by the chief flight instructor and given the rank of cadet Captain. Starr had come from another large sibling group and was the second from her family to sign up for the Academy. Her twin sister, Jayne, had been accepted at the highly rated Sikorsky Academy and left her family and friends behind. Renee was much more level headed than her friend Alexis de Vida Brock. Renee knew when to attack and when to withdraw. Daniella Bragg had always considered Renee to be the smartest member of their group. Renee had studied boxing and martial arts as a young girl and was capable of handling herself in any situation. She had brown hair, light brown eyes, stood under six feet tall and had shapely legs and toned physique.

The three women looked up at Daniella Bragg when she cleared her throat.

"What is it?" Starr noticed the look in Bragg's eyes.

"Yuri Gorski and his friends are here."

"Are they messing with us?" Alexis de Vida Brock stood up with her fists clenched.

Bragg nodded in the affirmative, "They just kicked your brother's ass. Francois wants us ready in ten. Get ready for a rumble."

Reynita pulled her leather jacket back on and slammed her hand onto the table top. "Let's send all those pinche extranjeros back to where they came from."

Francois Zerbe waited at the base of the stair case as the Bragg Gang slowly assembled behind him. William Bragg was the first to arrive and he had his knife ready. He desperately wanted to sink his blade into Yuri Gorski's heart. Bragg smiled at Zerbe in anticipation of the brawl. Zerbe looked at the knife in Bragg's hand and pursed his lips. Although the Bragg and Gorski confrontations had been violent in the past, there had not been any violence such as that. Deadly force had not been used.

"Bill, put the knife away," Zerbe told him.

"But this is the Gorski Gang. We gotta teach them a lesson," Bragg protested. His hatred for the rival group had grown to the point where he was willing to do things to them to cause real harm. Stabbing one of them, sending him or her to the morgue, would suite Bill Bragg just fine.

"We don't need that kind of trouble," Zerbe said firmly. "We can kick each other's butts around and live to laugh about it later. You start resorting to that level of violence, really hurting someone with weapons, then they will do the same to us. You want one of your sisters to go home in a casket?"

William Bragg looked at the ground, "No."

"Then put the knife away," Zerbe instructed him.

Bragg put the knife back in his boot. He waited for when Zerbe was not watching him so he could pull it out again.

Azeem Nour was the next to join Zerbe. Nour had just finished pleasuring himself with one of the strippers that had been at their table. One of the girls had been so experienced that Nour gave her more money than they originally agreed upon. He had been raised by his wealthy family to tip those in the service industries that did a better than average job. Nour learned from experience that lesson was especially true with the ladies of the night. When he overpaid a prostitute they would brag to their friends about how much he gave. The word would spread and the most attractive ladies of the night would seek him out so that they could be the one to pocket the extra money that he would compensate them in return for their company.

Daniella and Lisa Bragg were close behind with Reynita Calderon, Alexis de Vida Brock and Renee Starr following a few feet back. Carletto de Vida Brock, Jeffrey Cobb and Pierre Zerbe showed up a few minutes later. Pierre Zerbe was the younger brother of Francois. He had similar facial features to his older brother but lacked his willingness to fight over nothing. His older brother had been attempting to get him to join up with the Bragg Gang. The younger Zerbe did not understand how making other cadets eat Poggie dung would make him a better man. Pierre was a freshman pilot cadet at that time and had avoided taking part in any of the hazing rituals instigated by his older brother.

Harvey "Granite" Grutzmacher joined the gathering of Bragg Gang faithful. He had been given the name Granite due to his massive muscles that covered his seven feet three inch tall body. He had blonde hair and blue eyes and spoke with a heavy accent. Grutzmacher was a fanatic in the gymnasium and took all forms of steroids, both legal and illegal, to gain the muscle mass he had attained. His parents were immigrants from Austria of Old Earth and owned their own construction company. Grutzmacher was a senior student of the history of warfare and a capable hand with modern weaponry. He loved to fight and rumble which was what led Francois Zerbe to recruit the man to the group. With Granite Grutzmacher by his side, Zerbe was assured that he had the best chance in any brawl.

The last three to arrive were the Yutong brothers, Zou, Guo and Dong. Zou was a senior at the Academy, Guo a junior and Dong a sophomore. Zou nodded at Francois Zerbe to signify that he and his brothers were ready to rock and roll. The parents of the Yutong brothers had used the help of the fertility drugs out on the market. Zou had been born with four sisters. Guo had been born with two sisters and Dong had three sisters from his birth. Their parents gave birth to an additional five younger siblings. The Yutong brothers were martial arts black belts and shared Bill Bragg's hatred of the Gorski Gang. They specifically hated Drew Harrison as he had been accused of impregnating one of their sisters. When confronted with the prospect that he had fathered a child with the girl, Harrison had asked for DNA testing which the entire Yutong family felt was an insult to them all. Further, two of the other sisters had become groupies to the Clovis City Futbol team in which Marco and Dominic Andolini were stars. Zou, Guo and Dong were certain that the Andolini brothers had disrespected their sisters by taking them to bed for casual sexual activity. That was not acceptable behavior by the strict and disciplined Yutong family. The Yutong brothers were all about five feet six inches tall, slender in build and had shaved heads. Each had numerous tattoos of dragons and swords all over their torsos and arms.

When Lisa Bragg told the Yutong brothers that the Andolini's and Harrison were upstairs, they were ready to exact some revenge.

"Do nothing until I give the signal," Francois Zerbe instructed them. He waited for all of the gang to nod in agreement before he led them up the stairs.

The wedding guests were dancing to a catchy disco tune when Francois Zerbe stepped onto the second floor. He looked over the massive ballroom and estimated that there were a little over one hundred in attendance. He saw that Yuri Gorski and Mary Lincoln were on the dance floor next to Frank and Orellia Glenn. Drew Harrison and Julia Steiner were sitting at the bar located on the far west side of the ballroom. Marco and Dominic Andolini were flirting with a table full of groupies near the back. The five younger teen age Andolini's were at another round table playing cards and laughing. Joe Kander and Michel Evart were sitting at a table, holding hands and in a conversation that Zerbe could not make out. The two brides, Felicia Essex and Dia Cho were dancing to the music. Aura Lynda Glenn was carrying a wine bottle to a table full of Essex family members. Drayton Love-Easter was kissing Yesenia Guevara at a table in the corner. Piotr Gorski and Stella Andolini were sharing a red colored smoothie.

Gillis was all alone at another table watching something on his holo-com device. But he immediately noticed when the Bragg Gang began to strut their presence on the second floor ball room.

Francois Zerbe walked over toward the large wedding vanilla frosting strawberry cake and noticed that it had already been cut and most of it was eaten. He reached down with his left hand and took a handful of cake and began eating. Nour and Granite Grutzmacher stood next to Zerbe and watched with smiles on their faces as an old man in a priest outfit approached them.

Felix Essex noticed the rough looking crowd enter the ballroom from his table. He excused himself from his table and approached them. He was certain they were not there by invitation. "Young men, may I be of service to you?" Felix Essex asked them.

Francois Zerbe answered with his mouth full of the strawberry flavored cake, "Great cake, old man. You need to get me the recipe."

Felix Essex wiped the cake crumbs that Zerbe had spit in his face. "Do you and your friends have an invitation to be here?"

Nour laughed and swung at Felix Essex with his left arm. He struck the elderly priest in the face with the back of his hand. Essex fell backwards and landed on the dance floor. "That is our invitation old man," Nour said with a loud, booming voice.

The music stopped and the crowd ceased dancing. Dia Cho and Felicia Essex both ran to the side of Felix Essex and lifted him to his feet.

"You are not welcome here," Dia Cho yelled at them. "This is a private party. Get out!"

Gillis was on his feet after witnessing that the elderly priest had been hurt by the uninvited Bragg Gang. Out of the corner of his eye he could see Love-Easter and Guevara standing up. From the bar, Harrison and Steiner were walking toward the dance floor. Harrison's fists were balled up.

Gorski put his arm around Lincoln and whispered into her ear, "You ready?"

Lincoln nodded, "They have twelve blocking the stair well exit. Three in the room. The Yutong brothers and Reynita are here. Bill Bragg has a knife in his hand. Shit."

"We've taken them before," Gorski said to calm her and focused on the knife in Bragg's hand.

Steiner was the first to address the intruding Bragg Gang, "Francois, your little brother is over there. Is this the sort of thing that you want to teach him? You want him to grow up and think it is acceptable to crash a private party? Do you?"

Francois Zerbe laughed at Steiner, "If it is a party for one of you, yes, that is exactly what I want him to learn."

Pierre Zerbe walked over to his brother from where he had been standing at the stairwell. "Francois, let's leave. The lady is right, we should not be here. They just got married and it should be a happy time for them."

Francois Zerbe glared down at his younger brother, "You can leave whenever you want to little brother."

With sad eyes, Pierre Zerbe looked at Steiner, "I apologize, miss. I am sorry my older brother is a horse's ass. I am leaving."

The Bragg Gang members blocking the stairwell did not budge until Francois Zerbe barked at them to let his brother leave. Pierre Zerbe left the Mouse Trap Bar and never looked back.

"My little brother was never cut out for real manhood," Francois Zerbe said as he began to walk around the ballroom full of silent guests. Grutzmacher and Nour followed behind him as he walked. Their eyes stared down threateningly at the other people.

"Actually, you could learn some manners from your little brother," Steiner said as she followed the three men. Harrison stayed by her side, ever her protector.

Zerbe stopped at the table full of the five younger Andolini siblings. His eyes looked over the three girls. He smiled at Giola Andolini who smiled back at him.

"And how old are you?" Zerbe inquired as he could see in her eyes that she was drawn to him. Zerbe found that the three Andolini girls were perhaps the most beautiful women he ever laid eyes on. He hoped they were all legal age for consent.

"Fourteen. But I will be fifteen really soon," Giola said nervously. For some odd reason she found herself physically attracted to Francois Zerbe. Although he was acting like a brute without any social skills he was devastatingly handsome.

"Stand up, let me get a good look at the merchandise," Nour barked at Giola.

Dominic and Marco Andolini did not give Giola a chance to obey Nour's order. Dominic rushed in first and smashed a beer bottle over the back of the head of Granite Grutzmacher. As the large giant of a man crumpled to the floor, Marco leaped into the air, with his left foot leading and kicked Nour in the side. Nour fell to his left into Zerbe. Both men staggered and fell to the ground.

"Stay the hell away from our sisters!" Dominic yelled as he stood in a typical martial arts stance.

That was when all hell broke loose.

The Yutong brothers charged in and were met by Gorski, Lincoln and Lynda Glenn. The three immediately avoided karate style kicks from the Yutong's and began swinging their fists and legs at the men themselves. The Yutong's parried their attempts and went on the offensive, only to have their efforts thwarted by their opponents.

The three Bragg siblings were running into the fray, knocking down guests with punches and kicks. Even the elderly and women that were not members of the rival gang were shoved or hit to the ground. The Bragg's always told people that they hated everyone equal. Their rude actions proved them true to their motto. They were soon face to face with Evart, Kander, Dia Cho and Felicia Essex.

"Two fags and two lesbians!" William Bragg laughed and charged in swinging at them wildly. Kander calmly delivered a punch to William Bragg's face and sent the younger man falling to the floor. Bragg dropped his knife which went sliding across the dance floor. He clutched his nose to stop the bleeding.

Cho delivered three rapid punches into the face of Lisa Bragg which broke her nose and caused her to stagger to her knees. Cho showed no mercy and kicked the female Bragg in the face with her right foot. Bragg flipped over backwards from the impact and landed face first on the ballroom floor. As Bragg struggled to regain her footing, Cho kicked her hard in her left side. Bragg cried out as she rolled to avoid the onslaught that her opponent was about to unleash on her.

Daniella Bragg kicked Felicia Essex in the chest and then blocked the right cross attempt by Evart. Bill Bragg spun and took Evart's legs out from under him with her right leg. Evart sprawled to the floor with a thud.

Guevara, Frank Glenn, Love-Easter and other wedding guests began to fight with the de Vida Brock siblings, Jeffrey Cobb and Renee Starr. The melee was out of control. Tables were being crashed, chairs broken as people were being knocked to the floors.

Zerbe, Nour and Grutzmacher were back on their feet and fighting with Dominic, Marco, Harrison, Steiner and Orellia Li. Soon the younger five Andolini kids and Piotr Gorski were jumping in to help. Grutzmacher lifted Harrison over his head and threw him face first into Lucius Andolini. Nour laughed as he kicked Marco in his abdomen and then turned in one movement and punched Stella Andolini in the face. Piotr Gorski growled angrily when he saw Stella hurt, leaped onto Nour's back and began to punch the large man in the side of his face. Nour flipped Gorski to the floor in one fluid movement.

Gillis was attempting to move toward the Yutong brothers as they seemed to be the most talented fighters on the Bragg Gang side. Gillis had studied martial arts extensively and determined the Yutong's would be a good test for his skills. Gillis never made it to that area of the brawl. He stopped as Reynita Calderon jumped in front of him.

Gillis looked her over and found that he was immediately attracted to the woman. She had a very pretty face and nice body. Gillis watched as Calderon began putting on some gloves that had the finger coverings cut off.

"What are those for?" Gillis pointed at her gloves.

"So I don't hurt my knuckles while I am kicking your foreigner ass," Reynita said as she ducked down to avoid a flying table that was thrown in her direction.

"Why do you call me a foreigner?" Gillis asked innocently.

"Because you are not from here," she put her fists up. "You talk funny and dress weird. My father says you people come from Old Earth to steal our jobs and take our lands. Now put up your fists! Time to get it on!"

"You mean my accent is funny?" Gillis frowned. "That is how we speak in Ireland."

"Put up your hands pinche bolillo!" Reynita began circling him. "I am going to beat you so bad your mother back in Ire, or whatever you said, will cry."

Gillis shook his head as he heard some cries as Gorski and Lincoln began connecting some kicks on their Yutong brother opponents.

"No. I don't want to fight you. You are too pretty for me to hit you."

Reynita growled at that and kicked Gillis in the chest. He fell to the floor and rolled to his right as she tried to kick him while he was down. He narrowly avoided contact from her steel reinforced boot.

Gillis jumped back onto his feet as Reynita stepped into him and swung at his face with her right fist. Gillis caught her arm in his hand, pulled her close to him and then kissed her on the lips. Her eyes widened with fury and she pushed him away.

"Hey, cabron! Now your ass kicking will commence in spades!" Reynita had never experienced that before. An opponent kissing her as she was attempting to cause him harm was something she had never even heard of.

She charged at Gillis and he stepped to her left and wrapped his arms around her torso. He trapped both of her arms and held her as she struggled.

"Let me go and fight!" She growled.

"I don't want to fight you," Gillis said calmly and dipped her backwards and kissed her again. At first she struggled to get free.

After a few seconds, she slowly relaxed in his arms and stopped fighting with him. She softly kissed him back. Reynita realized that she was attracted to the man and found him to be a good kisser.

"I want to make love to you," Gillis boldly told her.

Reynita shook herself free and fell to the floor on her buttocks. She was stunned by his words. "You want to do what?"

"You and me. Let's get out of here." Gillis held out his hand to her. "I can tell that you like me. Take my hand. Come on. Making love is much more enjoyable than beating the crap out of each other."

Reynita looked around her as the Bragg Gang and Gorski Gang were tearing the place down. It was only a matter of time before the Military Intelligence soldiers under the command of the dreaded General Tan arrived and began making arrests. Besides, she found the white looking foreigner with the funny accent to be handsome and it had been a month since she had last been with a man. She smiled at Gillis.

"It takes juevos to do what you just did. Okay bolillo. I may not kick your ass tonight but I plan on rocking your world."

She reached out and took his hand. He lifted her up

and pulled her into his arms and gave her a long lingering kiss. She put her arms around Gillis and began kissing him back.

"If I am going to let you play hide the chorizo with me, I need to know your name first," Reynita whispered into his ear.

"Les. Les Gillis. And you?"

"Reynita Calderon."

"Little Queen? That is a very nice name," Gillis told her.

"Thank you," she responded and she realized she was looking forward to being alone with the handsome foreigner. "Who told you what my name means?"

"No one. I speak Spanish fluently."

"Really? Do all you pinche extranjeros know how to speak Spanish?"

"No, I just loved the language and studied it when I was younger."

"My motorcycle is out front," Reynita looked at Gillis and wondered what other surprises he had regarding his life before moving to New Edinburgh.

"Lead the way my little queen."

She led Gillis by the hand as they fled the brawl, ducking under a thrown chair as they ran. None of the other combatants noticed the two make their hasty exit. They ran down the stairs and through the first floor bar area as several of General Tan's Military Intelligence soldiers began storming the bar. Gillis and Calderon got past the female soldiers and ran toward the parking area. She jumped onto one of the solid black motorcycles, ran her fingers over the security sensor and the engine erupted.

"I have never seen one of these before," Gillis remarked.

"Get on the back and wrap your arms around my mid-section," Reynita instructed him. "Hold on tight. If you want to feel me out while I am driving, feel free. I like a man's hands on my body."

Gillis laughed and sat down behind her and wrapped his arms around her. He moved his hands up to her breasts and began fondling them.

"Very nice," Gillis whispered into her ear as she gunned the throttle and they sped away from the parking lot.   She drove as fast as she could as she felt his hands roam over her body. She would giggle as Gillis kissed her neck. She found a set of Raumschiff space craft in the docking area that seemed to be unoccupied. She spun her motorcycle in a circle, turned off the engine and jumped off.

"Here," she pointed toward the pitch black space between the two large space craft.

"You want to do it here?" Gillis slid off the back of the motorcycle. "Aren't there any hotel rooms around?"

"No chingas, bolillo. You want me? Si o no?" Reynita laughed and began walking backwards and pulled off her leather jacket. She beckoned Gillis with her index finger to follow her. Gillis shrugged and ran to her. He pulled her into his arms and they began kissing passionately. They made love for the first time there between the two large ships, not caring if anyone caught them.

Gillis and Reynita would continue their lust filled relationship for several months. They were the gossip of the Academy student body. The fact that a devoted Bragg girl and a Gorski member could find romance together was unheard of before then. The relationship was one that Gillis treasured as Calderon excited him in every way. She was a great lover and taught him so many things about his new environment. Calderon never looked at her sexual exploits with Gillis as a committed relationship. She assumed he was like the other New Edinburgh men that would want to bed her for a time and then move on to another woman, just as Francois Zerbe had done to her.

Everything was wonderful for the two of them until it abruptly ended. Although the circumstances of their breakup were bad, both would later realize that they had been each other's first love. Calderon would always regret that she had been the one to cause the break up. Due to the loss she seemed to lose some of her brash personality. She privately had hoped one day Gillis would forgive her and they would reconcile. But then in their sophomore year, Sophia DuBravac arrived on campus. When DuBravac and Gillis became inseparable lovers, Calderon gave up her hope that she could one day rekindle the spark she had shared with Les Gillis.

Through that experience, Gillis learned that some things were not meant to be.

Each time Gillis would walk past a bakery and he would see white bread for sale he would remember how Calderon used to refer to him as bolillo. For her, each time she would be near a location that she and Gillis had shared a special moment she would get a lump in her throat. The memories they shared would forever follow them. Through their sharing of time together they had helped each other grow as individuals. They learned from each other and gave to one another experiences that made them become better people. In the end their relationship was not to be one that lasted.

As for the rest of the Bragg and Gorski gang members that were involved in the wedding day rumble, most of them escaped General Tan's soldiers. Some were arrested and only released after Tan was bribed to release them. Over the following years, the membership of each gang altered. The Yutong brothers, Francois Zerbe, Nour, the Bragg sisters, the Brock siblings, Renee Starr and Grutzmacher graduated and moved on to their careers. William Bragg ascended to become the leader of the gang. Frank and Orellia Glenn were assigned to serve on the Battle Cruiser *Cortez* while Cho and Felicia Essex were sent to the Second Fleet. Kander bid Evart farewell after learning he was to join the crew of Admiral Yamamoto. Aura Lynda Glenn remained on the planet as a fighter pilot in the Planetary Defense Corps. Although many of the members changed, the hatred between the gangs continued over the years to follow.

CHAPTER ONE

The trip down the spiral staircase took all of a minute. She ran as fast as her legs would allow her, even leaping over some of the grey metal steps as she ran. Penelope Rosenburg had grown weary, no, she was livid at her father and step-mother for the unprovoked attack on Space Station Cy-7. She had filled herself with the resolve that it was time for her to do something about the situation. The stairs began at a secret entrance that was behind her office wall and only opened to her voice command. The entire journey downward was about four flights and led to a secret storage area that had been converted into a scientific laboratory by two of Penelope's sisters.

Penelope landed on the metal floor with both feet slamming flat on the surface. She was standing upright as she faced her sister, medical doctor Nicolette Rosenburg. Penelope surveyed the large storage room that was filled with hundreds of metal and glass tubes that were each ten feet tall and four feet wide. Some were mounted on the walls; the majority were lying flat on the floors and on tops of metal tables that were placed over the canisters on the floors. In each of the containers there were dormant bodies, duplicates or clones as some referred to them, that Nicolette had created using alien technology from a race known as the Danaraja.

Nicolette nodded to acknowledge Penelope's

presence as did another sister named Kristen, who was also a medical doctor. The two sisters had joined Penelope in the space station so that they could work on a possible coup of their father and step-mother in an effort to put an end to the cover up over brother Caine and his sadistic killings. Since that alliance had been forged between the three sisters, more events came about that hastened the need to stand up to their father.

Penelope was still wearing the long sleeved sweats from the previous day when Junior Ragnarsson and his employees attacked the space station. There were still patched of blood stains present, left by some of the injured children she had assisted during the aftermath of the attack. She walked around the large chamber, looking over the several tables filled with medical instruments and computer panels. Nicolette and Kristen were dressed in their light blue hospital jackets that were light in weight and possessed numerous pockets for their various instruments for quick retrieval when necessary.

"Did you hear?" Penelope asked as she inspected the dormant clones in the tubes.

"What happened now?" Kristen asked from her position next to a green and yellow Danaraja computer panel that stood over twelve feet tall and fifteen feet wide. She was in the process of downloading the mental patterns and memories of a man that they were able to scan just before he had died. The three sisters decided that the deceased man would be one of the brains that they would utilize in building their small brigade of clones.

"Junior Ragnarsson is dead," Penelope told them. Her face looked dour as she reported the news. Each of the sisters stopped what they were doing and faced her.

"Are you certain?" Nicolette set a computer disc down on the medical table to her right.

"Yes, it came through the satellite broadcast only moments ago. You all know that his father will be coming for revenge." Penelope shuddered as she inspected the face of one of the duplicate bodies of her long deceased brother named Cush. The face looked exactly as she remembered her older brother. He seemed so peaceful in the canister, his eyes were closed and his body not yet activated.

"We might have to put out plans on hold for a while until this all blows over," Kristen suggested meekly.

"No, we cannot wait. If Dell returns to the Rosenburg Ranch then getting my father and Magdalena will be nearly impossible. We have to take father out immediately." Penelope shook her head at Kristen for making the suggestion. "The only problem is that father has disappeared."

"What do you mean he has disappeared?" Nicolette walked over toward her.

"I mean that our father and one of our brothers, David, have vanished. They must have fled the Ranch using one of the underground tunnels. They could be anywhere."

"Penny, you were always the smartest of us. Give us your educated guess. Where would father run off to when he has Sean Collins obtaining indictments against most of the family and sending in soldiers to search our entire property? Father would not leave the others behind to fend for themselves. What if he found out what we are doing up here? He might be on his way to kill the three of us, just like he did to Cush." Kristen was crossing her arms as she spoke. The apprehension on her face was evident.

"No, I monitor all of the people coming and going on this station. David and father are not here with us. They have something else in mind. You want my guess? I think they might be on their way to see the Glorious Leader himself to obtain permission to kill Collins and Colonel Gorski. I cannot think of any other reason that they would leave when their presence is so badly needed on the Ranch." Penelope put her hand on Kristen's shoulder and squeezed it gently. "They are not here; I can assure you of that."

Kristen swallowed and her eyes darted back and forth as she forced herself to breathe. She had seen the way Cush died and still had nightmares in which she could hear his screams. She did not want to die in such a horrible manner.

"So, if father is not around what are we going to do with all of these Replicants that we have created?" Nicolette motioned with her arm around the room.

Penelope leaned up against one of the tables and crossed her arms. "I have given that question quite a bit of thought."

"And what is your answer?" Kristen shrugged at her.

"Perhaps we need to think of using these Replicants on a larger scale attack," Penelope responded.

"How much larger?" Nicolette frowned at her.

"Perhaps it is time to stop thinking of only ourselves and consider making a difference on a more universal scale."

Kristen looked down at the tubes on the ground, "I really do not like the sound of that, Penny."

"Think about it for a moment. Those that were once considered untouchable are being eliminated. Felix Ragnarsson was found dead in his home with no evidence of forced entry and all of his valuable paintings and jewelry were not stolen. Since robbery was not the motive, Felix was killed for some personal vendetta. His son, Sigurd, vanished after the Darktober assassinations. No evidence was located that proved Sigurd had left the planet. I managed his financials and he never made any withdrawals after the hits. I think it is safe to assume that Sigurd was killed that night. Then Darryl is killed by cadet Elektra, Caine and his friends are injured by Gorski and his friends. So, father sends in the best and the most experienced assassins to get revenge. But they fail and fail again and in the process they lose Montrose, Prescott and many others. The death of Junior proves that the tide is turning, the untouchables are being killed and the people dispensing justice against them are cadets at an academy. Caine opened a can of worms due to his twisted mind games and Collins now has indictments filed against most of our family. It is only a matter of time before Collins traces the corruption all the way up."

"All the way up to who?" Nicolette was still frowning.

"To the rest of the Royal Family and ultimately the Glorious Leader. If Collins is able to connect the dots, and I believe he is intelligent enough to do so, then the darkest secrets of humanity might be exposed to the general public."

"But, Penny! We are members of the Royal Family!" Kristen blurted out. "Are you saying we are all going to be tracked down and arrested?"

Penelope paced back toward the staircase, "I have many personal sins I need to pay for, Kristen. When this is all over I will have to turn myself in for prosecution and I will gladly take the punishment that is coming. You two never did anything wrong, so you will be in the clear. We need to be ready, ladies. Father has something planned and Dell Ragnarsson will no doubt be a part of those plans."

"So what do we do in the short term and long term?" Nicolette wanted to know.

"Remember the man that you took the memories of while you were posing as an ER doctor here on the station?"

"Yes. What about him, Penny?"

"Are his copies ready?"

"Yes, Penny. I have twenty-five clones of Orville William Garrison ready. All I need to do is download his memories into the blank brains and they will be activated."

Penelope smiled and placed her hand on the guardrail on the staircase. "And the DNA I gave you of Ella?"

"I have twenty-five of her body ready as well. The only problem is that we do not have her brain patterns to download into the clones. Who would you suggest that we use for that?"

Penelope sighed and looked up the stairs as she gave the question some thought. She turned her head back at Nicolette, "Use the scans that you did of my memories and download them into the clones of Ella."

"You sure you want to do that?" Kristen chimed in.

"Do it quickly. We have very little time. Things are going to happen and we need to have some muscle to watch out backs."

Doctor Nicolette Rosenburg had been working diligently in the basement of the Baroness Hotel for the past few months. She had started off with fifty small petri dishes and had used the DNA cultures in them to produce fifty works of perfection. She later added fifty more specimens and fifty more after that. She looked at the first fifty glass tubes, all were ten feet tall and four feet wide. Inside each tube was a human specimen that Nicolette Rosenburg had been able to recreate. All that she needed to do was download the memories into the brains and they would all become living people. Exact duplicates of the host of the DNA used by her in what many would term as a mad experiment.

Religious leaders would say that Doctor Nicolette Rosenburg was blasphemous or that her work was that of demonic possession. She did not care what others would say. All she knew was that her sister Penelope was in trouble and she needed an army. She required the protection by the best against the best.

Nicolette was thirty-seven years old. She had short blonde hair and green eyes. She was Penelope's oldest full blood sibling. The two sisters had always been close and kept secrets from the rest of the family. Nicolette hated her father and her step-mother. She never forgave them for killing her beloved older brother Cush. Now she and Penelope would make them all answer for what they had done.

Nicolette walked over to her work bench and picked up the first computer disk. "You died very young, Drayton Love-Easter," she read the name on it. "I am going to give you another chance to get it right, to make amends to anyone that you may have wronged. My brother Caine and his friends have much to answer for, your murder being one of them. Time to live again and take your revenge."

There was going to be a reckoning and past abuses would be avenged. Nicolette began the process of downloading the memories from the disk into twenty-five of the replicated humans in the large glass tubes.

CHAPTER TWO

"I need this one in the ER! Let's move people!" Doctor Grace Kai yelled out loud so that the three orderlies near her could hear over the noise of the other medical personnel that were diligently working to save the lives of the wounded that were arriving each minute. The medical staff at the Cordell Hull Hospital were not used to such a mass of emergency room admissions. Doctors, nurses, orderlies and search and rescue staff were wheeling in the injured for treatment.

Doctor Freya Doernitz Cardenas had called in all cadets that were studying medicine to help out. She had received the news reports of the attack and concluded the hospital would be under-staffed. Answering Freya Cardenas' pleas for assistance were cadets Julia Steiner, Robert Windfohr, Lynn Goldsmith, Clark Blundell, Siobhan Collins, Candy Farinelli and several others. Most of the wounded were their fellow cadets from the Clovis Academy.

The casualties from the ambush perpetrated by Junior Ragnarsson and his small band of killers were estimated at over three hundred. The wounded outnumbered the casualties and the lobby of the hospital was cluttered with prone soldiers, cadets and a few civilians that had been victims of the attack.

Steiner gasped when she saw the badly burned and

torn body of Elektra Papanikolaou brought in by the search and rescue medics. Steiner fought back tears as she observed the missing right arm, the cuts, bruises and burns on the sweet girl. Steiner looked to one of the search and rescue officers, a Captain with her name tag reading Yang.

"How are her vital signs?" Steiner asked.

"Not good," Captain Yang replied quickly. "She needs immediate attention. Move her to the front of the line."

Steiner directed the other orderlies to wheel Papanikolaou to the emergency room entrance. They followed her to one of the waiting operating rooms where surgeons were ready to begin the attempt to save as many lives as possible. Steiner saw other injured cadets in beds, being pushed into operating rooms. She noticed that Lupita Calderon was among the injured. She was sitting on the floor, holding her blood stained side, waiting for medical attention. Steiner swallowed and tried to keep her mind on the task at hand. The injured needed assistance.

In the lobby area, Jack Harcourt was pacing back and forth. He had rushed Papanikolaou to the search and rescue team so they would take her first. Harcourt wondered what became of the rest of his friends. Although Jack Harcourt was a major player in the Gorski Gang, he did not drink much. But after everything he had been exposed to, Harcourt felt a stiff drink would be the only remedy for his frayed nerves. He continued pacing.

Jack heard the voices of Jurgen Doernitz and Lila Zapata asking for help. Harcourt began walking toward their position and saw that Doernitz had the unconscious Michel Evart in his arms. Jack ran to them and helped Doernitz with Evart.

"Is he okay?" Jack was concerned for his roommate. Over the past three years, Evart had grown to become his best friend.

"He needs help," Zapata answered. "He must have

hit his head hard on the pilot control dashboard. Smelling salts won't wake him."

Doctor Harding appeared as if from nowhere. She checked Evart over, using a small hand held metallic scanner. She read the three dimensional green pop up from her instrument. "This man needs to go to the E.R., immediately. Looks like blunt force trauma to the head. He has a hematoma and his breathing is irregular. Let's move."

Harcourt and Doernitz allowed the orderlies to relieve them of Evart and carry him to the back where surgeons were waiting.

"How bad was it out there?" Jack asked as he watched the orderlies carry his friend away.

"Two cadet pilots were killed," Doernitz said with regret in his voice. "Starr and Martinson. There were many more casualties on the ground, mostly Army and Marines. Fortunately their escape ship did not get away. It crashed on top of the Great Wall."

"Yuri?" Jack pressed.

"He is alive and well," Doernitz said. "The assassins were not as fortunate. Gorski and Evart really were heroes today."

Harcourt detected admiration in Doernitz' voice when he mentioned Evart and Gorski. He observed Zapata holding Doernitz' hand with hers, her eyes were red, possibly from crying. What Harcourt did not know was that Zapata was feeling guilty for firing on a Raumschiff that had two of her friends on board. Doernitz had been doing his best to convince her that anyone else would have done the same had they been in their shoes. Although Zapata knew Doernitz was correct, she still felt sick to her stomach. Had the rockets hit the Blitzkrieg in a different area, Gorski or Evart or both could have been killed.

"Come on. Let me treat you two to a cup of coffee downstairs." Harcourt offered.

Zapata smiled, "Thank you. Coffee would be very nice right now."

Dirk Fenster had been able to get Theodora to his personal transport, a Fenster Corporation eight man courier Model 7. It had four side doors and a larger rear sliding entrance. Fenster placed Theodora in the back of his ship and ran to the front and sat in the pilot seat. He flew his ship to the nearest Veterinarian clinic and landed haphazardly, in a rush to get treatment for his injured wolf. He rushed into the small clinic and found a fellow cadet working, Danielle Day. She was a pretty young woman, twenty years old, blonde, blue eyes and slender. She was from a large family that lived on planet New Edinburgh in Gellar's Province. Her father and mother were small business owners, hardworking and honest folks. But they had very little money to pay for things. As a result, Danielle Day and her siblings had to work part time to help out with expenses. She had a twin sister at the Academy named Dorothy.

"I need help!" Fenster said abruptly.

"Dirk Fenster?" Daniella Day said as she frowned and stood up from behind her desk. Fenster knew he was not liked by Daniella Day. They had shared a short history in their freshman year, sleeping together a few times until Fenster moved on with another woman. His actions had not set well with cadet Day as she had envisioned a future with him.

"Theodora is hurt and needs a doctor," Fenster told her.

Daniella Day, despite any residual anger she may have had for Fenster, maintained positive memories of Theordora. She rushed from behind her counter and ran to the back. She returned with a veterinarian doctor and a stretcher. They followed Fenster outside and to his small ship and they found the injured wolf inside. The doctor and Day lifted Theodora onto the stretcher and rushed her inside the clinic.

"We'll take it from here," Day told him.

"Thank you," Fenster called out to them. He sat down in one of the chairs in the waiting room. He looked out the windows and wondered of the fate of his friends. As soon as he was sure Theodora was safe, he would leave to find out what had befallen the others. He pulled out his holo-com device and tried contacting Arch Frazier. His friend did not respond which was out of character. Fenster was concerned for his friend's welfare.

"Be okay, Arch." Fenster said to himself.

Yuri Gorski was covered with bruises, scrapes and cuts from his hand to hand encounter with Junior Ragnarsson. His muscles were soar, as was his jaw and ribs due to some of the punches and kicks he had sustained. His knuckles on his right hand were gashed open. He had reluctantly left the scene of the crash on top of the Great Wall. He had wanted to stay and help the military and the CID in the investigation, but his father insisted that he be treated by a physician.

Gorski, Staszko, Harrison, Lincoln, Marco Andolini, and Zerbe arrived together at the Cordell Hull Hospital. They were taken aback by the scene of hundreds of family members and friends in the downstairs Lobby. There was fast paced activity as search and rescue officers continued to arrive with the injured and the dying.

Gorski saw many members of the Calderon family huddled together in a corner, all of them were clearly upset by the injuries to Lupita. Reynita Calderon made eye contact with Gorski for only a brief moment. He noted the redness in her eyes and the tracks of tears on her cheeks.

Clark Blundell approached the group and walked toward Gorski. "Yuri, you are hurt. Let me look at you."

Gorski recognized Blundell as one of the cadets that had helped out during the sand storm incident. Gorski nodded and let Blundell scan over him with a similar medical instrument that Doctor Harding had used on Evart.

"You have a few strained muscles," Blundell was smiling at him. "You'll live. Word is you really took care of business. I will get you a room so we can patch up your cuts. You might need a sling for your left arm for a few days. Sit tight."

Gorski thanked him as Blundell turned his attention to the others. "Everyone else okay? Jen? You have a considerable amount of blood on you."

Staszko smiled, "Not my blood. It is from one of the assassins."

"So I was told. She is really angry."

"Who is angry?" Staszko demanded.

"Ella Ragnarsson. She was just brought in and is in surgery. They cuffed her to the hospital bed so she won't be going anywhere." Blundell walked off, speaking instructions into a hand held communication device.

Staszko looked at Gorski with a look of surprise. Staszko had been certain she killed the Ragnarsson woman. Gorski wrapped his arms around her and held her close. He could tell Staszko was worried by the news.

Staszko shuddered and buried her head in Gorski's chest. If Ella Ragnarsson fully recovered, she would return and hunt Jen Staszko down for revenge. Staszko dreaded that she failed to finish her rival off.

"I should have slit her throat, like they did to Dray." Staszko whispered to Gorski.

Harrison pointed over to the far corner of the room, "Over there."

Gorski looked to see his little brother, Piotr Gorski, standing with Mia Nguyen, Flora Evart, Supreet Patel and Ann Harcourt. They were not talking much; Patel had her arm around Flora Evart's shoulder and was trying to console her. Gorski motioned for the group to join them. It was good to see that they were safe, Yuri Gorski thought to himself.

On the second floor recovery room, Les Gillis woke up and found himself in a hospital bed with an IV tube in his right arm. He felt dehydrated, which was a common drawback from having been stunned by a laser. His vision was still blurry. He tried looking around to see if anyone else was nearby.

Lying on a hospital bed next to Gillis was Corporal Frank Preston. He also had an IV in his arm, receiving fluid to hydrate his body.

Preston smiled at Gillis, "You finally woke up."

"My head is pounding," Gillis remarked as he slowly sat up in the bed. He looked around at the others. He saw Arch Frazier lying still in another bed. Sara Stewart was also asleep, her eye lids fluttering every so often. LaShondra Lewis was also in a state of calm, her chest rising and falling as she breathed. Brandon Harcourt was also there, sleeping off the stun blast he received in the battle. Gillis began to panic as he did not see DuBravac among the patients. "Where is Sophia?"

"Not to worry," Preston said after drinking a glass of vitamin fortified plantana juice. "She was up in no time. For some reason, women seem to wake up faster than men after being hit by a laser. She was running around like a chatter box, getting the scoop on what happened after we got hit. She went to help out her friend, Steiner, with some of the incoming patients."

Gillis rubbed his eyes with his right hand. That would be just like her. She always was the first to volunteer and lend a hand when needed.

"What did happen after we were shot?" Gillis wanted to know.

Preston leaned over and faced Gillis. "All hell broke loose, my friend." Preston began to fill Gillis in on the few tidbits of information he had learned since he woke up. Gillis laid back down as he heard how Staszko took on the former security chief at the Baroness Hotel in a confrontation with knives. That was the only story Preston had heard from the orderlies since he had regained consciousness.

Elektra Papanikolaou was on the operating table as Doctor Harding and Doctor Doernitz Cardenas were attempting to mend her wounds. The two surgeons knew they were fighting to save the young woman's life. The right arm was gone, her ribs were broken, her left leg was broken just above the knee and her skin was burned on the right side of her body. Her right lung had been punctured by a broken rib. She had suffered some trauma to the head in the explosion. Although it was not hopeless, Harding gave Doernitz Cardenas a look of despair as Papanikolaou went into cardiac arrest.

The resident heart surgeon on duty, Doctor Zhennipher Bass, applied electric shocks to the patient. The nurses and doctors watched silently as Papanikolaou's body arched up with each electrical treatment. Bass tried again and her heart responded, beating again.

"Inject her with some adrenaline," Bass instructed a nurse, her voice had an urgent tone.

Both Harding and Freya Doernitz Cardenas stood back as the nurse did as Bass had instructed.

In the back of the operating room stood Julia Steiner. She had come in to deliver some more bandages and supplies. She saw how close her friend Elektra had come to passing on the operating table. Steiner bit her lip and walked out. She leaned against the wall in the long hallway and crossed her arms. She began crying.

Sophia DuBravac approached Steiner and hugged her.

"Come on, Julia," DuBravac whispered in her ear. "Pull yourself together. There are many people here that need you."

Steiner nodded and wiped the tears out of her eyes. "If they save Elektra, the hospital won't replace her arm.

They won't give her skin grafts to repair her burned skin."

"Why the hell not?" DuBravac felt he blood pressure rising. "We are all cadets. We are supposed to receive the best medical care when we enter the service of the Empire."

"You are right about that if and when we are in the service," Steiner said. "Elektra is only a cadet. The military will not waste the resources on a cadet."

"What? So they are going to leave her like that?" DuBravac was ready to go find someone with authority and light them up with a barrage well-chosen four letter words.

"She is not the only one," Steiner went on. "Lupita Calderon might lose the use of one of her arms. Dorothy Day is going to need a leg replacement. Donald Harcourt lost a hand. Several civilians were critically hurt as well. They are going to patch them up and that is it. Elektra needs a new arm. They have the technology to help her and the others, but they say it costs too much money."

"Get back to work," DuBravac said abruptly. She had heard enough bad news. "All of our classmates are going to get everything that they need or the powers that be will answer for it."

"What are you going to do?" Steiner watched as DuBravac was walking away from her.

"What I do best. I'm going to raise hell."

DuBravac made her was to the first floor where the Financial Office was located. She instructed the computer to open the door, but the door was locked shut. DuBravac could hear voices inside the Financial Office. There were people laughing and carrying on.

DuBravac began kicking the door as hard as she could.

The door opened after about ten kicks. An elderly man, overweight, with a grey beard and wearing a white lab coat stepped toward DuBravac. "Can I help you?"

DuBravac looked at the man's name plate. It read

"Ramsey."

"Are you in charge of the finances?" DuBravac demanded.

"And who are you?" Doctor Ramsey asked, his voice sounded as if he was annoyed by the intrusion.

"I am a friend of all of the injured cadets being treated here at this facility," DuBravac said rapidly. "I was just told that anyone that lost a limb or that needed skin grafts would not receive them? Is that true?"

Ramsey nodded, "I am sorry, but yes, that is true. Only actual service men and women get replacement limbs for free. Cadets are considered private citizens and must pay. That is the way the world works, young lady."

"How much for an arm?" DuBravac demanded. She could see two young female nurses getting dressed in Ramsey's office. That would explain all the laughter and other noises she had heard.

"An arm?" Ramsey thought for a moment. "Normally a top of the line arm, say one of our Allen Corporation or Brackenridge Corporation models, made with tungsten, iron and other heavy metals, guaranteed for life, would run around, say four hundred thousand Empire Dollars."

DuBravac swallowed. That was more expensive than she had thought it would be. DuBravac had thought about giving all of her money from her savings, but she did not have that kind of money. Not even close to half that. "And a skin graft?"

Ramsey pursed his lips in thought, "A skin graft, with nerve connections so the feelings and sensations would be exactly as the original skin, you are looking at another three to four hundred thousand Empire Dollars. Do you have that kind of money?"

DuBravac looked down at the floor, ashamed she could not help her friends. "No. I do not. But this is not fair! All of these cadets will be officers one day. How can they function if they are not treated for their necessities now?"

Ramsey chuckled, "Hardly my concern, young lady. Now, if you will excuse me, I was in the middle of something before you rudely interrupted me."

Ramsey walked back to his door where the young, nubile nurses were waiting for him. He was about to mount one of them when DuBravac started kicking his door. He did not make it to the door. He felt a hand on his arm and was spun around. He expected to see the rude female cadet but he saw a male cadet instead. The female was standing behind the new man, with her hands on her hips.

"Get your hands off me!" Ramsey ordered. "I will have you arrested!"

"You do not arrest a Fenster," Dirk Fenster said in a low, threatening tone. "You deal with a Fenster, you negotiate and come to an understanding with us. The question on the table is about the bottom line. My family only understands the language of business and money."

"I am supposed to believe you are a Fenster?" Doctor Ramsey was laughing. Ramsey considered himself well connected. He had never been told that a Fenster was either living on or visiting planet New Edinburgh. That was a piece of gossip that Ramsey was certain he would have heard at some point.

"Damn right I am," Fenster said as he pushed Ramsey against the wall. "Now, my friend Sophia asked you nicely how much. I want to know how much to make patient Elektra Papanikolaou as good as new."

"Arm, skin graft, new ribs, new lung, repaired leg?" Ramsey asked.

"Everything," Fenster said.

"About a million and a half Empire Dollars," Ramsey said. "That is a rough estimate."

"And Dorothy Day?"

"I would have to check the computer to see what

her exact injuries are," Ramsey said.

"Check Donald Harcourt, Lupita Calderon and any other cadet patient that needs a limb replacement or other cosmetic assistance." Fenster instructed. He released his grip on the elder Doctor. "Do it."

Ramsey ran, not walked, back to his office. He consulted his computer and began coming up with prices for different types of limb replacements, and varying treatments. The nurses in the Financial office were buttoning up their blouses and giving Fenster the eye.

DuBravac moved close to Fenster, "How did you know to come here?"

"I was at a veterinarian hospital," Fenster whispered. "Dorothy's twin sister, Daniella, works there. The hospital contacted her and was demanding more money than she or her family could afford. I told her not to worry, that I would straighten out the situation."

"Those nurses are really checking you out," DuBravac warned him. "They are both kind of cute."

"Gold diggers," Fenster dismissed the thought of the nurses. "They heard my name. That's all they are interested in is my name and the money they think they can get from my family."

"How can you tell?" DuBravac wanted to know.

"Being rich is a curse," Fenster told her. "Not all men and women are good people like you and Les. I have had uncles and aunts scammed by gold diggers. After seeing how some of my family members got used, I learned to be wary."

Ramsey returned with a small print out of expenses for the four patients Fenster had mentioned. "Total cost to replace all limbs and skin grafts, would come to four million two hundred thousand Empire Dollars."

"And you will be using Allen Corporation limbs?" Fenster demanded. His family and the Allen's hated each other. But the Allen family was the top of the line in medical supplies and limb replacement.

"Yes, yes. Only the best," Ramsey assured him. "Why are you helping these cadets? They are not from your stock? They are peasants compared to you. Why would you waste your time on them?"

"Because ever since I moved here I found friendships are hard to come by. Elektra, she is like family to me," Fenster responded as he was pulling out his hand held holo-com device. The amount quoted was about a third of Fenster's trust fund, but he did not care about the money. All that mattered to him was that his injured friends received the best medical treatment possible. He knew his parents would be furious if they found out he spent that much of his Trust. But Fenster did not worry because he knew that he would make more in the future. "Where do I route the money to?"

"Follow me," Ramsey motioned for Fenster to go down the hallway to the left.

DuBravac watched in silence as Fenster voluntarily gave up a small fortune to help out his injured classmates. She remembered when Gorski and Gillis recruited Fenster to be in the Gang. None of them knew where Fenster had come from nor did they know his family ties. They saw a quality in the young lad that they liked. It seemed Gillis and Gorski had very good instincts when it came to judging others. What Fenster did that day would never be forgotten by many families.

DuBravac walked away from the scene. She wanted to find Les Gillis to thank him for finding Dirk Fenster and convincing him to become their friend.

At the Happy Wedding Chapel, Dominic Andolini and Harumi Shigeta had finished all of their computerized signatures and agreements. All was ready for the wedding in the morning. Dominic Andolini pulled out his small solar powered holo-com device and asked for a person to person with his brother, Marco. He had his arm around

Harumi Shigeta when Marco's three dimensional life size image appeared before them.

"Marco!" Dominic said with joy. "It is done! All of the arrangements are made for the wedding tomorrow!"

"Dominic," Marco said softly. "We have been trying to contact you for some time now. Get down to the hospital."

"What is going on?" Shigeta was alarmed by the tone of Marco's voice.

"We were attacked again," Marco told them bluntly. "It was that damn Junior Ragnarsson. He came back with a super powered space ship that was loaded with firepower. A lot of people are dead, Dom. Elektra might not make it. Get over here quick."

"Damn," Dominic said, thinking of the good hearted Elektra. He had gone from being the happiest man alive, getting ready to marry the most wonderful woman he had ever met, to deflated in hearing the distressing news. He could see the reaction in Shigeta's face that she was going through the same emotional turmoil. He softly told her, "Let's go."

Shigeta did not hide her emotions. As she followed Dominic out of the wedding chapel, she wept for her friends. Elektra had become her closest friend and the thought of losing her was something that she did not want to face. Dominic put a consoling arm over her shoulders and whispered in her ear that he loved her. Shigeta smiled bravely at him as they walked for the nearby solar powered light rail station. Her wedding plans would be placed on an indefinite hold until Elektra recovered. If she recovered.

Dominic moved her through the crowds of civilians that were waiting to leap onto one of the many ground level rail cars. There were more that were underground and above ground as well. The commerce of Clovis City was fast paced and the tourism industry was in full swing. Dominic estimated that several hundred of the folks waiting at the rail tracks were not citizens of planet New Edinburgh. Their manner of dress was different, many had odd tattoos on their faces and bodies and other sported brands. Some of the brightly colored dyes in the hair of many of the commuters gave them away as Cootronians, Athenians and New Berliners. He heard the digitized voice announce that Train One was arriving on track seven. Before he could alert Shigeta to start moving toward that track, she was already pulling him by the hand to follow her.

The couple arrived at the seventh ground level track and Train One arrived. It was silver with streaks of black and purple on the sides. It had fifteen cars, each able to comfortable seat fifty passengers. The side doors slid open after the train came to an abrupt stop. Dominic and Shigeta waited impatiently as the passengers departed. As soon as they thought they had a chance to board, they moved in quickly. Shigeta found a set of seats in the rear of the car and led Dominic in that direction. After she sat down she pulled out her small eight inch by six inch wide computer and ordered it to turn on.

"What are you hoping to learn?" Dominic inquired.

"I want to find out how badly our friends were hurt," she said softly.

Fifteen eleven inch by twelve inch holographic screens appeared before Shigeta. Her computer was security sensitive to her retinal identification and blocked any other person from being able to view the screens. Any other person would see a grey screen and nothing else, while Shigeta could watch the news reports from all over the planet without any rude passengers looking over her shoulder. She realized that Dominic was unable to view the news reports so she verbally instructed her computer to scan his eyes and authorize him to view the screens. She cuddled up in his arms as the train began to move. They watched the reports of the ambush in silence. When the names of the deceased were presented on the eleventh screen, Shigeta and Dominic blocked out the others and listened intently.

"Li Mingjuan was killed," Shigeta said sadly after she heard her name. "She was such a sweet girl."

Dominic nodded in agreement. His parents had been friends with the Mingjuan family for several years. Li had always been a kind person and had no enemies.

"Why did this happen to us?" Shigeta asked to no one in particular. She did not expect an answer. She knew if Yuri Gorski was sitting next to them, he would have responded with his usual: "The universe is a dangerous place."

"I am certain that Collins and his lawyers will indict the killers and bring them to justice," Dominic said softly.

Shigeta looked at her future husband and scowled, "You know you really put too much faith in the law. The law means nothing to those animals that did this. Sometimes you just have to throw down and kick some ass. Sometimes it comes down to a matter of family honor."

Dominic nodded, "The problem is determining whose ass to kick. But I am with you, Harumi. I grew up with the Mingjuan family. They are all good people. I would like nothing better than to get those responsible in my sniper scope and blow their heads off."

CHAPTER THREE

Caine Rosenburg was elated when he opened a satellite message while perusing his messages on his hand held computer. He had received information that his father had arrived at his campus. The encrypted e-mail to Caine read: "Son, arriving today. Come meet me at the Dean's office, we have business to discuss with him. Love father."

Caine immediately dressed and ran, not walked, to the Administration Offices of his Academy. Being late for father was not an option. He arrived at the fifty-two floor Administration Building and bolted up the stair case. The Dean's offices were located on the ninth floor. Caine had kept himself in excellent shape through the physical training requirements of the Academy. He would run a minimum of five kilometers a day. Sometimes he would conquer ten or twenty kilometers.

Caine was barely winded when he arrived to the ninth floor. He saw the attractive blonde at the reception desk. He smiled and approached her. Caine thought it would be so easy to rape and kill the receptionist. He could wait for her to leave work, follow her and kidnap her when she least expected it. But today was not a day to consider such things unless father authorized it.

"I am here to meet with my father and the Dean," Caine announced, smiling at the woman. One of the best perks to being a Rosenburg was that no one knew your real name until it was necessary to reveal it. Caine had been using the last name of "Smith" ever since he applied to the Academy.

The Receptionist pointed to a door and barely gave Caine a second look, "They are expecting you."

Caine felt slighted by the woman in the manner she dismissed him. He walked toward the sliding door, which slid open for him. He saw that Bill Ford, the Dean of the University, his father Alfred Rosenburg, II, and one of his older brothers, David Rosenburg, were all sitting around a glass rectangular meeting table. The floor of the office was rectangular black and white tile which matched the similar pattern on the walls.

"Ahh," Dean Ford said when Caine arrived. "Please come in and have a seat."

Dean Bill Ford was in good condition for a man in his eighties. He had a full head of grey hair, blue eyes, wrinkles on his face and was tall and lanky. He was considered a no nonsense leader of the Achilles Academy, he was well liked and rarely exacted any tough punishment on cadets for infractions.

Caine sat down next to his older brother, David. Although the brothers had a strained relationship, they shook hands.

David Rosenburg was seven feet tall, mostly due to the metallic improvements made to his body. He had his legs, spine, neck and arms surgically altered so that he went from six feet tall to seven feet. He was a marksman with laser weapons and a master of advanced laser technology. David had killed many human slaves before, mainly for sport and other times to study the reactions on their faces as they died. He was a brilliant engineer, obtaining his doctorate at the Sikorsky Academy and working as an understudy to his uncle John on several projects. David had also been heavily involved in the formation of the

Rosenburg Ranch. He helped in the construction of the protective walls around the over one hundred kilometers of land and designed many of the power plants and mansions occupied by his siblings and some of the Ragnarsson's. His age was forty-seven, but he looked twenty. David had long dark hair, down below his shoulders and deep blue eyes. His face was perfect, due to the numerous cosmetic operations he had taken over the years. His internal organs were also new as he had taken new body parts to make himself immortal, just like father had.

"Your father and brother are very charming and delightful men," Dean Ford said and tapped a large duffle bag on the table.

Caine glanced at the black leather bag on the table that was lying in front of Ford. The bag looked stuffed, no doubt with Empire Dollars. He deduced that his father was attempting to bribe the Dean for some purpose.

"Yes sir," Caine smiled at the outright acknowledgment of the monetary bribe on the table. "I am very proud of my father and brother."

"And they are proud of you," Ford announced. "Your father wants me to appoint you, Caine, to lead the Achilles Academy Tournament Team on the Blood Moon. I am inclined to agree with him."

Ford was looking at the large duffle bag as he spoke. Caine deduced that was the reason for the money, but the amount paid was a mystery. Based on what Caine could tell, his father had decided to back up his scheme to eliminate the Clovis Academy cadets at the Tournament. At first his father was not supportive. Caine pleaded with his father and did his best to convince him that the best way to kill Gorski and his friends was to ambush them on the Blood Moon. That his father had changed his mind on the plan meant that something must have gone terribly wrong with the hired killers that the family normally relied on.

"Thank you, sir." Caine responded.

"We would also like for my son to select the entire team that will serve with him on the Tournament," Alfred Rosenburg, II, added in. "I do hope that will not be a problem."

"None at all," Dean Ford assured the men. "If he is to lead the team, he should select the members that he feels most comfortable with. Do you have any names in mind?"

Caine had been prepared for the question and had previously discussed the opportunity with many of his friends at his Academy. He had promised the students that he had recruited a large sum of cash in addition to the chance to look another person in the eyes before they killed them. Caine cleared his throat, "Yes, I do, sir. I need Avery Jackson to be my second in command. I need Peter Lomax as chief pilot. I also need cadet pilots Clive Doornink, Keith Austin, Neal Giamatti and Rutger Stenerud. To round out the team, I need Kai Chin, Cleon Alexander and Burton Stapler."

Dean Ford was silent for a second, as if he was contemplating the names given to him. "I think all of those names will be just fine. I will submit them to the competition committee. Is there anything else I can do today for you gentlemen?"

"No, we are very satisfied," Alfred told the Dean as he stood and extended his hand. The two men shook hands, smiling at each other. "We would like to take some time with my son, Caine, to walk around the campus."

"Please, help yourselves." Ford told them. "I hope you enjoy the campus."

The three Rosenburg men walked out of the Dean's office and out into the hallway and maintained their silence until they had descended the stairs and exited the Administration Building.

"Son, this is an important event for the family." Alfred Rosenburg, II, said. "I will be meeting with the Glorious Leader later today and make the necessary arrangements."

"Yes father," Caine responded as he walked in the middle of his brother and father. "We obviously will target all of the cadets from Clovis Academy. But what about the Referees and the Teams from Newton and Tyr Academies? How do we keep them off of the Blood Moon?"

"We do not," David Rosenburg finally spoke. "They are all going to die, regrettably. You will be the only ones to survive the betrayal and cowardly attack of the Clovis Academy cadets."

"But they are not the aggressors, we are." Caine frowned in confusion.

"No. They are," David continued. "The rest of the Eight Solar Systems will be watching the competition live. The people will see the Clovis Academy cadets attack and kill the referees and at least one of the other teams. The people will believe that Yuri Gorski and his friends went rogue and decided to embark on a killing spree. They will then be killed by you and your team, all in self-defense. The bottom line is that Clovis Academy will be disgraced, Gorski and his friends will die as villains and you and your friends will become heroes overnight."

Caine smiled as he listened to his brother. "And weapons? No deadly weapons are allowed at the Tournament. How do we fight, or should I say, how do we kill the others?"

"Weapons will be there as well as a good amount of help," Caine's father responded. "We will have ships that have been painted in the colors of the Clovis Academy and fully loaded with armor piercing rockets and laser batteries. We will have a few large lockers of extra weapons waiting on the surface of the moon for you and your team. You should have no problem killing them all. And by all I mean the cadets on the other teams as well. You must leave no witnesses."

"The broadcast feed to the planetary audiences?"

Caine wanted to know.

"We will jam the broadcast feed from the source, at the satellite towers on the surface of the Moon," David explained. "We will let the world of humanity see the Clovis Cadets attack and kill in the beginning. After the first attack or two, we will cut the broadcast. The audiences will demand repairs and moan about the lack of service. They will send in a group of Space Command ships to investigate. The closest ship will be Colonel Jamal Lincoln's, which we estimate will be about seven to ten days flight from the moon when the shit hits the fan. More than enough time for us to kill everyone there and dispose of the evidence of our involvement."

"Which of the cadets from Clovis will be there?" Caine stopped walking.

"Yuri Gorski, Les Gillis and Michel Evart are confirmed," his father told him. "The others are just insects, pests to be stepped on. After we finish this off, you should be in the clear. There will be no more eye witnesses to identify you for your culpability on the space station."

"Any women?" Caine hoped the answer was yes. It had been too long since he had been able to satisfy his sadistic urges.

Alfred Rosenburg, II put his arm around his younger son. "There will be some women. But I need for you to remember that your nasty habit is what got all of us in this predicament in the first place. You are to not commit any rapes or tortures until after we cut the broadcast. Do you understand me?"

"Yes sir. I understand," Caine responded softly. He could feel his father's fingers digging into his shoulder. Father was not too pleased with young Caine, mainly due to the fact that his actions had gotten Darryl killed.

His father stopped walking and turned to face him. He grasped Caine on his shoulders and held him still. "You better understand, son. You better. If you screw this up, the

Glorious Leader will be furious and will order your execution. You got Darryl killed and because of that you are currently my least favorite son. If you fail in this mission, I will make sure that you die a death that will be ten times more painful than the way Cush died. You understand me?"

Caine nodded and swallowed, "Yes, father. I promise that I will not fail. Yuri Gorski and his pals will all die. I swear it."

CHAPTER FOUR

The Cordell Hull Hospital had slowly returned to normalcy. All of the emergencies had been dealt with and the necessary surgeries to repair the injured were done. Now, the injured cadets and military personal had to recover.

Dean Harvard announced that the Tournament Team celebration would be delayed a week until the injured could participate.

There were funerals for the dead. The cadet graveyard had to be repaired and manicured to cover up the blood and repair the damaged headstones. The services for Cadet Tina Martinson drew the largest crowd. She had been well liked by all that knew her. Her family members were touched by the showing of support by the cadets that honored Tina.

Roy Starr's services drew the fewest attendees. His time in the Bragg Gang did little to endear himself to the other cadets. The Bragg Gang was present in total to pay their final respects for their friend. There were seventeen members of the Starr family weeping for him, including his father and his three wives.

Two days after the attack at the graveyard, Ella Ragnarsson woke up in a hospital bed and found she was secured by metallic binds on her wrists and ankles. She deduced that she had been taken to a second surgery to repair the wounds she suffered at the hands of Jen Staszko. How she arrived was a mystery to her as she had been unconscious after she had been stabbed by Staszko. She looked around her and noticed the IV's in her arm and other fluids that the medical staff were pumping into her. She reached down with her hand and felt the bandages in her abdominal area and concluded that she was lucky to be alive. She moved her tongue over her molar and discovered that her suicide capsule had been removed. Her eyes darted all over the room as she wondered whether or not Junior had escaped or died. She attempted to obtain information from the medical staff treating her, but none of them would answer her questions.

Ella considered her situation and desperately needed more information before she could devise a plan to escape. She surveyed her surroundings and she saw several plain clothes CID agents at her door and three uniformed Marines. The powers that be were taking no chances with her this time. Attorney Sean Collins had already visited her for a statement. Predictably, Ella refused to speak with him. The lawyer informed her that her brother, Junior, and all of his men were dead. Collins added that the charges against her were severe. One of the more serious charges facing her was murder and illegal possession of weapons. Collins told the woman that they had searched the ship after it had been legally seized by court order. During the search and inventory they found hundreds of illegal weapons. Ella showed no reaction to the lawyer, her face was stone cold and expressionless.

Collins also explained to her that they had located some nuclear devices on board the space craft, which were subject to the death penalty sanction under the laws of the United Nations. Ella Ragnarsson still refused to speak. Silently, she wished that she and Junior had just used the nuclear weapons and vaporized all of the people in Clovis City. Had they done so, Junior would still be alive and she would not be subject to charges that most likely would net her a death penalty verdict.

Collins had been calm in his short conversation with her. He made it clear that there would be no escape. Ella hoped her that her lawyer brother, Ellis, could work out some legal miracle for her. Collins was about to depart her hospital room since the woman was seemingly unwilling to say anything to him. As he approached the doorway he heard her speak to him.

"Your children will all die, Sean Collins."

Collins stopped walking and turned to face the woman and he glared at her for a few seconds. She was smiling at him as if she knew something that he did not.

"You sound sure of yourself, Ella. Unfortunately for you, my family is well protected."

"No one is safe from my father," she said with a tone of surety in her voice. "He will come for revenge against you and all of your friends and family. When you die, it will not be a quick death."

Collins shrugged, "We all die at some point. If you see your father, tell him that I look forward to meeting him in person so that we can find out which one of us is the better man."

"He will kill you."

Collins smiled back at her as if he was the one that had some knowledge that she did not. "When he arrives, we shall see who walks away."

Ella frowned as Collins walked out of her room, leaving her to wonder what it was that he meant by his parting comment.

CHAPTER FIVE

When a parent is informed of the death of one of their children, they react in many different ways. Some give out an emotional outburst, wailing and crying. Others ask the Gods why while others take the news with stunned disbelief. No parent contemplates out living their offspring. Dell Ragnarsson took the news of Junior's death with quiet calm. He learned of Junior's demise while resting in the command station area of his personal Super Raumschiff which was at a full stop on the outer reached of the New Edinburgh solar system. He ordered his ship's computer to download the satellite feeds of the event and watched the scene of his son being thrown into the Forbidden Region by Cadet Yuri Gorski.

Dell did not notice that his meager crew of five women left the command station to allow him privacy. While watching the recording of Junior's death over and over again, the assassin memorized Gorski's face.

"I will take my revenge on you, cadet. But not now. Revenge can wait."

Dell poured himself a sixteen ounce black metal cup of juice mixed with energy enhancements and drank it in a long, prolonged gulp. He had received several recorded satellite messages from his main employer, Alfred Rosenburg, II, demanding that he immediately contact him. Dell pondered the pompous demands of the man and could not wait for the date that he was eliminated. Dell waited on contacting him and decided that he would first check in on his co-conspirator, Magdalena Rosenburg, and find out whether she had completed her mission on Space Station Cy-7. Dell asked his ship computer to access the communication system and contact Magdalena.

After a wait of ten minutes, the computer alerted Dell that contact had been initiated and he smiled as the three dimensional view screen lit up with Magdalena's image. She smiled at him.

"I wanted to check in on your progress," Dell greeted her in his no nonsense manner. "Have you eliminated Penelope Rosenburg yet?"

"Dell, I am so sorry about your son. I am here for you if you need anything from me." Magdalena was not one to care for others. Although she was married to Alfred Rosenburg, II, she did not love the man and she despised all of his children save the ones that she had by him. Dell was the closest man that she had ever felt any romantic feelings for. Sex had always been a means to an end and her marriage to the Rosenburg patriarch had been a sham from the very beginning.

"Please do not mention what happened to my son. Although I appreciate your concern, we have business to attend to. Have you killed Penelope?"

"No, I am still a few minutes away from the space station. Once I arrive there, the girl has agreed to meet with me. I will wait til I get her in a vulnerable position and take her out. When she is out of the way, we will have only the stupid children to contend with."

"Keep me informed of your progress. I want to know when you have killed her."

"You will be the first one I contact."

"Fine. I look forward to hearing from you then. Computer, cease the communication."

Magdalena's image faded away and Dell sighed, wondering whether or not to contact Alfred Rosenburg, II, at that moment or to wait until after Penelope was removed.

Magdalena Rosenburg observed dozens of engineers and technicians in enviro-suits out in space, working on the hull breaches of Space Station Cy-7. She beamed with pride that Junior had been able to assault the station with precision strikes, hitting it in the exact locations necessary to cripple her defenses and eliminate the military presence on board. Of all the Ragnarsson assassins that had been killed in the past, she would miss Junior the most. He was the most professional and capable killer that she had ever worked with, even better than his father in many ways. She cleared security and landed her Raunschiff in the docking area of Space Station Cy-7.

Her lone intent was to begin the extermination of the Rosenburg family so that she could take over the Rosenburg Corporation as the widow of Alfred, II. Penelope Rosenburg was brilliant, especially when it came to quickly learning foreign languages and determining the financial weaknesses of business endeavors. Magdalena feared that if Penelope was left alive and learned of the demise of her siblings, that she would be the one that could formulate a plan of action to fight back. That fact alone demanded that Penelope die first.

Magdalena contacted Penelope using her ship's internal communication system. Penelope seemed happy to hear from Magdalena and promised that she would meet her at the docking area and get her a suite at the hotel. Magdalena concluded that her step-daughter suspected nothing. She hated that Penelope had to die, but with her death a new direction at the Rosenburg Corporation would begin, with Magdalena as the new Chairman of the Board of Directors.

She had a few last chores to finish before she revealed all that she knew. Penelope Rosenburg entered the lobby of her hotel and saw two men wearing black trench coats and hoods at the entrance waiting for her. She motioned with her left hand for the two men to follow her. She walked from the Baroness Hotel with the two men following behind her. She was filled with the solace that the two men would watch her back. They were created for that purpose and her safety as their top concern. The two mystery men had laser pistol weapons hidden under their coats in case the person that they were going to meet provided any resistance.

Penelope Rosenburg kept a brisk gait toward the Docking Bay of the space station. After she had been contacted by Magdalena Powers Rosenburg, one of her mothers, that she was arriving at the station and wanted to stay the night, Penelope selected the two men to accompany her. Technically, Magdalena Rosenburg was not Penelope's mother, but a step-mother. Penelope felt no love for the woman. Penelope knew that Magdalena was a dangerous woman, a ruthless killer, a trained sicario. Magdalena had probably killed hundreds by her own hand. That was the reason Penelope had decided to initiate her secret plan sooner than she had planned. Over the years, Penelope and her sister, Nicolette, had stolen technology from their father. Both Penelope and Nicolette were greatly disturbed by the way their father murdered their older brother, Cush. So the sisters developed a secret pact. They agreed to steal from their father and prepare for the day they might have to defend themselves.

Penelope had determined that day had arrived. She had contacted her sister, Doctor Nicolette Rosenburg to join her on the space station many months ago. Penelope and Nicolette had used the basement area of the Baroness Hotel to construct and design their means of defense, using stolen machinery from their father with the ability to make duplicate humans from DNA specimens. Nicolette had been the one to first suggest the idea to Penelope. About a year ago, Penelope decided that her sister was correct; they had to be prepared for the eventuality that their father could not be trusted any longer.

When the decision had been made to proceed, Penelope had the basement area of the Baroness Hotel cleared out and gave the space to Nicolette to begin the process of creating a small defense team. The procedure was highly technical and the majority of the machinery had been stolen from another alien race. The scientists and doctors working for the Sikorsky's and Rosenburg's were able to reproduce the structural designs and copy the engineering. The part that amazed Penelope was that they could grow, or create, a new person in a week from DNA sample to a live human in a week.

But the aging process was only one step since the new organism needed intelligence. Nicolette and other experts created new technological advancements of their own. They found a way to download a person's memories directly from the brain to a microchip. The download was a safe action since the donor human would lose no memory and suffer no ill effects. The stored data could be transferred to the brain of the scientifically created human, giving them all of the memories, abilities, desires, urges, hopes, dreams, values and knowledge of the pirated brain.

Nicolette had discovered that the Glorious Leader, Vladimir Sikorsky, had used this brain scan, also called the memory download, several times. She revealed to Penelope that there were several Vladimir Sikorsky's, as well as several copies of his children and grandchildren, populating the planets of the Earth Empire.

Over the span of one year, Nicolette had visited the Baroness Hotel numerous times and she worked on creating a small yet elite army of duplicate humans to protect and fight for her and Penelope. The sisters agreed they would not use the duplicated humans until it was time.

Penelope resolved in her mind that the time had come. She contacted her sister Nicolette and confided in her all of the past events and the sisters came to a meeting of the minds. They concurred that the reign of Alfred Rosenburg, II, should end. But, there was the issue of the hired killers, the Ragnarsson's. Fortunately, Yuri Gorski, Jen Staszko, Les Gillis and their friends had eliminated several of the Ragnarsson family for Penelope and Nicolette.

But the lead assassin, Dell Ragnarsson Senior was still alive. He was perhaps the single most dangerous person in the galaxy. He was cold, calculating, efficient, and highly intelligent. Penelope determined that the best way to get to Dell Ragnarsson was to cut him off at the knees. Eliminate his payers, kill off his followers and his small band of assassins, and he would be powerless.

Dell Ragnarsson's most important and influential benefactor was Magdalena Rosenburg. Nicolette had been given reliable information that their dear step-mother had been carrying out a long term love affair with Dell Ragnarsson. Magdalena had secretly funneled millions in Rosenburg Empire Dollars to Ragnarsson. If Magdalena were out of the picture, Ragnarsson would be crippled. His flow of money would end, at least temporarily, and with Magdalena gone, father Alfred, II, would be vulnerable to a coup.

With the plan designed by the two sisters, Nicolette awakened two of the copied humans and downloaded memories into the bodies. The two duplicated humans were men that would follow Penelope's directions given how they had died. Once the two men were ready to perform, Penelope dressed them up in trench coats and hoods, to conceal their identity from passers-by on the space station. The two men were instructed by Nicolette and Penelope that if they followed them, they could obtain revenge for how they had died. They could exact punishment on all of the people that had harmed them.

The two men agreed to support Penelope in her quest to bring justice to those that had caused harm to others.

Penelope led her two men out onto the large docking bay of Space Station Cy-7. There was a minor military presence in the area due to the majority of the soldiers being utilized for the repair effort. She saw the large Raumschiff belonging to Magdalena Rosenburg entering the Docking Bay and slowly come to a stop on the metal floor. Penelope motioned to her two escorts to flank her on the left and right as she stopped at the bottom of the Raumschiff.

She waited.

Penelope surveyed the rest of the docking bay. Most of the activity was from the military and engineering, delivering supplies to continue the repairs of the station. About fifty feet to her left was Charles Bennington and seven of his remaining CID officers. She had contacted Bennington hours earlier and invited him to meet her at the docking bay, telling him that she needed him to support her and arrest the passengers that exited the Raumschiff. He had reluctantly agreed after receiving further information and evidence from Penelope that the occupants to the arriving Raumschiff had ties to the killers that had ambushed the space station. Penelope promised she would explain everything to Bennington in more detail once the passengers of the space craft were safely in custody.

Magdalena Rosenburg stretched her legs. Her flight had been long and uneventful. Her crew had performed well. Magdalena had enjoyed her brief time with Dell Ragnarsson. She was looking forward to returning to her husband, Alfred, II, and thrusting a large steak knife into his heart. She was aware that her husband was insane. He was a loose end that needed to go. Magdalena had plans of her own. She had schemed with Ragnarsson in their time in bed together. She would kill her husband after arriving on the Rosenburg Ranch, take over the entire Territory and the Rosenburg Corporation and she would also kill her sister wives and all of their children. Penelope was one of the other children that would have to die in the next forty-eight hours. Regrettable, but necessary. No child of Alfred Rosenburg, II, could be left alive to challenge her authority.

Magdalena slowly walked down the plank of the Raumschiff as it lowered to the floor of the docking bay. She saw the ever prompt Penelope waiting for her. Magdalena had a laser pistol ready, hidden under her jacket with the controls on the highest power setting. She had planned it all out; she would hug her step-daughter and fire the weapon at point blank range. In a micro-second, Penelope would be vaporized. Magdalena slowly walked down the ramp of her vessel, not wanting to come across as to eager to greet the lovely Penelope.

Magdalena stepped foot onto the space station and she walked in the direction of Penelope. She watched as the younger woman nodded to her left and right. Magdalena frowned, wondering what the odd head gesture was about. She noticed, to her chagrin, that Penelope had come prepared, and had drawn a hand laser of her own. Magdalena stopped in her tracks, staring at the weapon pointing at her.

Magdalena laughed out loud and began clapping her hands together. "Well played, little one. You think you can play the game? Did your father order this?"

The two hooded men rushed Magdalena and took hold of her arms. They searched her thoroughly, finding three hand lasers, four knives, a few vials of poison, some stun darts and flame darts. Magdalena stood still, looking bored, as the two men used binding ties to secure her arms and legs.

"Not only am I going to play this game, I am going to win it. For years my siblings and I have endured your abusive treatment. We all stood by silently and watched as you helped butcher Cush. I will never forget your laugh, that evil sounding cackle that came from your mouth as

Cush died. I swore that one day I would make you pay for it. Today is the day I will make my oath a reality. You will never kill again." Penelope nodded at her two body guards as she spoke.

"You have no idea who you are fucking with, Penelope."

Bennington and his squad of CID detectives watched with interest. When the two strange men began removing weapons from the woman, Bennington ordered his detectives to move in. They ran to the side of Penelope Rosenburg.

"Why are you detaining this woman?" Bennington wanted to know.

Penelope looked into Bennington's eyes, "She is the one that ordered the deaths of Gorski and his friends. Ella and Junior Ragnarsson worked for her. The transport explosions, the attack on the space station, the recent attacks on the cadets living in Clovis City, are due to her directions."

Bennington was skeptical. He had always felt the Penelope Smith had been holding back information. "Can you prove those accusations? How would you know these things?"

"Because she is my step-mother," Penelope told him. "My name is not Penelope Smith. I am a Rosenburg. Smith is my cover name. Your men should search this ship of hers as I am certain that there will be dangerous mercenaries on board and you will find many illegal weapons. So be cautious."

"Why are you doing this?" Magdalena demanded of her step-daughter. She was livid that Penelope would willingly give out so much family information to a law enforcement officer. "Shut your mouth! You are a traitor! Wait until your father learns of this! Remember what happened to Cush! Your father will do the same to you! No, he will do worse!"

Bennington watched with amusement as Penelope rushed the bound woman and slapped her across the face. "This is Magdalena Powers Rosenburg. She is a mercenary for hire that has killed people in every solar system that humanity has ventured into. I have documentary proof of all I say. Her actions would warrant dozens of indictments."

Bennington pointed to the two hooded men, "And who are your guards?"

"Remove your hoods," Penelope instructed the two men.

The two men complied, pulling their hoods back. Bennington gasped when he saw Lieutenant Garrison and Drayton Love-Easter standing before him. Both alive and well.

"Holy crap!" Bennington's jaw dropped. "How in the name of the Stars are you two still alive?"

"We have much to discuss," Penelope told him.

"I would say so," Bennington was looking over the two men that had been killed. It was impossible, but yet, here they both were.

The replica of Garrison smiled and reached out with his right hand, "Good afternoon Mister Bennington. It is certainly good to see you again."

Bennington had a look of bewilderment on his face as the clone of Garrison shook his hand. Bennington looked over at the woman he had known as Penelope Smith, now revealed to be Penelope Rosenburg and she smiled at him.

"Come with us, Mister Bennington," Penelope said. "I have a business proposition for you and some of your investigators."

"What kind of business?" Bennington was still looking over Garrison and Love-Easter in awe.

"The kind of business that leads to fundamental change in how we all live." Penelope motioned with her head to the docking bay entrance to the main body of the space station. "Shall we?"

Bennington followed the woman and the two copies of Garrison and Love-Easter. He did not want to miss the explanation as to how this miracle had been accomplished.

CHAPTER SIX

The body bags had been collected and three days following the attack that had been labeled the "Blitzkrieg Invasion" the Clovis Academy student body and faculty had returned to normal. Colonel Nikolai Gorski had the unenviable task of informing General Welker on an emergency three dimensional communication of the death toll to the Marine and Army forces. Welker, who commanded the United Nations Marines from his headquarters on Sikorsky's Planet, went into a tirade with Gorski and threatened to fire him unless stability was restored to Clovis City. Gorski promised the General that his forces would be arresting all of those involved in the violence so that peace would be soon restored. Welker cursed and kicked his chair as if he were a three year old throwing a tantrum. Gorski kept his composure by constantly calling the General by his rank, or calling him "sir" and answering only yes and no to his demands.

Classes began on time that Monday morning without incident. Dean Golden Harvard and Admiral Seward had received a bad news report that needed to be addressed. The two men decided to call in the three top cadets for the Tournament Team to inform them that there would have to be a change in the selected cadets. The change had become necessary due to the injuries suffered by Michel Darcel Evart during his heroics on board the *Blitzkrieg*. Fortunately, Seward had a list of cadets that he felt would make suitable replacements. He hoped that the three cadets that they had summoned would be able to mutually decided on the replacement and build on that collaboration as a team building exercise.

It was an average Monday morning for planet New Edinburgh. The sun was rising over Clovis City, the red-orange sky was slowly reaching its' normal glow. There were no clouds in the sky and the wind was blowing slightly to the west. The air was cool. It was the perfect morning for a jog or a bicycle ride.

Construction crews were busy repairing the structural damage to the Great Protective Wall that surrounded Clovis City. The demolished statues of the Glorious Leader, Robert Andrews, Judy Andrews and Thomas DeMartino were being replaced with new stone carvings of the four heroes of the past wars. Extra snipers had been assigned to protect the laborers from Cawler attacks.

Cadet Eamon O'Grady received his summons via his holo-com device, requesting that he report immediately to the office of Dean Golden Harvard. O'Grady lived in the married cadets housing area with his wife, Ginger. She was still asleep as he slid out of their bed. The married couple had spent the evening at a nearby computer game competition and Ginger had finished in second place in the single elimination tournament of the holographic game called "Soldiers of Fortune." The game had been created twenty years ago and was now in its' seventh edition release. Ginger loved that particular game due to the realistic holographic images. The laser battles and explosions in the game gave the accuracy of presentation such that the person involved in the game would feel as if they were in the actual battle. She had told her husband that she could smell the burning bodies and feel the heat from the explosions. It was the most realistic of the computer games she had played. Since Ginger had made it to the final round, they had been up until two a.m.

O'Grady quietly dressed in his Class-C uniform and walked out of his home, careful to make as little noise as possible. He wanted his wife to get her sleep. He was happy that she had decided not to join the ranks of the military and pursue a career in the civil service instead. As a graduate in computer technology, Ginger O'Grady was allowed to choose military or civilian service. That option was only available to scientists, engineers, medical personnel and computer technicians. By order of the Glorious Leader, all of the other Academy graduates had to serve in the military ranks.

Once the doors of his quarters slid shut behind him, O'Grady took in a deep breath and he savored the fresh air. He began running double time the entire four kilometers to Harvard's office. On his run he saw Cadet Porfirio Cardenas ahead of him. The cadet pilot was also running to the meeting requested by Seward and Harvard.

"Hey! Wait up a second!" O'Grady called out to Cardenas.

Cardenas turned and saw who was beckoning for his attention. He noticed the large, muscular frame of O'Grady approaching. Cardenas immediately began jogging in place so that the other cadet could catch up to him. Cardenas had left his home just a few moments before. His wife, Freya, had been up getting their two children prepared for day care. Cardenas had a full day scheduled at the Academy and the evening was booked for his training for the Tournament. Freya Doernitz Cardenas had a twenty-four hour shift to work at the hospital. After cooking breakfast for his family, Cardenas dressed in his dark blue Class-C uniform and was out the door.

"You receive the summons, too?" Cardenas asked as he gave O'Grady a salute. O'Grady outranked Cardenas and it was still the custom to salute superior officers while outside. The cadet corps maintained that discipline. While in uniform and outdoors it was required to salute as a sign of respect to the rank, to the individual and to the cadet corps.

O'Grady returned the salute as he caught up to Cardenas and both men began running side by side. "Yes. I wonder if we were the only ones. Where is your brother-in-law, Jurgen?"

"He has a new girlfriend. We can't get the kid to leave her. They have spent the entire weekend together, including the last three nights." Cardenas smiled as he ran.

"She is very intelligent and pretty," O'Grady observed. "Very naive, as well. My wife knows Lila. They have spent some time together socially."

"Jurgen is inexperienced also," Cardenas told him. "At least in the ways of love and relationships. My wife and I had dinner with them the other night and Freya thinks they are already sleeping together."

"How would she know?"

"They were holding hands, cuddling, sneaking little kisses here and there," Cardenas recalled. "I have never seen Jurgen look at a woman the way he looks at her."

"I know her, not well, but enough to know she is a good person." O'Grady jumped over a gold colored cocker-spaniel that was running in his path. "She has her own slang terms. Kind of funny. She gets excited about things that most would consider no big deal."

Cardenas laughed at the comment, "Yes, she said Jurgen was 'super-hot' to Freya when asked why she liked him. Super-hot? Who talks like that?"

O'Grady laughed, "I think it is cute."

"Me too," Cardenas said, breathing a little heavier. "I hope it works out for the two of them. Jurgen got burned by one of the Harcourt women about a month ago. He wasn't in love with her or anything. He just did not understand the concept of people wanting multiple sex partners."

O'Grady looked at the tattoo of the cross on

Cardenas face. "If he shares your beliefs, then that would explain it, I mean Jurgen's feelings and his perceptions."

Cardenas noticed that O'Grady had been looking at the tattoo. "Are you a believer?"

O'Grady thought about the question for a moment, "I am not a follower of Pastor Love-Easter, if that is what you mean. I am Catholic. I come from a long line of Irish-Americans from Boston, Massachusetts. I was raised to follow the Papacy and all of the teachings from there."

Cardenas knew that Pastor Love-Easter was extremely caustic toward Catholicism. In many of his sermons, Love-Easter referred to Catholicism as a false religion, even though both ultimately believed in almost the same things. Cardenas never really understood the logic in the Christian faiths attacking one another.

"So your family is still in Boston?" Cardenas wanted to change the subject.

"Some are," O'Grady answered. "After the United States collapsed financially and was splintered into separate Territories, we became citizens of one of the North-East Territories. My family was always in law enforcement and firemen. But the new Nations that rose out of the ashes of the old United States, well, some of the laws that were passed were a bit draconian. So we started moving around. My father and mother are still in Boston. Most of my siblings have gotten away to other planets, just like me."

The two men continued jogging. They saw some other cadets out, running. The other cadets would salute them. O'Grady was the highest ranking cadet at Clovis Academy.   Lila Zapata woke up on her bed in her dormitory room. She felt the sunlight coming through her windows. She stretched her arms above her head and looked to the bed of Sophia DuBravac, which was empty. No doubt DuBravac had slept over at Les Gillis' dorm room.

Zapata looked to her other side and saw Jurgen

Doernitz asleep. She looked over his naked body. Over the weekend they had made love five times. She had received some instructions from DuBravac on what to do in the bed with a man. After the incident with the Blitzkrieg, DuBravac told Zapata to make it clear to Doernitz that she wanted to be with him. Zapata asked how and DuBravac taught her a few moves, like backing into the man and moving her buttocks against his sex organ. Zapata did just as she had been told and it worked. Doernitz was all over her and instinct took them both as they spent the rest of the evening enjoying each other's bodies and the passion of consummating their relationship.

Zapata never felt so strongly for any man in her life. She had only been with Doernitz for four days now and was certain that she was in love with him. He was smart, respected, fun to be with, laughed at her jokes, handsome and made her feel ways she never had when they made love.

"I never want to lose you," Zapata whispered, not wanting to wake the man up. She silently slipped out of bed and tip-toed to her shower. She wanted to talk to her friend Sophia DuBravac and ask her when two people should say the "L" word. Zapata did not want to scare Doernitz away. She had heard of men leaving women when they would tell them they were in love. She jumped in the shower and sang softly as she felt the warm water hit her body.

At about ten o'clock the previous night, Yuri Gorski had received his summons to appear before the Dean. Gorski had been asleep when the order was sent to him. He was trying to rest his muscles as he was still healing from his fight with Ragnarsson and the crash landing of the Blitzkrieg. Gorski's personal holo-com device started beeping at four in the morning. He sat up and checked the encrypted message which was a reminder from Seward of the time and location of the meeting.

Lying next to Gorski was Jen Staszko who was sound asleep. She had given Gorski a massage with some body oils that she explained would help relax his strained muscles. Gorski allowed her to do as she wished. The massage seemed to have helped as Gorski felt better. He did not feel as sore as he had the night before.

On the other bed were Drew Harrison and LaShondra Lewis. The beeping noise had not disturbed Harrison as he had drank a fifth of his favorite whiskey the night before and failed to fall asleep until the early hours of the morning. Lewis had one eye open and was watching as Gorski slid out of bed. Lewis was a light sleeper due to her military training. Any small sound such as a Holo-com chime or a closing door would cause her to wake up.

"It's okay," Gorski whispered to Lewis. "Go back to sleep."

Lewis nodded and closed her eye.

Gorski slid out of bed and made his way to the shower. After stepping into the area he commanded the computer to turn on cold water. He let the cold water fall over him. The cascade of the cool water woke him up. He used the dispenser on the wall and got some liquid soap in his hands. He lathered his body from head to toe before rinsing off. He grabbed his towel from the opposite wall and dried himself off. He hoped whatever the Dean and Seward wanted was worth getting up so early.

"Better get used to it, the military has your ass twenty-four hours a day and seven days a week," Gorski muttered to himself, remembering the admonishment he received from his father before joining the Academy.

Gorski dressed quickly into his cadet Class-C uniform. He combed his hair and looked at himself in the mirror. He still had bruises on his face from his fight against Ragnarsson. Gorski still felt sore and hoped that he would heal soon. He looked back over at Staszko when he walked out of the bathroom to the sleeping area of his dormitory room. She had not moved from her position on the bed and he did not have the heart to wake her as she put a high premium on her sleep time.

"I'll tell her you had to go," Lewis whispered to Gorski, as if reading his mind.

"Thank you," Gorski said as he left his dormitory room. He was happy for Harrison that Lewis was in his life. She was attractive, loyal, smart and seemed to really care for him. The only impediment to Harrison and Lewis maintaining any long term relationship would be her status as an enlisted Marine/Military Intelligence operative and Harrison receiving a commission as an officer upon graduation.

Such relationships were frowned upon in the Space Command. Even though sexual relations between enlisted soldiers and officers was commonplace, it was officially prohibited by the Code of Military Justice for officers to sleep with enlisted personnel.

Gorski walked quickly in the direction of the Administration Building which was only a kilometer away. Gorski noted that none of the other cadets were awake as he moved down the hallway to the stairwell. He ran down stairs and was out on the paved walkway in seconds. He took a deep breath of the fresh air. For a Monday, the weather sure seemed promising. He began his kilometer long walk to see the Dean of the Academy.

CHAPTER SEVEN

After concluding his communication with Alfred Rosenburg, II, Dell Ragnarsson had ordered his on board computer to set course for planet Semiramis. The elder assassin had received notification of the death of his son by way of the Satellite System News Service and had watched the image of his son falling to his death from the safety of the Great Protective Wall. The news reporter announced that Junior had "fallen to his death." The elder Ragnarsson knew from other sources that report was not true.

His son had been thrown to his death by cadet Yuri Gorski. Dell Ragnarsson learned that tidbit of information from his other son, Ellis, as well as the original recordings that he had retrieved from the satellites.

Although angered by the death of his son, Ragnarsson understood it was a risk that all in their field takes. He quashed his rushing feeling for revenge, to find this Yuri Gorski and kill him. In a way, the older assassin admired the Gorski kid. Ragnarsson had personally trained and taught his son to be one of the best hand to hand fighters in the galaxy and yet a senior cadet was able to defeat his son. Ragnarsson felt that fate would allow him to cross the path of Yuri Gorski one day. When that day came, Ragnarsson would take his vengeance. Perhaps Gorski would be a father one day and Ragnarsson could kill Gorski's child as a form of poetic justice. But the idea of revenge would have to wait and Ragnarsson would mourn the loss of his son in his own manner. He would have plenty of time to deal with Gorski. Ragnarsson had other issues to deal with.

He had been ordered, not requested, not asked, but ordered by Alfred Rosenburg, II, to get to planet Semiramis immediately. Ragnarsson had become a wealthy man thanks to the work he received from the Rosenburg clan. But in the mind of the assassin, the time had come for a change. He felt he could better manage the Rosenburg Ranch as Alfred Rosenburg, II, had gotten too careless and was prone to take too many risks. That kind of carelessness brought down empires and Ragnarsson did not want to go down with a sinking ship.

Further, Ragnarsson blamed Rosenburg for the death of his son. It had been the Rosenburgs that started the debacle with Cadet Yuri Gorski in the first place. Now, because Alfred Rosenburg had a desire for revenge for the death of his son, Ragnarsson had lost many of his own children. Ella and Emma were most likely dead or incarcerated. His youngest son, Ivar, was also in a jail somewhere and Junior, was certainly dead. The Rosenburgs had lost all objectivity in the matter. They had ordered unacceptable risks to be taken and the results had been negative. Too many innocents were murdered while the actual targets were all still alive.

Ragnarsson had made plans with Magdalena Rosenburg to take over the Ranch on New Edinburgh which would require wiping out the entire Rosenburg clan, including Alfred's brother and his children. If Ragnarsson was in charge of the Ranch, he could control the Rosenburg Corporation, which was worth trillions of Empire Dollars. But for now, Ragnarsson had to pretend to be the loyal lackey. He fired up the engines of his space craft and ordered his computer to make haste to Semiramis. He hoped that the Rosenburgs had something interesting planned for him there.

Hot coffee was waiting for the three cadets when

they arrived at Dean Harvard's offices. The Dean and Admiral Seward were already waiting for the men. Yuri Gorski was the last to arrive. He poured himself a twenty ounce cup without any cream or sugar and walked into the large conference room. He saw Dean Harvard seated at the head of the conference table. To his right was Admiral Seward. To his left were Eamon O'Grady and Porfirio Cardenas. They were all laughing about some joke that someone had told.

Seward looked exhausted. He had been up for almost two days without sleep and his uniform was wrinkled and his hair had not been combed. His eyes had dark rings forming under them. He had been the one given the unenviable responsibility to inform the families of the deceased of their loss. The Martinson family took the loss of their daughter Tina the hardest. The Starr family had taken the news of the death of their son quietly. Seward believed that their lack of tears demonstrated they had expected that Roy Starr was destined to die young. It was a silent acceptance of the inevitable.

Seward and the others saw Gorski enter the room.

"So glad you could join us," O'Grady said sarcastically. Due to their differences, O'Grady and Gorski did not like each other very much.

Gorski sat down next to Cardenas.

"Good, we are all here," Harvard said with a touch of annoyance in his voice. "I had to get this cleared up immediately since the training begins today. One of your team cannot participate in the Tournament."

"Who?" O'Grady wanted to know.

"Michel Darcel Evart," Seward responded. "In the crash landing on the Blitzkrieg he suffered whiplash and blunt force trauma to the head. Doctor Harding refuses to clear him for any kind of strenuous activity for the next few months. Poor guy is going to be in a neck brace for a month."

Gorski cursed under his breath. He knew that Evart was so excited about being chosen to compete on the Tournament team. Evart did a heroic act when he climbed on the escaping ship with Gorski and because Evart was willing to take such a risk he would miss the chance to be on the team. Gorski felt terrible for Evart. Gorski recalled his childhood when his father was always telling him: "No good deed goes unpunished." That statement would be appropriate for Gorski's friend in this case.

"Has Michel been told?" Gorski asked breaking the silence.

"Yes, I told him yesterday," Seward affirmed. "The question now is who to replace Evart with. It has to be a senior cadet and has to be a pilot. The unfortunate reality is that the best senior pilots are already on the Team."

"Blossom Li," Cardenas said, trying to be helpful. Li was very talented and worked well with others. Cardenas thought she would be a natural fit for the Team.

"No good," Seward waived his left arm, dismissing the idea. "She is a junior. I thought of her and Jack Harcourt, but he is also a year back. I have gone through the roster of pilots that are seniors. None of them really stand out. They are all capable, but I wanted this Team and all of the members, to be extraordinary. The best of the best."

Dean Harvard looked at O'Grady, "Eamon, do you have any recommendations?"

"Well, I think Gorski and Cardenas might be in a better position to address that sir. I am not a pilot, never even studied the introductory course. There may be one or two of the cadet seniors that they could recommend."

The Dean looked over at Gorski and Cardenas and raised his eyebrows. "Well?"

"There was one," Gorski spoke up. "He helped out in downing the Blitzkrieg. He never really calls attention to himself. His name is Pierre Zerbe. He followed Marco and

Mary without question when he was asked to helped out. He even thought to warn the snipers on the Protective Wall to get to safety."

"I know him," Cardenas chimed in. "He is always on time. He never disobeys orders and he will lend a hand when needed. I think he just keeps to himself. He never really interacts with any of the other cadets."

Seward was thinking over the suggestion as the cadets spoke. He had also considered Zerbe but hesitated due to the young lad's reputation for being involved in kinky sexual activities.

There was silence for a few minutes.

"All right," Seward finally announced, decided that he would overlook Zerbe's sexual activities. "I will invite Zerbe to be a part of the Team. If he refuses, do you have any alternates?"

"You could try Juana Flores," Cardenas suggested. "She is a senior and seems pretty steady."

"Thank you for your input," Seward told the group. "Remember, weight training and conditioning at four and pilots training at six p.m. Be there."

"Yes sir," O'Grady said.

"Dismissed," Seward stood up and walked out of the room, followed by Dean Harvard. Seward was ready for bed. He could feel the fatigue taking over his body.

"I feel horrible for Michel," Cardenas said. "My wife was treating him and she told me Evart kept asking her if the stiffness in his neck would keep him from going with us to the Tournament. He really wanted to go."

"He said the same things to me," Gorski told them. "He really wanted to be a part of this. I need to go see him. He will be very hurt by the bad news."

"Yes, I am sure he will be," O'Grady said. "But from my perspective this is a good thing. One less Gorski Gang member on the team. Too bad I am still stuck with you, Gorski, and your friends Harrison and Andolini. You all are troublemakers. They should never have selected any of you in the first place."

"Good," Gorski sipped his coffee and set his cup on the table. "Honesty. I like that. You know the feeling is mutual Eamon. I don't like you either. I think you are a stuffy and pretentious jerk. You are an ass kisser first class."

"And you have no respect for rules, regulations or common decency," O'Grady pointed his right index finger angrily in Gorski's direction. "Everyone here was shocked when Love-Easter was killed. You know what? I wasn't. My only question was why it took so long before one of you got into some danger you could not get out of!"

"You son of a bitch!" Gorski jumped to his feet, his chair sliding backwards against the wall. Gorski's fists were balled up, ready for a fight. "You were not there! Dray did not ask for what happened! I should kick your ass right now!"

"Bring it on!" O'Grady stood up, clenching his fists. He had been waiting for the chance to teach Gorski a lesson by beating some sense into him.

"Guys!" Cardenas stood up in between them, holding his arms out to keep the two men at bay. "Calm down! We have to work together on this! Stop it!"

Gorski and O'Grady were glaring at one another. Each one waiting for the other to make the first move.

After about a tension filled minute, O'Grady relaxed his arms. "All right, Porfirio, you are right. We should be working together. I still dislike you, Gorski, and your friends. I hope that you all prove me wrong about my perceptions on this Tournament."

"When this is all over," Gorski said, letting his guard down, "you will thank the Stars that my friends and I were there with you."

"You better not screw it up," O'Grady warned. "Or I will personally kick your Russian ass. You read me,

Mister?"

"I am Russian-Estonian," Gorski corrected him. "And when this is over, I will kick your ass, regardless of how things go. So, truce until we get back?" Gorski held out his hand to shake with O'Grady, a sign of ending the hostilities.

O'Grady grunted and reached out with his hand and shook Gorski's. Their eyes were locked and Cardenas felt he could cut the tension between them with a knife.

"That is better," Cardenas said to the two cadets. In his mind, he was wondering just how this was going to work when the team leader and the second in command despised each other. I must have faith, Cardenas told himself. There had to be a reason they were all brought together for this Team. Have faith.

Pierre Zerbe was asleep at one of the local brothels located on the south side of Clovis City. Prostitution was legal in the Eight Solar Systems and was regulated and taxed by the local governments as a revenue source to fund local projects. Zerbe was an average looking man and in decent shape due to his Academy physical training. He had girl friends in the past and each time he got involved they wanted a commitment which prematurely ended the interaction. Zerbe preferred sex without commitment so the women would come and go. He also liked to engage in what was considered by the majority as abnormal sex. He enjoyed sex with multiple women at the same time and found pleasure and pain mixed together pleasurable. He enjoyed being hit, whipped and spanked. And he paid for his sexual desires whenever his family on Earth would deposit money into his trust account.

Zerbe woke up that Monday morning next to a female Kotek, a cat-human hybrid. Zerbe lusted for the raw animal aspect of having sex with the female Kotek that he only knew as "Mara." Zerbe was certain Mara was not her real name. Mara was five feet tall, covered with orange and white fur. Her body was basically shaped like a human, with the exceptions of the cat's eyes, claws, fur, fangs and cat ears. Her hind legs were also shaped like a cat's legs. He had sought out a female Kotek after he had a brief sexual relationship with a pilot named Reesha Bedrosian that had been killed in an unfortunate transport explosion. Reesha had made a strong impression on Zerbe and he longed to find a woman that could give him the same pleasure she had.

Zerbe had wanted to find one woman that would share his sex drive. Zerbe had always heard of women that desired sex as he did. Zerbe just seemed to never meet one. Thus, he had to resort to the brothels and would rent two, three even four women at a time to satisfy his lust.

Zerbe woke up when his holo-com device began beeping. He sat up and accessed his satellite mail. It was from Admiral Seward. Zerbe speculated that he must be in some kind of trouble. He looked for his clothes. His body had scratches, mostly on his back and chest, from Mara's claws. Zerbe loved the feel of pain while making love and was proud of the cuts in his body.

Zerbe dressed quickly. He had to get back to his dormitory room, shower and dress before meeting the Admiral. It must be something important for the Admiral to call on him so early in the morning. Zerbe hoped it had nothing to do with his deviant sexual activities.

Sean Collins and his legal team were diligently working on solutions to the news that the arrest warrants for Alfred Rosenburg, II, could not be served. Collins learned that although he had been warned to remain at the Rosenburg Ranch pending the legal motions to be ruled on by the judge, Alfred Rosenburg, II, fled. The Marines on the scene reported that no space faring vessels had lifted off from the port in the last week. It was as if the head of the Rosenburg family had vanished into thin air.

Upon receiving the bad news, Collins asked for a

meeting with the Rosenburg family lawyers. To Collins' surprise, Ellis Ragnarsson and Alfred Rosenburg, III, were willing to talk. Collins waited for the lawyers to arrive at the United Nations Administrative Building at the mutually agreed time. He ordered his staff to prepare the main legal conference room with coffee, pastries, colas, juices and fruit trays. As he waited for the legal teams to assemble, his office secretary buzzed him on his intercom.

"Mr. Collins, you have someone on the computer broadcast wishing to speak with you. She says it is urgent."

"Who is she?" Collins poured himself a cup of coffee.

"A Penelope Rosenburg. She says she has information for you and wants to arrange a face to face meeting with you."

A Rosenburg contacting him was not something he had expected. It was odd that she would want to meet with the lead lawyer prosecuting the family. That was nothing short of unusual. Plus, it was not wise for a potential defendant in a criminal matter to contact an opposing lawyer. Collins was intrigued. "Put her through three dimensional viewer."

Collins waited as the center of his office brightened with the image of the attractive and desirable image of Penelope Rosenburg. She was wearing a dark colored pants suit with black boots. Her long hair was pulled back into a twisty and tied off over her left shoulder. She smiled when she saw the image of Sean Collins appear before her.

"Mr. Collins? My name is Penelope Rosenburg," She announced. "I am in my office at the Baroness Hotel located on Space Station Cy-7. Here with me are my two sisters, Nicolette and Kristin. Both of them are licensed medical professionals. Also here is the director of the Criminal Investigation Division, Mr. Bennington."

Nicolette and Kristin bowed their heads slightly as they were introduced. Both of the women were wearing light blue hospital uniforms.

Bennington was wearing Class C fatigues with black boots. He had a web belt with a hand laser attached to it and several knives and thermite grenades.

"And what do I owe the pleasure of this unexpected call?" Collins walked around the image of the three attractive sisters and Bennington. He saw two men with hoods on in the background. The faces of the two men were completely obscured. He wondered why this Penelope Rosenburg had not introduced the mystery men.

"I am contacting you to help you and the innocent people of planet New Edinburgh and the rest of the Eight Solar Systems." Penelope told him. "Do not worry, counselor, this communication is being blocked from any MI Hacking by some of the most advanced technology of humanity. My two sisters and I are the only three Rosenburg's with any form of a conscience. We are tired of watching our family harm others and we wish to help put an end to the killings and the slave trade."

"Go on, I am interested." Collins stated as he wondered if he was going to be set up with false information from this woman. Her entire family were criminals and by now were fully aware that Collins and his staff were working overtime to bring them all to justice. He sat down in his chair and took hold of his ever present coffee cup.

Penelope walked around the room as she spoke, "Mr. Collins, I hear you are a good and honorable man. Humanity will soon be in need of men and women such as you. Very soon. A war is coming and many will die. Possibly millions or even billions. Things will get much worse before they get better."

"War?" Alarmed by the word, Collins sat up in his chair. "Who said anything about a war?"

"I did," Penelope said boldly. "You see, you have little knowledge of the extent of how high your investigation could go. Powerful people are involved, Mr. Collins. Extremely powerful. I do not want to go into details now, but rest assured that I have raised a small army, with the help of my sisters and some alien technology that was found on planet New Edinburgh over twenty years ago. Sir, the reason my family wanted the lands that now are known as Rosenburg Ranch is because an ancient alien civilization once lived there. They all died off when some organisms began to kill them."

She paused, drinking a glass of water. "They tried to escape death, sending ships out into the cosmos. One of your friends, Marine Corps Colonel Gorski, lost his wife because of those creatures. She was ordered to board one of those ships and was attacked by those beings. The Space Command had to kill Melita Gorski and her platoon because the ship they boarded had technology that the leadership on Sikorsky's Planet wanted to keep secret."

"What kind of technology?" Collins was now hooked on her story. The lawyer never fully understood why the Space Command ordered that Derelict ship blown up, when Lieutenant Melita Gorski and her Marines had been winning the battle. If the Rosenburg woman was telling the truth, then the order to blow up the ship made sense. The Sikorsky's were covering up something that they did not wish the rest of humanity to learn about. Collins knew there always had to be another explanation. "Can I bring in Colonel Gorski to hear this?"

"No!" Penelope responded quickly. "He would want retribution, which would get him killed. We need you, Colonel Gorski and men and women of good will like you, alive. When the smoke clears, you and men like Colonel Gorski will be needed to chart a new direction for humanity. Trust me; it would be best to wait on revealing the truth to him. The technology found on Rosenburg's Ranch was legion. One of the discoveries was an intricate underground transportation system, built by this alien race called the Danaraja's. These advanced beings also had many amazing new complex medical machines, deadly weaponry and space ship designs. My deceased brother, Cush Rosenburg, helped in cracking the codes, so to speak, on how to use the alien medical systems. Another of my brothers named David was able to begin translating the alien language into our native tongue.

"My sisters here, Nicolette and Kristin, learned how to use the machinery that Cush worked so diligently on. We have stolen some of the Danaraja items from our family. That is how we were able to build a small army. Mr. Collins, I said a war is coming and I meant it. My family kills people without question. I witnessed children, little children, suffering. They were turned into orphans by my family and then enslaved. Their parents were either murdered or used for sport. And for what? To maintain power for the few? We are going to stop the madness. History records that many politicians on ancient earth would campaign for election saying elect me for fundamental change and then they would never deliver. I will deliver. In one years' time, the United Nations form of government will change for the better."

"Wait!" Collins shook his head. "How are you going to change the government?" His voice was full of disbelief. Collins had expected a Rosenburg to give him false information. This woman was speaking of insurrection against her own family.

"We are going to cut off the head of the snake," Penelope assured him. "You probably are thinking you should indict me for treason. You would be correct for that belief for I do speak of treason. I speak of outright insurrection. But I also speak of basic human rights, Mr. Collins. The right to live, the right to freedom, the right to free elections, the right to free speech and the right to restrict government interference in one's life. I intend to start a new direction so your children and grandchildren can live in a world of true freedom.

"I wanted you to know that I am sending you a gift. It will be delivered to you in person by a man that you will immediately recognize. He will be arriving soon at your office. You need him and he needs you. He will have information on a diskette that you will find very useful. The disk will be road map for your prosecution against my family members. The man that will bring you this evidence will need you to take him in and go undercover to see a cadet named Yesenia Guevara. With all the tragedy and death of the last few months, I wanted to at least give someone a happy future. You will be startled when you see him. He will tell you all you need to do to help out."

"Wait!" Collins stood up, sensing the woman was ready to end her conversation. "Your other brother, Alfred, the lawyer. How much does he know?"

Penelope paused before answering him, thinking. To protect Collins she would have to reveal that her brother was a full participant in the ugly events of the past few months. "He knows everything. Do not trust him and especially watch out for his law partner, Ellis Ragnarsson. Ragnarsson is a murderer. He will cut your throat in a second and smile while doing it. Watch your back Mr. Collins. Both of them knew that my father was going to flee the jurisdiction. Both know of the slave trade and both knew of the assassination attempts on the cadets at the Academy. They are evil. The information I am sending to you will assist you in indicting and prosecuting Ellis and Alfred as well."

"Typical defense lawyers, lying to the court." Collins mumbled. "What specifically did they know?"

"Not only did Ellis know of the conspiracy, he participated in it. He personally killed Mister Kharkov, the patsy, in the Love-Easter murder. Ellis was paid well by my father for that assassination. My brother Alfred was in the loop in all of the discussions and plans. In the disk I am sending you it is all there for your review. You should arrest them both now before they kill anyone else."

"When you begin your... war, how will I know? How will I know which side to be on?"

"You will know, Mister Collins. Oh, before I forget, the CID director here is going with us. You will need a replacement."

"You are in on this, Charles?" Collins addressed Bennington.

"Yes sir. These three Rosenburg women have convinced me that we need to begin to alter the status quo. I am sorry to abandon my post. But I can be of better service to humanity following the three ladies here. I have children, some are officers in the service and I want them to have a better world. So, I bid you farewell, my friend," Bennington said with emotion in his voice. He and Collins had known each other for several years. Most of their interaction had been conferring on criminal investigations and trial preparation. Bennington had gained a deep respect for the work ethic that Collins brought to each case. It was rare in the era that they lived in to find a prosecutor that would not succumb to bribery, threats or corruption. Collins was a man of ethics and honesty and Bennington would miss interacting with him. Due to his many friendships and acquaintances, Bennington's decision to join a mutiny had not been an easy one.

"I could contact Colonel Gorski and have him stop all of you," Collins told them.

"Yes, you could." Penelope responded softly. "But you won't. You will remain quiet because you are a man of higher ethics. You are a man that has values and deep in your heart, you know change is needed. Do not trust my lawyer brother. If you can find a way to arrest him and Ragnarsson, do it."

"So, this is good bye?" Collins asked.

"No, Mr. Collins. It is, shall we say, til we meet

again? If I survive this, I will return and voluntarily accept whatever punishment you and the courts deem appropriate for my past actions. Please take care of my gift. Use the data he brings to you. I wish you and all of your friends and family the best."

Collins asked her to give him more information as he watched as her image faded away. The communication was over. She promised him that a war is coming and Collins wondered what kind of war. She was so vague but the tone of her voice made it seem like she envisioned some kind of violent rebellion. He sipped his coffee as he wondered why her name never came up in his vast investigation. This Penelope Rosenburg seemed to be in possession of information that Collins had not yet uncovered. He continued to drink his coffee and speculated as to what events could have occurred to cause this woman to betray her family.

Collins had been widowed now for some time and had been raising all of his children as a single parent. He had not allowed himself the luxury of dating women as his work and parenting requirements left him with precious little spare time. But the woman named Penelope Rosenburg was fascinating to Collins. He realized he found her to be both desirable and mysterious. He hoped to one day meet her in person.

Collins' secretary walked into his office and interrupted his thoughts. "Sir, the lawyers are here to see you."

Collins stood up and he ate a breath mint as he walked toward his conference room. He looked forward to the excuses he would hear from the two defense lawyers. Collins hoped that the additional information the Rosenburg woman was sending to him would prove to be relevant in his attempt to prosecute the conspiracy. Collins had already gathered enough information against Ellis Ragnarsson and Alfred Rosenburg, III, from the interrogations of the captured assassins. Collins was prepared to take the two lawyers into custody and prosecute them to the fullest extent of the law.

At the space station, Penelope Rosenburg and her two sisters rushed to the docking bay. They were followed by Charles Bennington and fifty men, all wearing grey outfits with hoods covering their faces. They quickly boarded a Super Raumschiff which was almost double the size of a normal Raumschiff. The name painted on the side of the vessel was "The Peacemaker."

The Rosenburg women stepped up onto the loading ramp and were followed by their entourage. Penelope moved up the stairs to the second level then to the third and then climbed up the metal ladder to the two seat pilots section. She sat in the pilot's seat and put on a pair of earphones that had a tear drop extension for her to speak into to give orders to the rest of the crew. She cleared her large space craft for departure with the sparse security on Space Station Cy-7. She began flipping switches on the control panels above her and on the flight command desk before her.

The path she had chosen would be dangerous. At first her immediate family would begin to hunt her and they would most certainly put a large price on her head. The much larger risk for her and her crew was when they began to challenge the rest of the Sikorsky's and the Royal Family. Penelope was one of them and she was aware that there were over several hundred thousand Royal descendants out there in the many solar systems controlled by the Glorious Leader. They would all want her dead when her war against them began in earnest.

"Good bye, Cy-7 and farewell Baroness Hotel," Penelope whispered to herself. She fought back the urge to cry. She had made arrangements for the safety of all of the children she had cared for after the attack. She would miss the young orphans more than anything. The fear in the eyes of those children had made a lasting impression on her. She had left the children in the charge of Captain Tierney who was in temporary command of the military operations on the space station. She had no doubt that Tierney would do right by all of the orphans.

She had also taken precautions so that no one would ever know she had departed the space station. Penelope had her sister, Nicolette, create a Replicant of her. Anyone visiting the Baroness Hotel would find a Penelope Smith in charge. Unfortunately, there would be a huge difference between the real Penelope Rosenburg and the copy. The Replicant was a duplicate of Penelope Rosenburg as she looked before all of her corrective surgery. It would be easy for someone that knew her to tell the difference between the real Penelope Rosenburg and the Replicant. Since the duplication process was based on blood DNA, there was not any way to make a Penelope Rosenburg as she appeared now.

The only mystery left behind by Penelope Rosenburg and her two sisters was the decapitated female body in room number 222. Penelope had used a large sword and chopped off the head of Magdalena Rosenburg. She committed that violent act after Nicolette Rosenburg used a small sword to rupture Magdelana Rosenburg's heart. The body would be found by the hotel cleaning crew the following day, long after the perpetrators had gotten away. The head would not be found as Penelope had sent it in a box, via transport mail, to her father on the Rosenburg Ranch. The message was simple, prepare to die. Death by decapitation was considered the most insulting way to kill a fellow human. Sending the head to a specific person was a way of communicating that the recipient of the head would be the next to die. But for the Royal Family, decapitation was the form of death most feared.

Penelope smiled as Drayton Love-Easter #21 sat next to her in the co-pilot seat. All of the Replicants of

Love-Easter and Garrison understood the mission and agreed to participate. Penelope and her two sisters gave the twenty-five Love-Easter's and twenty-five Garrison's a choice. They could join the revolution or go out and live their lives. They all elected to fight against the Glorious Leader. And all were prepared to begin that battle.

All save one.

Nicolette Rosenburg had convinced one of the duplicates that they named Drayton Love-Easter #2 to go to the planet New Edinburgh and seek out the lawyer Sean Collins. His mission was to be the messenger for the necessary information Collins would need to break the power of the Rosenburg's forever. Drayton Love-Easter #2 had been given a second mission, which was to assume the life of the original Drayton Love-Easter. He was to graduate from the Academy, marry Yesenia Guevara and raise a family with her. The clone of Love-Easter was willing to take on that mission as he had inherited all of the brain patterns and emotions of the original. The love that Drayton Love-Easter felt for Yesenia Guevara had been transferred to all of the Replicants with his DNA and memories. One would go to regain the lost relationship with Guevara while the remaining Love-Easter Replicants would go to fight a war to protect Guevara from a distance.

After the way Penelope Rosenburg had failed to do the right thing in the past, it was the least that she felt she could do.

In addition to the Love-Easter and Garrison clones, Nicolette had created fifty clones of Cush Rosenburg and imprinted the memories of Love-Easter in each of their brains. In addition, Nicolette used the alien machinery to expand the mental abilities of each of those fifty clones of Cush and downloaded dozens of terabytes of information regarding military tactics, past wars and history.

Sean Collins walked into the large conference room to find Alfred Rosenburg, III, and Ellis Ragnarsson waiting for him. Both of the defense lawyers had black leather bound briefcases sitting next to their feet. They both were in black business suits, with open collared white dress shirts. They were both sampling from the food Collins' staff had prepared for them. Collins motioned for his five associate lawyers to follow him inside the conference area. They all sat down around the rectangular cherry wood table in pre-designated seats.

Ellis was certain that Collins would dismiss the indictments against the Rosenburg family. He had filed dozens of pre-trial motions and many more requests for dismissals with prejudice. Ragnarsson had dealt with government lawyers before and found the majority of them to be lazy and unmotivated.

Collins smiled pleasantly at the opposing lawyers and placed his hands on the table, left on top of the right. "I think that you know my associates Miss Li, Miss Zhanders, Miss Fowlkes, Miss Ward and Mister Goldsmith. Thank you gentlemen for coming today."

Ellis smiled back at him, "Our pleasure. We are hoping that we can work this out amicably. The Rosenburg family is expecting us to leave this meeting with dismissals on all of the charges pled. We would also like to express our belief that a written apology is appropriate for the slander and libel your office has committed against the good family name of Rosenburg."

Collins, still smiling, looked to his lawyers seated to his left and his right. Collins had been around long enough to know when a defense lawyer was just too stupid for their own good, or when they were out right liars. Collins knew Ragnarsson and Rosenburg were lying to him. Collins knew it from the very first time he met them in court. After the truth serum interrogations of Junior, Ivar and Ella Ragnarsson had been completed, Collins learned that the two lawyers before him were willing participants in the entire criminal enterprise scheme.

"Well, then I am very sorry that this meeting may very well be a waste of your time," Collins began. "You must understand that when evidence is received in this office, it may take some time to collate it, categorize it and to determine the relevance of each piece of evidence. It is not easy when we deal with the potential of prosecuting multiple defendants in a conspiracy. I am a cautious man and I had no intention of pursuing any case against the Rosenburg family unless there was solid evidence to back up such a charge."

"And you have shown us nothing to substantiate such charge!" Alfred Rosenburg, III, cut Collins off. "My family wants justice."

Collins, still smiling, drank some of his coffee and pondered that statement. "The family of Tina Martinson deserves justice, counselor. The families of Roy Starr and Li Mingjuan deserves justice. The family of Drayton Love-Easter deserves it as well. What do I tell the families of Bill Hodges and Starr and Martinson if I dismiss my case? I do not have it within me to consider it. How about the families of the Transport that was blown up from the space station? What about the families of all that died on the space station attack? What do I tell them?"

"You have to do justice!" Ellis bellowed.

"Justice?" Collins leaned forward as he spoke the word. He saw that the squad of Marines he requested from Colonel Gorski the night before were arriving just in time. Collins had orchestrated the whole charade of luring the two lawyers over to the United Nations Building for the purpose of arresting them. It was much safer to arrest the two men in the building as opposed to attempting to take them into custody elsewhere. The two men were about to learn that their reign of death was coming to an end.

"What justice was there when your sister Ella was rescued by your brother Junior in which a judge a prosecutor and several men and women died? What about all of the men and women that served the Space Command that were murdered in that cowardly attack on Cy-7? Where is the justice for all of the children that are now orphaned?"

"Now wait a minute! We did not come over here to discuss those matters!" Alfred Rosenburg, III, complained. "You have not charged for those things. Junior is dead as are his three henchmen. Ella is incarcerated and you have not even charged her yet. Those acts have nothing to do with the indictments against the Rosenburg family. You are out of line."

"I think not," Collins stood up and waived in the Marines. "Ellis Ragnarsson, Alfred Rosenburg, III, you are both under arrest for over one hundred felony conspiracy counts to commit murder. You are both under arrest for over one hundred felony murders that you assisted in. May I remind both of you gentlemen that each felony murder charge is punishable by death. I will be seeking the death penalty."

"What the hell!" Ellis screamed as he struggled with two female Marines that had grabbed his arms and cuffed him.

Alfred Rosenburg, III, tried to run. He did not get far. Two of the other Marines tackled and hand cuffed Rosenburg. Both men were thoroughly searched and the Marines found laser pistols on each of the lawyers.

"Tag the weapons," Collins instructed the Marines. "That is another felony, bringing deadly weapons into a United Nations building. Tsk. Tsk. As lawyers, you should have known better than that. I hope the two of you hire really good lawyers. You will need all the help you can get because I will personally present your case to the jury. And you should know that I never lose."

Ellis began screaming obscenities as he was dragged away. Rosenburg was silent as the Marines took him to be transported to jail. Collins had played them. Alfred Rosenburg, III, had thought a government lawyer would not be as smart an adversary as Collins had proven to be. Collins had lured them into a trap.

"Well done," Collins told his staff. He turned to the Marines that were still present. "There is an executive assistant in the building named Rebecca Rosenburg. Please find her and arrest her for conspiracy."

The Marines nodded in unison and departed the conference room. Collins smiled at his staff and noted that they were all stunned by the events. Collins had not warned them as he was uncertain if any of them were working under the table for the Rosenburg family. Collins stood and calmly walked out of the room, leaving his speechless staff behind. Collins wondered if the laser pistols that were on the persons of Ragnarsson and Rosenburg were meant to be used on him and his staff. The answer to that question did not matter to him. The only important fact was that one by one, the rats were being trapped.

CHAPTER EIGHT

The simulator room was empty when Jürgen Doernitz and Profirio Cardenas arrived at fifteen minutes til six p.m. They were early and eager to begin to learn the terrain of the Moon over Semiramis, or the "Blood Moon" as it had been called. They sat down in the theater where they were going to be shown the entire surface, over and over again. Admiral Seward instructed them to memorize every inch, as it would be an advantage over the other three teams of cadets.

"We haven't seen you around the house lately," Cardenas said to his brother-in-law.

Doernitz nodded and looked at his feet. He was not sure how Cardenas would take it if he knew that his little brother-in-law was living in sin.

"I am not going to judge you," Cardenas told him. "Your sister and I, well, we were active before we got married. It is natural."

Doernitz looked up at Cardenas, "She makes me feel so wonderful. I can't explain it. I think about her all the time. I want to be with her every minute. She makes me laugh. It, feels so, so right. Like I was meant to find her and be with her. Does that make sense?"

Cardenas smiled. Young Jurgen was in love. "It makes all the sense in the world. When I first met your sister, I never would have believed that such a smart, humorous and lovely woman would ever find me interesting. But she did and all the things you are feeling, I still feel them for Freya. The first time she kissed me, I thought I had died and gone to heaven."

"Yes!" Doernitz nodded. "Is it wrong for me to want Lila so badly, I mean to always be with her?"

"No, it is good that you feel that for her," Cardenas slapped his hand on Doernitz' leg. "I hope she feels the same for you. She is a good girl. I can tell she is smarter than almost everyone. You just be good to her and I think she will do right by you as well."

"So, then it's okay when I stay the night with her and don't come home?"

Cardenas laughed, "Jurgen, I am your brother-in-law, not your father and if I was your father, I would tell you it is fine for you to be with Lila. I think the two of you are good for each other. Whoever set you up with her was a genius."

"Sophia DuBravac did it," Doernitz said. "She told me Lila and I should be friends."

"And so you two should be friends," Cardenas stood up. "Always remember the qualities in Lila that first got your attention. Never forget the things that first attracted you. If you do that, you will be friends and lovers for life."

Doernitz stood up as he noticed Marco Andolini, Mary Lincoln, Yuri Gorski and Pierre Zerbe entering the auditorium.

"For life?" Doernitz repeated. "What about after this life? I could not go through eternity without her."

"Have faith, Jurgen. You need to have faith," Cardenas said, patting him on the back.

"Have faith in what?" Marco asked as he hugged Cardenas and them Doernitz.

"Faith in the Lord," Cardenas told him.

Gorski sat down and motioned for the others to do the same. "We can talk religion and politics on our long flight to Semiramis. Right now, I have a date waiting so let's start our terrain movies."

The room went dark and the large floor to ceiling and wall to wall screen lit up with a picture of the Moon of Semiramis. Also known as the Blood Moon.

The camera zoomed in on the light side of the moon. The six cadet pilots watched in silence as the camera showed the surface, the orange dust, the chlorine green gas over the top four to five feet of the surface, small geysers erupting green rocks and chlorine gas onto the lunar surface. The cadets observed many canals that might have had water or some other form of liquid river in them centuries ago. There was a baritone voiced narrator throughout the two hour long film. The night's lesson was to go over the canal system of the moon. Their locations on the grid maps were gone over ad nauseam.

Near one of the empty 'rivers' was a five story facility and about as wide as one hundred yards. It was completely covered in a form of dark blue metal. No windows were visible to the viewers. The building had five smoke stacks that were each varying in height from fifty feet to one hundred feet high. The narrator stated those were for oxygen to be released out onto the surface of the moon. In addition there were two dishes on the grounds nearby the building that seemed to be for some form of electro-magnetic purpose. The narrator indicated it had been one of the dozen terra-forming constructions built on the moon. The function was to produce an atmosphere that would make possible the retention of oxygen.

The camera zoomed inside the five floor terra-forming building. It was still operational and producing oxygen. The building had cryo-sleep tubes, quarters for engineers and technicians, a small eating area with freeze-dried food and plenty of frozen water. The dozen terra-forming buildings were attached under the ground by manmade catacombs. The catacombs were nicknamed the "catacombs of despair" as there was a collapse many years ago and the chlorine gas was able to billow in which killed twenty engineers and fourteen computer technicians from the exposure. There were light rail trains in the underground so that the workers of the terra-forming effort could go from facility to facility quickly.

The narrator named the rivers to the cadets and once again reviewed them. Gorski stretched his arms over his head. The narrator changed the subject matter and the screen showed the cadets four other structures which were the home bases of the cadet teams. They had been built sixteen years ago after the oxygen levels began to increase. Each structure was two floors high and had a basement. The outside had four small space faring fighter ships from the Fenster Corporation. Each of the small craft was painted in the colors of the Academy. The film concentrated on the Clovis Academy facility. The upper level had some beds, computers, food processing stations, communications and satellite capability. The lower level had a dozen sleeping rooms and a medical area for up to seven patients.

The film ended and the lights in the auditorium came back on.

"And this is the first night," Zerbe said as he stretched his arms and legs. "We have to watch these films for the next two weeks? I need a drink."

"That sounds like a really good idea," Lincoln agreed as she stood to stretch her legs. "Why would we even need to know about the catacombs of despair? We just need to get in there and capture as many of the other cadets as possible."

"Well, those catacombs could be used as a hiding place," Cardenas observed. "If one team wanted to sneak up on us, they could use the underground light rail to go to a station close to us and then sneak attack. I see it as useful information."

"If one of the teams hides in those buildings, we

would have to search them all," Marco seemed to agree with Cardenas. "But, now its' time for drinks at O'Malley's. Jurgen, you are with us. Sophia is taking Lila there."

Doernitz was on his feet when he heard Lila's name. "Let's go."

Cardenas waived to the group as he walked toward the door, "You all have a good time. I have to go get the children from day care. Stay out of trouble."

The others respected Cardenas for the fact that he was a great pilot and a good father. Some would say he was a far better father and husband than a pilot.

"I'll catch up to you," Gorski told the group as they began walking out of the auditorium. He waited until he was alone. "Computer, can you replay the presentation for me?"

"Yes," the computer replied.

"Please proceed," Gorski ordered and sat back down. "Please show me the architectural designs of the individual cadet Headquarters again."

Marco had his arm around Lincoln's waist as they walked through streets, lit up by the solar powered lamps. Doernitz and Zerbe were keeping up with them.

"In two weeks we leave for the moon?" Zerbe asked with excitement in his voice. "We can win this, right?"

"We will win," Lincoln said with conviction. "Les, Julia, Drew, Yuri and Eamon will have a plan to beat the other teams. You can bet on that."

"Never in my wildest dreams did I think I would be chosen for this," Zerbe told them.

The four continued their walk toward the bar O'Malley's. In the distance they could see a crowd of about one hundred cadets at the entrance of the large multi-level bar. The other cadets had changed into civilian clothing and were ready to party and dance.

Les Gillis and Julia Steiner were already on the fifth

floor at O'Malley's. Gillis had down loaded and printed out color photographs of the opposing cadet headquarters. He had large, poster size color prints of each the three opposing team's locations. Gillis and Steiner had black markers and were pinpointing the entrances of each.

As they were working on their maps and pictures, Eamon O'Grady and Drew Harrison arrived. Harrison sat down next to Steiner and gave her a weak smile. Gillis watched Steiner to see if being so close to her former lover was a distraction. If there was a problem, Steiner seemed to show no reaction. Gillis hoped the past feeling between Harrison and Steiner would not be an issue on the flight to the moon and the time they would spend together during the competition.

"So what have you come up with?" O'Grady inquired as he sat down.

"Each of the headquarters have a front and back entrance," Steiner reported. "The roof tops can be accessed as well. The roof has an entrance in the middle, like a hatch. See here?" She was pointing to one of Gillis' color prints that focused on the roof.

"So," Gillis continued, "Julia and I feel that we can create diversions for the occupants on the outside of their headquarters. We use flares. We have a team dropped on the roof top by one of our small fighter ships to enter the HQ by stealth and then take out the enemy from the inside. Any of the opposing cadets that attempt to flee will be picked off by the rest of us that are waiting on the outside at the two entrances."

"How do we get people there on a small fighter?" O'Grady wanted to know. "Only two people can fit. That means a pilot and one other person."

"We use the tow cables," Steiner said simply. "Those cables can hold tons. We can put say three of us on a cable and slide down to the roof. They would never know we were there until it was much too late."

O'Grady scratched his head, "I like it. But once we do this trick on one set of cadets, the other two teams will know our tactic. And how would the flares distract them? They would expect some attempt at diversion like that."

"Not if we use the natural elements to our advantage," Gillis said.

"How do you plan on doing that?" Harrison chimed in.

"The planet surface is full of chlorine gas," Gillis explained as the waitress arrived with a pitcher of beer and began pouring it for them. "I saw that our headquarters have some turpentine and ammonia bottles."

"And how does that help us?" O'Grady asked as he drank from his ice cold glass of beer.

"Chlorine gas will react explosively with turpentine and ammonia," Steiner told him. "We create a diversion in the form of a nice big explosion. They run out to investigate and our three cadets drop in from the roof to capture whoever stayed behind."

Harrison drank from his beer. He noticed a look of disapproval from Steiner.

"You see, no past tournament team has ever used the natural elements to their advantage," Gillis told them. "We will. I read up on each and every past competition. I was surprised no one else thought of it. Chlorine gas has been used as an offensive weapon. In the history of warfare, it has been used in many ways since all the way back to 1915 in the First World War. The French soldiers in Ypres, Belgium got attacked with it by the German army. It is horrible stuff. It causes tearing in the eyes, vomiting, blurred vision, difficulty breathing and nausea."

"And it is heavier than oxygen," Steiner explained. "That is why you see the olive-green clouds on the surface of the moon but about four to five feet above the surface we have oxygen. Constant exposure to chlorine gas can cause pulmonary edema in two to four hours. Horrible way to die. You have fluid buildup in your lungs. It can be quite the weapon, as Les pointed out.”

“And in World War One, over a million men died due to the gas warfare,” Gillis added.

“A million three hundred thousand,” Steiner corrected him.

“But we are not allowed to take offensive weapons with us,” O’Grady reminded them of the rules of the Tournament.

“And we are not,” Steiner shot back at him. “We are using what is there already. We bring nothing new to the equation. It is there to be exploited.”

O’Grady laughed and drank some more, “Remind me to never get the two of you pissed off at me. I feel sorry for anyone that gets in the cross hairs of team Steiner/Gillis.”

Gillis drank some of his beer and then looked his team leader in the eye. “So, you approve?”

“I absolutely approve,” O’Grady said. “And speaking of approval, my drop dead beautiful wife just walked in with some equally appealing women.”

Harrison, Gillis and Steiner followed O’Grady’s gaze to see Ginger Collins O’Grady walking toward them with Sophia DuBravac, Lila Zapata, Bao Mingjuan and Cara Perez Guerrero following. All five of the women were dressed provocatively. Gillis and O’Grady rose to their feet and greeted their other halves with hugs and kisses.

They all sat down at the table to share in the food and drinks. Gillis motioned for the waitress to bring more glasses and another pitcher of beer.

DuBravac sat on Gillis’ lap and playfully bit his ear, “Miss me?”

“All day long,” Gillis told her.

Steiner and Harrison began rolling up the color prints so they would be out of the way. It was time to relax.

“We still need a few other plans,” Harrison

whispered to Steiner, hoping to get her attention.

"True," Steiner agreed. "But enough work, it is time to relax some."

LaShondra Lewis had been standing next to the bar watching over Harrison. She observed the interaction between Steiner and Harrison and felt a tinge of jealousy. Harrison had told Lewis that his relationship with Steiner had ended, but the look in his eyes said otherwise. Lewis decided she needed to defend her turf and walked over to join the table. She sat next to Harrison and smiled at Steiner. Steiner smiled back at Lewis and introduced herself. The move placated Lewis to some extent. As Lewis viewed the rest of the interaction of the group she was able to conclude that Steiner was no longer interested in Harrison. Steiner hardly spoke five words to Harrison the entire evening.

Zapata was sitting close to DuBravac and Gillis, "Ask him, Sophia. Please. Ask him. Ask him."

"Ask me what?" Gillis wanted to know.

DuBravac ran her fingers through Gillis' hair, "She wants to know whether it is too soon to tell a man she is in love with him. She is afraid of scaring him off."

Gillis looked at Zapata and saw that her eyes were wide, like a deer in the headlights. "Well, the answer is not simple."

Zapata's facial expression showed disappointment. She was hoping for a clear cut answer.

"Look," Gillis told her as the new pitcher of beer arrived. "You are worried about how Jurgen will react if you tell him how you feel?"

"Yes. I don't want to ruin it. I love him so much, but I can't lose him. I just can't." Zapata sounded like a scared high school girl.

"Look, I am not Jurgen." Gillis told her. "But, speaking for myself, I love to hear Sophia tell me she loves me."

"You better," DuBravac interjected.

"Now Jurgen is not me," Gillis continued. "Let me watch the way he looks at you when he walks in. I will give you a thumbs up if I think he is ready, or a thumbs down if he is not. Deal?"

"You can tell by the way he looks at me?" Zapata was not sold.

"More than the way he looks at you. The way he greets you. The whole package." Gillis kissed DuBravac on the lips. "If he loves you, he will come in here and will have eyes only for you. What I mean is, he will walk around looking for you specifically. And then the way he acts when he finds you, very critical."

"Okay," Zapata was shaking her head up and down. "I will wait for the thumbs."

Dominic Andolini came bursting through the doors with Harumi Shigeta in his arms. He carried her to the table and was singing an Italian love song to her. Everyone in the bar began clapping for his performance. The Andolini brothers always seemed to have a flair for the dramatic entrances. Following behind them was the regular Gorski Gang members, April Mejia, the Rhinehard brothers, Dirk Fenster, Jack Harcourt and Arch Frazier.

O'Grady grimaced slightly when he saw them all approaching. It was no secret that O'Grady despised the Gorski Gang members. O'Grady could not shake his opinion that the friends of Yuri Gorski disrespected the uniform and the cadet corps. He had promised his wife he would behave so he remained silent and said nothing. He concentrated his attention on his wife by asking her how her day had been.

Dominic was hugging everyone, as was his customary way of greeting others.

Klaus sat down next to Mejia, his arms were still wrapped in the plastic castes. The couple shared smiles, laughing together.

Marco and Lincoln arrived a few minutes later. Following behind them were Zerbe and Doernitz.

Zapata watched Doernitz eyes, as Gillis instructed. DuBravac and Gillis were silently observing the interaction so that he could give Zapata an accurate assessment. They could see Doernitz looking around the bar and then his eyes met Zapata's. They watched Doernitz smile and walk to her as fast as he could. Zapata and Doernitz embraced like lovers that had been separated for too long. Their kiss was passionate and he held Zapata tight in his arms.

Gillis looked into DuBravac's eyes, "I'd say the boy is in love."

"I would say you are correct," DuBravac was smiling. "Just call me the little miracle working matchmaker. I knew those two should be together."

Gillis waited until Zapata looked over at him. He gave her a thumbs up. Zapata smiled back at him. Hand in hand, Zapata and Doernitz joined the table.

Yuri Gorski continued to have the auditorium computer play, replay and replay again certain segments of the film. He had sent Jen Staszko a text from his Holo-com letting her know where he was. She had joined him and was standing behind Gorski, massaging his neck and shoulders. Gorski loved it when she gave him massages. It relaxed him. In the back of the auditorium was Gorski's undercover shadow, Sergeant First Class Mark Lund. Even though the Ragnarsson assassins were seemingly eliminated, Gorski's father was taking no chances. When the Marines and the Military Intelligence were able to incarcerate the rest of the Rosenburg's, Colonel Gorski would end the shadow coverage for his son and his friends.

"What are you looking for?" Staszko whispered in his ear.

"I think I found something that might give us a tactical advantage," Gorski said, leaning his head back and looking up at her. "There are four cadet headquarters on the

Moon of Semiramis. There are four judge's towers and twelve terra-forming buildings. Connecting the twelve terra-forming buildings are these catacombs." Gorski was pointing at the screen.

"I follow," Staszko was nodding.

"Well, the catacombs seem to run underneath the four cadet headquarters. There is no entrance from the catacombs to the cadet buildings." Gorski stroked his chin with his right hand. "Why did they put the cadet headquarters over the man-made tunnels with no access point? That makes no sense."

"How do you plan on using this information?"

"I think we could dig upwards, from the tunnels and into the opposing cadet's headquarters. They would never expect us." Gorski told her. "Computer, print the schematics of the catacombs. Also, give me a print out for the exact coordinates where the catacombs intersect the cadet headquarters."

"Printing," the computer answered.

"You are pretty observant," Staszko kissed him on the cheek. "Are you ready?"

"Yes, let me get the prints and we can go join the others at O'Malley's." Gorski stood up. "I am craving a filet mignon cooked medium rare with steak fries, sautéed mushrooms and some red wine. You alright? You seem tense."

"Steak sounds fantastic. I am craving the O'Malley's cabbage soup."

"And you are dodging my question, Jen. What's wrong?"

Staszko looked away from him and paused before making eye contact with him again. "Yuri, I love you more than anything. But I am worried about you."

"Why are you worried about me?"

Staszko took his hands in hers, "You killed a man. Yes, he was an assassin and yes he had it coming. But I know what it is like, the guilt, the sick feeling in the gut, the self-doubt and the constant internal turmoil with the ongoing question as to whether you did the right thing. I am here for you, Yuri. I am willing to listen. You need to talk it out. Holding in the feelings that you must have cannot be kept inside. You have me and dozens of friends that will listen to you."

Gorski nodded, "I appreciate your concern for me, Jen. I really do. But I do not feel guilty about killing Ragnarsson at all. Like you pointed out, he had it coming. When I threw him to his death, I knew that it was the right thing to do. I do not regret it. But, if I do start feeling some of the things you just mentioned, you will be the one I confide in. Okay?"

She smiled, "I just wanted you to know that I am here for you."

"I know and I love you for it," Gorski pointed toward the exit. "Now come on. We have a warm meal waiting for us and a lot of friends that want to spend some quality time in our presence."

Staszko followed Gorski toward the printers in the back of the auditorium.

Gorski began collecting the color copies that the computer made for him. He turned to Staszko and kissed her. "I want to show these to Arch. Some of these rock and metallic formations look odd to me. Perhaps he can make some sense of it."

"It's good to have a friend that likes studying rocks," Staszko said of Frazier and helped Gorski roll up the large prints.

Within twenty minutes, Staszko and Gorski arrived at O'Malley's. Lund was behind them, shadowing their every move. Lund watched as the couple shared hugs with the Andolini brothers and the majority of the other cadets on the fifth floor of the popular restaurant-bar. Lund noticed that there were several musicians on a stage against the wall, tuning their electric and acoustic guitars, an electric bass guitar, a harp, flutes, accordions, banjos, a synthesized keyboard machine, a piano, three electric violins, a saxophone, bouzoukis, mandolins and fiddles. There was a drum set in the very back of the stage. Lund deduced that there was going to be live music of some sort.

Gorski handed his print outs to O'Grady. "You might want to take a look at these. The catacombs under the moon's surface might be used as an offensive threat."

"How so?" O'Grady took the color prints and spread them out on his table.

His wife, Ginger, was looking over the computer generated photographs and nodded. "Honey, look. The tunnels go underneath these buildings here, but there are no entrances from the tunnel to the building. That is very odd."

O'Grady grunted, "I see it. What are you proposing, Gorski?"

"That we tunnel under the buildings of our adversaries." Gorski pointed to the Headquarters of the opposing cadets. "There seems to be only about five feet of distance between the top of the catacomb and the bottom of the headquarters."

"And how do we cut through the rock of the moon and the sheet rock, metal and concrete of the cadet headquarters?" O'Grady more demanded than asked. "That could take a whole day with the proper tools. What if the other cadets hear what we are doing? Our team would be sitting ducks. I don't see this as a workable plan at all."

"I disagree," Ginger O'Grady shook her head at her husband. "I think we need a geologist to let us know what kind of impediments exist, what kind of rock formations are in the way and what kind of tools are necessary to dig underneath. I am not saying it is easy, but it could work."

Gorski was a bit surprised that the elder Collins sibling, Ginger, would defend him. He recalled that Ginger never approved of his involvement with the younger sister,

Siobhan. "Yes, I was planning on letting my friend Arch Frazier look it over. He is a rock lover. I think he could give us some insight on those issues."

"Do it," O'Grady ordered. "But not tonight. Relax. Have a beer on me."

Gorski and Staszko both were taken aback by O'Grady's offer. Gorski had told Staszko what had happened earlier in the day when he nearly ended up in a fist fight with O'Grady.

"Thank you," Staszko said for Gorski. She took a glass and poured from one of the pitchers on the table. "Where are Les and Sophia?"

"They went dancing downstairs," Ginger told them. "Jurgen, Lila, Julia and my brother Cormac are there as well."

"If you go find them, tell Cormac and Les that the band is about to play," O'Grady added. The campus of cadets knew that the O'Malley family performed for one hour each evening, singing old Irish tunes. For some of the numbers, the band would invite the customers to join them on stage and sing along. Cormac Collins and Gillis were decent musicians and enjoyed singing with the group.

Gorski and Staszko took their beers and left the O'Grady's to find Gillis and DuBravac on the lower levels. Gorski noticed that Harrison was at the bar with Lewis sharing drinks with Dominic Andolini and Harumi Shigeta. Gorski raised his glass to the four and they responded with the same gesture.

Pierre Zerbe watched as Gorski and Staszko walked toward the stairs. Zerbe felt a bit out of place since he was not a part of the Collins group and he was never a Gorski Gang member. In fact, for a very short time in his first year at the Academy, Zerbe had been a member of the Bragg Gang. But here he was, drinking with both of the cadet clicks. Zerbe had the urge to leave and find a woman to spend the night with. That was his plan until Cara Perez

Guerrero approached him. She wrapped her arms around his left arm and pushed her slender body against him.

"So, Cadet Zerbe, you are on the team?" She whispered in his ear. She had been eying Zerbe ever since he had arrived at O'Malley's. Perez Guerrero had slept with many men to include cadets, random pilots and two of her professors. She enjoyed sex and liked having many partners. Most of the other female cadets referred to her as the "Resident Nympho" due to her past sexual exploits. Perez-Guerrero cared little how others perceived her as she wanted to experience life and do the things she enjoyed. Picking up men for a night of passion was a hobby to her. She wanted to become involved with one of the tournament team members. The problem was that all of the men seemed to have a woman already. Except Zerbe. She decided she wanted to be with the man and Cara Perez Guerrero had never been one to shy away from a challenge.

Zerbe felt her athletic body against his arm. There seemed to be no body fat on the woman at all and her light brown skin was soft to the touch. He looked at her beautiful face and into her light brown eyes. He had always found her attractive. As fellow cadet pilots, he saw her often but they never really said more than ten words to each other. Zerbe had believed Perez Guerrero was one of those very attractive women that were out of his league. Due to his own lack of confidence, Zerbe had never attempted to pursue Perez Guerrero.

"Yes, I was put on the team," Zerbe finally answered.

"Let's get some drinks," Perez Guerrero suggested to him.

"Yes, great idea." Zerbe was more than agreeable.

She led Zerbe to the bar, holding his arm and rubbing her body against his. Perez Guerrero wanted to make sure Zerbe would be hers for the night.

Gorski and Staszko located Gillis and the others on

the third floor of O'Malley's. They watched as DuBravac was dancing seductively against Gillis to the throbbing beat of the music. Steiner and her boyfriend, Cormac Collins, were also on the dance floor. Gorski noticed that some of the Bragg faction were there as well. Bret Bragg and James Cobb were sharing a pitcher of beer with some of the other group members. Juanito Calderon was at one of the bars purchasing a round of tequila shots. Reynita Calderon was on the dance floor with some other cadet that Gorski had never seen before. Bragg made an obscene gesture in the direction of Gorski and Staszko. Gorski ignored him. He did not want to get into any fights. The tournament team was a good addition to his resume and Gorski did not want to let a fist fight jeopardize the opportunity.

Gillis saw Gorski and Staszko across the dance floor. DuBravac was grinding her buttocks in Gillis' crotch area and turning to face him and kiss him.

"I love it when you grind against me," Gillis told her.

DuBravac laughed and kissed him. "I will grind against you every night and day because I love you."

"I love you too," Gillis kissed her back.

Gorski and Staszko began dancing to the musical mixture of rock and disco. They moved through the crowd together to get close to Gillis and DuBravac.

Staszko bumped into Zapata, who was dancing with Doernitz. Zapata saw it was Staszko that had bumped into her and hugged her. "Wow! Everyone is here tonight!"

"Almost," Staszko answered. She was amazed how young Zapata could find everything so eventful. She was the most excitable person Staszko had ever met. "How do you like your new boyfriend?" Staszko pointed to Doernitz.

"I love him!" Zapata said loudly.

"Well, if you want, we know some other men that would like to meet you," Staszko said, just to see the reaction.

"No way!" Zapata looked at Staszko as if she were crazy. "Why would I do that?"

Staszko laughed, "Just checking, Lila. Have a good time."

Staszko and Gorski made their way to the center of the dance floor where they met Gillis and DuBravac. The four exchanged hugs.

"Eamon said the band is getting ready to play!" Gorski yelled over the music.

"I love listening to Les sing!" DuBravac stopped dancing and was in Gillis' arms. "Let's go! I haven't heard you sing in months!"

Gillis smiled and waived to cadet Cormac Collins and Julia Steiner. Collins shrugged at Gillis as if to ask "What?" Gillis pointed up at the ceiling. Collins and Steiner knew immediately that was Gillis' sign that the band was ready to play. Steiner enjoyed hearing the Collins family and Gillis sing with the O'Malley family band. The majority of the lyrics generally seemed to have a humorous twist to it, with the exception of one of the tunes, "Loch Lomond" which Steiner thought was a romantic tragedy, almost like a "Romeo and Juliet" twist. The three couples made their way through the crowd. DuBravac grabbed Zapata by the arm and motioned for her and Doernitz to follow.

Bret Bragg and James Cobb watched the four couples leaving. Bragg was still angry at the death of his older brother. Cobb just wanted to beat Doernitz to a pulp and steal Zapata away from him. Some of the other Bragg members were wanting some retribution for the Gorski's getting their friend Roy Starr killed. Bragg nodded to the other end of the bar where two dozen cadet Bragg gang members were sitting. They stood, all knowing what was going to happen.

"Tonight, the Gorski Gang is going down," Cobb said to Bragg. Johann LeSkaysner grunted in agreement.

"Damn right," Bragg agreed.

Bragg led his group toward the stairs. Unknown to them, Lund and Preston were watching. They were both still protecting Gillis and Gorski. Although Zhao and Stewart were at the hospital watching over Michel Evart and Elektra Papanikolaou, Lund was confident that the two of them could diffuse the pending confrontation with a few stun shots. The cadets in the rival gang would wilt like dying flower petals. Lund and Preston followed at a safe distance, all the way to the fifth floor.

Pierre Zerbe and Cara Perez Guerrero decided to skip out and go to her dormitory room for the night. She was glad he was in an agreeable mood to spend the rest of the evening with her. As they were walking on to the stair case, they passed Gorski and Staszko. Zerbe told them good night and then took Perez Guerrero by the hand and led her out of O'Malley's.

DuBravac whispered to Gillis when she saw Zerbe with the other woman. "That Cara, she sure gets around."

"Are you jealous that she has so many men?" Gillis asked.

DuBravac laughed, "Are you kidding? With your sex drive? My mother never told me a man was capable of doing the things you do to me."

Gillis put an arm around her, "That's because I am so much in lust for you. I can't get enough."

"Well, Cara has talked to the rest of us girls, bragging about her men," DuBravac said. "She said she had three men in one night, all taking turns with her. She claimed it was the greatest night of her life. I hope Pierre knows what he is getting himself into. Cara is a wild one."

Gillis thought to himself for a moment, "I think Pierre will rise to the challenge."

DuBravac laughed.

They made it to the fifth floor and found the band was already playing. The O'Malley family of Clovis City was one of the largest in sheer numbers. There were seven brothers on stage, playing various instruments. Four of the sisters were there as well, playing along. A cousin was playing the drums and an aunt and uncle were singing. At the bar there were another twelve cousins of the O'Malley family clapping to the music. The other seven sisters and twelve cousins were working as bar tenders or waitresses at the popular bar.

Gillis and Cadet Sean Collins gave each other a high five.

"Tabhair dom do La'mh!" Collins said happily to Gillis.

"What?" Zapata asked, not understanding Collins.

"White, Orange and Green," Gillis translated for them. "The name of the song is "White, Orange and Green".

Zapata listened for a moment. "It sounds beautiful."

Cormac was suddenly grabbed away from Steiner by his younger brother, Liam. The two Collins boys ran to the stage and began singing with the band. Within moments, their sisters Ginger and Siobhan were on the stage. The band began playing "Green Sleeves" and the Collins siblings sang along. They were waiting for O'Grady and Gillis to join them.

"You know the words?" Zapata asked Gillis.

"Lila, my man has the best voice this side of the Solar System." DuBravac told her.

"Yes, they sing the songs of my homeland here," Gillis explained to Zapata. "I'll join them on the stage for the next number."

They all followed Gorski and Staszko to the table and sat down. Gillis drank a sip of dark beer.

"You going on stage?" Gorski knew the answer before he asked the question. Gillis always would join the band. Gorski had noticed that the Collins siblings seemed to not know all the words to some of the songs. Gillis had explained there was the music from the old country and then there were songs from the Irish immigrants in old New York and Boston. Similar sentiments in the music, but different. Gillis, hailing from the Emerald Isle and the Collins family from Boston, there were differences between them. Gillis' accent was the most noticeable. But they shared a common loyalty, a bond, that Gorski admired and respected. Gillis had told Gorski once that the Irish had suffered much oppression and starvation in their history. They had to fight just to survive the next day. That common history was important to them. It somehow defined them.

As the song "Green Sleeves" was coming to an end, Gillis kissed DuBravac and darted up onto the stage. The O'Malley siblings hugged him and gave him a guitar.

"You never told me Les could play music," Zapata said to DuBravac.

"My man has many talents," DuBravac whispered to her.

Gillis snapped his fingers and the band began playing "Rising Of The Moon." Gillis played his guitar along with the O'Malley family. Gillis stepped to the microphone and began singing:

"And come tell me Sean O'Farrell tell me why you hurry so

"Husha buachaill hush and listen and his cheeks were all a glow

"I bare orders from the captain get you ready quick and soon

"For the pikes must be together by the rising of the moon!"

The Collins siblings, O'Grady and O'Malleys joined in with Gillis, singing the chorus:

"By the rising of the moon, by the rising of the moon

"For the pikes must be together by the rising of the moon!"

Gillis began singing the next stanza. Steiner leaned over to DuBravac. "They could change the words, given where the tournament team is going."

"By the Rising of the Blood Moon?" DuBravac read Steiner's mind.

Gorski found he was thinking the same thing. He hoped that the team would have a safe time on the Moon of Semiramis.

Bret Bragg, James Cobb, Johann LeSkaysner, Juanito Calderon and their followers felt the time to strike was now. The two dozen cadets began to move toward Gorski's table. They never made it.

Lund, Preston and Lewis were ready with stun batons. The stun batons were three feet long metal rods that emitted electrical charges. The dose was not lethal, just enough to render the recipient unconscious. The three recognized Bragg and Cobb as the leaders and dropped them both by touching the end of the stun baton to their torsos.

Bragg and Cobb collapsed to the floor without incident. Cobb urinated in his pants when he felt the surge of electricity surge through him. Lewis stunned a third cadet. Their followers hesitated and then demonstrated some intellectual capacity by raising their arms up in a sign of surrender and slowly backed away, moving toward the stairs to avoid being stunned. The gang members left Bragg and the other two on the floor.

Gillis, O'Grady, the Collins and the O'Malley siblings did not miss a beat. Lund heard some words he liked from the singers: "Death to every foe and traitor! Whistle out the marching tune! And hurrah, me boys, for freedom, tis the rising of the moon!"

CHAPTER NINE

Obtaining an audience with the Glorious Leader was no easy task. Vladimir Sikorsky was protected by legions of armed soldiers, diplomats and high ranking officers that were all daughters and sons of his. He had several battalions of Marines surrounding his large one hundred thirty-five floor tower home with snipers on the rooftops and anti-aircraft laser canons mounted all around the radius of the structure. Naturally, Sikorsky officially stated his tower was one hundred floors high, in reality it was much higher. He used many floors for secret hiding places, all fully stocked with provisions, in case of insurrection. With all of the stocked provisions and food, Sikorsky could hide out for months in his tower. All of the commanders on Sikorsky's Planet were his children, grand-children, great grandchildren and great great grand-children. He trusted only his family to guard him. Over the past two centuries the Glorious Leader had survived several assassination attempts due to his family members thwarting the attempts.

Alfred Rosenburg, II, was one of Vladimir Sikorsky's descendants. The Rosenburg portion of the Sikorsky regime was trained and assigned to produce weapons, mostly weapons of mass destruction, so that the Glorious Leader could use them to strike fear in the hearts of any person that thought of rebellion. The Glorious Leader had always believed that men and women would be willing to die for liberty and freedom. But if there was the real threat of instant death to an entire family or race or nationality, that threat generally kept freedom fighters at bay. It was an altogether different analysis for a freedom seeking individual if they had the knowledge that their home town would be annihilated by a nuclear blast.

Rise up against the Glorious Leader, and all of your family and your people and your culture would surely perish. Vladimir Sikorsky had told the people of the Earth Empire that many times. Only once did Vladimir Sikorsky have to demonstrate that he meant what he said. Seventy years ago a military commander that had been a decorated General from Poland, decided to rise up against Sikorsky and his family. Sikorsky had the home town of the traitorous General vaporized with a nuclear blast. The Glorious Leader, Vladimir Sikorsky, was proud to report to the people that the explosion killed approximately two hundred thousand men, women and children. The General was caught and tortured to death on live broadcast for all of the citizens of the Eight Solar Systems to see.

The bomb that had been used was manufactured by the loyal Rosenburg Corporation.

Sikorsky considered the Rosenburg's some of his finest offspring. When Sikorsky took total military control of Sikorsky's Planet and began to initiate martial law on Earth, he met a lovely woman from New York named Esther Rosenburg. She had been a novelist and historian. She traveled to Sikorsky's Planet to write the biography of the Glorious Leader. The two began a love affair and soon married. Esther Rosenburg had been his third wife. Together they created several children and Sikorsky gave each child the surname of their mother. It was a practice he began with his second wife to protect his children from would be assassins or kidnappers.

The Rosenburg offspring had mastered the art of taking conquered alien technology and ruthlessly exploiting the new found knowledge to produce some of the most deadly weapons ever known. The Rosenburg creations had allowed the Glorious Leader to maintain power for over two hundred years and had also enabled humanity to expand its' reach in the universe. Conquering and wiping out new life forms was not easy. Genocide was a dirty business. It was more efficient to drop bombs from far away distances to accomplish the complete and deliberate murder of an entire race or species. Doing such acts face to face was difficult for the average human. Sikorsky believed that many humans possessed emotional weakness and could not follow through with mass murder. Sikorsky despised such weakness in the masses which led to the mass production of deadly weaponry. Pressing a button on a control panel on a Battle Cruiser from a few astronomical units distance was much less personal.

Alfred Rosenburg, II, and his son David were escorted by Army General William Welker to the Tower of the Glorious Leader. General Welker was a grandson of the Glorious Leader. They made some small talk on the way. They had met several times in the past when the Rosenburg's would present their newest creations and train the Royal Family on the proper use of the devices. Welker respected the Rosenburg's due to their ability to forge efficient weaponry for the troops.

Welker was wearing a Rosenburg manufactured laser pistol on his hip and no doubt had other weaponry hidden in the many pockets on his uniform.

The two Rosenburg men noted that all of the floors were white marble with some black streaks through it. Even the stairs were marble. The expense for that kind of decor was astronomical. The ceilings were seventeen feet high from the floor. It was the same height on each and every floor on the Sikorsky Tower. Welker led the two men to an elevator lift and ordered the computer to open the doors. The computer, after confirming Welker's voice print, slid the metal doors open. Rosenburg and his son followed the General onto the lift.

"Executive Suites," Welker said softly so that the building security system would know their ultimate destination.

The Rosenburgs stood motionless as the elevator rapidly shot upwards. The inside of the elevator was also floored and walled with white marble. David Rosenburg was impressed that the ascension took only a few seconds. The elevator door slid open and Welker motioned with his right arm for the two men to exit out onto the hallway. They stepped out and Welker quickly walked past them, motioning for them to follow. In about forty paces, the Rosenburg men found themselves entering a large room, adorned with expensive art work from ancient Earth. The Glorious Leader had acquired paintings, sculptures, drawings, original art work from various artists that had produced some of the most splendid works over the centuries. The floors were black marble with white swirls. There were several ancient weapons on the walls. The Rosenburg men noted old hand guns from the World Wars mounted on the walls. There were spears, swords and crossbows similarly mounted. In the center of the room was a pink round table, with twenty chairs sitting about the table. The center of the table had a large black capital "S" which presumably stood for Sikorsky.

David Rosenburg was amazed that the room was surrounded by glass windows. He could see for miles in all directions. He estimated that they were at least one hundred twenty floors high. He walked to the windows and looked out onto Sikorsky's Planet and smiled. He had dreamed one day that he would be here, in this room. The family had spoken of it in the past. Many had made statements of speculation regarding the top floors of the Sikorsky Towers. It was a majestic sight.

David Rosenburg and his father heard footsteps

approaching. They turned to see fifteen lovely women enter the room, all wearing see through purple dresses. All of the women were desirable. Some were brunette, some blonde, some with red hair. Two of the women were dark skinned, two were Latin and one was from the India region on Earth. Three of the women were Asian. One of the women was one of the so-called Children of Athena, a Harcourt. The other six were white. David enjoyed watching them walk in and offer him a seat.

David sat at the round table, next to his father. There was a naked woman shackled on top of the table. She had dark hair and nice curves. David noticed that she had a device in her throat that prohibited her from speaking. David was proud that his family had been the ones to perfect the voice nullifiers. The woman was young, probably in her late teens. She had tears running down her cheeks. David looked over her breasts and smiled. General Welker sat on the other side of David and noticed the lust in his eyes.

"Careful," Welker warned him in a low tone of voice. "These are all wives of the Glorious Leader."

"Why is she chained up?" David wanted to know.

"The Glorious Leader is going to cut her open for her heart and liver," Welker whispered to David. "He needs a transplant."

"But she is one of his wives?" David wanted to confirm.

"He has dozens of wives," Welker said of the Vladimir Sikorsky. "She was expendable due to her inability to carry a child to term for him."

"Sucks to be her," David whispered.

Alfred grinned as the Glorious Leader, Vladimir Sikorsky, walked into the room, wearing an outfit of flowing purple and gold silk. He had a gold cape over his right shoulder tied loosely around his neck with a purple sash. His tall six foot five inch frame moved gracefully. His short cut dark hair and dark eyes stood out due to his white skin. His muscular frame was obvious to all that saw him. He was handsome and beautiful to the beholder. He grinned as his wives led him to the round table. Sikorsky sat down in a large, throne chair that was similar to those of the kings and queens of ancient lore. He grinned as the women served wines, cheeses, fruits and meat slices to the men.

He looked fantastic for a man that was over two hundred forty years old.

Sikorsky ate a slice of cheese and motioned for Welker and the Rosenburg guests to eat. They did as directed.

"So, my children!" Sikorsky bellowed as he chewed his food. "What was so pressing that you needed to disturb my business of managing the vast empire of humanity?"

Alfred had instructed his son David to say nothing unless addressed directly.

"My Glorious Leader, we come to ask your permission to proceed with something that may be risky, but will certainly eliminate many enemies against you." Alfred began. "My Lord, we must kill all the cadet participants on the Tournament at the Moon of Semiramis. That is all save my son and his friends at his Academy. And we have a flawless plan to do it."

Sikorsky bit into a slice of beef as he considered the words of his descendant. "But I like all of the Tournaments!" The one on the planet Semiramis Moon was not the only tournament in the Eight Solar Systems. There were dozens that were performed each calendar year on various locations. "If I let you sour one, it would damage the others."

"Glorious Leader, I promise that we will not defame the Tournaments," Alfred responded calmly as he had anticipated that would be the main concern against their plan. "We will frame the cadets from Clovis Academy for the murders. It will be a blood bath that will be remembered for decades and only we will know the truth behind what had happened and why the contestants all died."

"Aaaahhhhhh," Sikorsky began clapping his hands. "I like this. So the world will believe the cadets from planet New Edinburgh killed everyone. But the broadcast feed? How will you fake the attacks? Everyone in the eight solar systems will be watching."

"We need permission to cut the broadcast, only for a day or two, while my son and his friends kill the others," Alfred said. "Once we clean it up, the broadcast will be reactivated. It will look as if my son and his team had to fight to the death in a defensive mode. We eliminate the Clovis trouble makers and come out like the heroes."

Sikorsky kept eating. He put some cheese slices on wheat crackers and was crunching on them. He said nothing for a few minutes. He had been informed by one of his daughters that the cadets at Clovis Academy had thwarted several attempts on their lives by the Ragnarsson assassins and were close to stumbling on the fact that the Rosenburg's were actually related to him. The connection could prove to be a political impediment and could lead to some anger among some of the citizens.

Sikorsky considered that the cadets had to be eliminated to ensure that his rule over humanity would not be interrupted. "Your request is granted. Kill the three teams. But, I want to be able to watch it live here, in my Towers." The Glorious Leader pointed to the marble floor as he spoke. "So, the broadcast feed must come directly here throughout the entire performance. I want to enjoy the entire show. Understood?"

"Yes Glorious Leader," Alfred readily agreed. The Royal Family knew how the Glorious Leader viewed humanity to exist for his own pleasure. Fights, wars, competitions were all performances for Sikorsky. "We will make sure you get to watch everything in gory detail. We promise there will be plenty of suffering and death."

Sikorsky laughed, "Good. My forty-seven wives and I will be watching everything. We love a good slaughter." He smiled at one of his wives that was massaging his neck. "You love to see men and women die, don't you my love?"

The young wife smiled and giggled in response.

General Welker said nothing throughout the conversation. He did not like what the Rosenburg's were proposing. Welker felt there were too many risks associated with their plan. As it was, there were many unhappy citizens and rumblings of rebellion were coming from several locations on old Earth. Welker and the other military siblings were on notice that some military leaders, not related to the Glorious Leader, were involved in plans for insurrection. Welker and his cousins, uncles, brothers, sisters nephews and nieces and all of their extended family were having to commit political assassinations throughout the Earth Empire.

Planet Cootron had to be cleansed recently; her leaders were all killed and replaced with those loyal to the Sikorsky's. The Martian Colonies also had to have a few of their elected officials and military officers eliminated.

The Sikorsky family viewed the majority of people as sheep. Freedom mattered little to the people as long as the policies of the Sikorsky family kept them dumb and fat. Welker feared the day when the free thinkers, the ones that secretly did not agree with the Glorious Leader, rose up in unison against the regime. An event such as that would be catastrophic and possibly challenge the two hundred year rule. Fortunately, the majority of the Battle Cruisers' Admirals and Captains and the other planetary leaders were descended from the Glorious Leader. For any treason to succeed, the Sikorsky family leadership would have to be eliminated first.

But one incident, just one, could be enough to send

the people into a frenzy. Welker feared the day that something would come to pass that would result in a domino effect and end up being the catalyst for all out civil war. He ate in silence, hoping that the Rosenburg family were not handing over to the freedom movement a justification, a rallying cry for freedom was all that was missing, to become the flame to light the fuse. Welker and his family feared that. Killing men and women was easy but an idea which gives way to a cause cannot be killed so easily. Men and women come and go.

But ideas last forever.

CHAPTER TEN

At seven a.m. sharp, class began at the Clovis Academy. It was another wonderful day on planet New Edinburgh. The red-orange hue hung over Clovis City as many cadets rushed to shower, dress in their cadet uniforms, eat their breakfast at the large cafeteria and make it to their courses in time. Some of the more dedicated cadets were at the large gymnasium before sunrise, putting in a solid workout before making their way to the showers.

Pierre Zerbe woke up next to Cara Perez Guerrero after falling asleep next to her the night before. She was stretching her naked body next to him. Zerbe had made love to her three times the night before. Perez Guerrero thought she had died and gone to Mount Olympus since most men could not satisfy her in such a manner. But Zerbe was unbelievable. She smiled at him.

"You are amazing, Pierre."

Zerbe smiled as he began running his hands over her body. She was the most beautiful woman he had ever slept with. She was one of the members of the lady track team and trained to run the twenty and forty-two kilometer runs. Her toned body and flat stomach had certainly kept Zerbe satisfied the prior evening "You are too. I am glad you enjoyed."

"Mmmmm," Perez Guerrero purred. "I love your hands on my body."

Zerbe rolled over on top of her and kissed her passionately. He made love to her again under the beams of sunlight coming through her dormitory window.

When they finished, he lifted her up and carried her to the showers.

"Why didn't we get together before this?" Perez Guerrero wondered aloud as they stepped into her shower together. "We could have been having a lot of fun together."

Zerbe ordered the computer to turn on the shower water. "I don't know, but I agree that we should have. I leave in two weeks for the tournament. If we make love four to five times each day, that means we can have sex about thirty times together. Think you can handle that?"

Perez Guerrero laughed and kissed him, "There is a God out there somewhere!"

"How is that?"

"I have been praying for a man like you for years!"

After the heavy drinking and night on the town, many of the cadets woke up and found themselves in compromising situations. Rolf Rhinehard was one of them and he found himself in the dormitory room of Supreet Patel and Flora Evart. The two first year cadets were naked on their floor, lying next to him. Rolf was also in the nude. A third woman, Zarnella Bedrosian, was also asleep on the floor and stark naked. Zarnella was a hybrid feline human. Her fur reminded Rolf of the pictures of the ancient white leopards of old Earth. Her tail was moving up and down slowly as she slept. Rolf was grateful that he remembered having sex with all three women in what was perhaps the wildest foursome of his young life. Flora had been timid at first, but got into the action when she saw how much Supreet enjoyed having intercourse with Rolf. Zarnella allowed Rolf to take her doggie style and during the passion of love making, she shredded the carpet of the dormitory room with her claws.

Rolf stood up and walked quietly over to where his cadet pilot uniform was lying. He was about to force his legs into the one piece outfit when he heard a voice.

"Leaving so soon?" Supreet Patel whispered.

"It is morning," Rolf whispered back.

She stood up and stepped over Flora and Zarnella. Rolf looked over her naked body as she moved closer to him. When she was close enough she took his manhood in her hands and kissed him on his chest. Patel was much shorter that Rolf and his chest was as high as she could reach with her lips while standing flat footed.

"You told me last night at O'Malley's that you had never made love to a woman from India before," Patel reminded him as she softly stroked his hardening penis. "Now that you have had me, what do you think?"

"You were quite amazing," Rolf leaned his head down and kissed her lips. The motion of her hands on him was turning his sex drive on again.

"Then don't leave," Patel said before kissing him back. "I liked how you felt inside of me and I really liked watching you let Flora and Zarnella have it. They both really needed to get laid and I am grateful that you serviced them both. It turned me on watching them as you let instinct take over."

"I rather enjoyed it myself," Rolf admitted as Patel got down on her knees and began kissing his erection.

Patel paused after a few seconds and smiled up at him, "I know you are a big player and that you will never commit to any of us girls. All I want is for you to take me over to my bed for one last great session of sex so I can remember you fondly."

Rolf found that he could never say no to an attractive woman that was performing oral sex on him. "Ja, Supreet. Ja. I would like nothing better than to bed you again."

"Then let's get it on," Patel giggled.

The cadets slid on top of one of the two beds and Rolf climbed on top of Patel. He made love to her with the same energy level he had the night before with the three women. The cadets climaxed and lay next to one another for a few moments, breathing heavily and occasionally glancing down at the floor to ensure that Bedrosian and Flora were still asleep.

"You are amazing," Patel complimented him.

"So are you," Rolf admitted.

"Look, um, I don't want you to feel pressured by the three of us. You have quite the reputation with the ladies here, Rolf. I hear that you have slept with a few dozen of us in the dorms and that you seem to sneak off some nights for clandestine meetings with women that are not attending the Academy."

"What are you getting at, Supreet?"

She rolled over on top of him and pulled her long dark hair back so that she could see his eyes as she spoke. "Rolf, I know you do not want a commitment with anyone. You like having sex with us and we like being with you. I am proposing that in the unlikely event that you are alone some night, you can come here and satisfy your needs. I know it might never happen because you are a very handsome man and in great physical condition so women will flock to you. Flora or I will gladly give it up to you anytime and anyplace. So, if you are alone and want to come over, our door is open to you."

Rolf smiled and kissed her lips. "Supreet, you are one beautiful woman. I like a woman that keeps her body toned like you do. So, I will keep your offer in mind. I am wondering something, however."

"What would that be?"

"Last night, when we started our foursome, you went down on Flora and got her all excited. It really turned me on watching you two."

Patel laughed, "What do you boys expect? There

are over eight women to each man. How are we girls supposed to handle our sexual needs with such bad odds? Flora and I have had sex together several times. We women know what another woman needs and we can satisfy each other quite well. But the majority of us would prefer to have a man like you fucking our lights out. I would say that for me, a man is far more preferable to share my bed with than another woman."

"So you like me better than Flora?"

"I like your bulging muscles, your eyes and the way you take charge of me during sex. There are so many advantages to having a man."

Rolf pursed his lips, "Including getting pregnant."

Patel nodded, "Yes, getting pregnant is important but not to the majority of us in the Academy. Perhaps later in life. But not now. My family expects me to build my career first and then work on a family. My family has high expectations of me."

Rolf rubbed his cheek, "If that is the case, then are you not worried that you could easily get pregnant by being so sexually active with me or some other man?"

Patel shook her head, "No worries my handsome future astronaut. Most of my family is in the medical field. I have connections. Do you remember the pink pills I shared with Flora and Zarnella last night? Those are birth control tablets that I get from my oldest sister. She's a doctor here in Clovis City. I know it is against the law to use any form of birth control, but to hell with the law. I like sex and I do not want any children right now. So, my dear Rolf, that means you can bed me and Flora with impunity. You will never have to worry about us chasing you down for support. But seriously, Rolf. You should be careful. I hear you have done this kind of thing before."

"What kind of thing?"

"Multiple women at the same time. People talk and they are talking about you."

Rolf grunted and sat up in his bed. Most of his sexual conquests had been with married women so that he could avoid any demands for a commitment. It was only recently that he had found that bedding multiple women at the same time was an amazing experience in and of itself. "I really do not like to talk about what I do with other women. I believe what happens behind closed doors should remain there."

Patel shrugged, "And I agree. But women gossip and in the past it was Marco Andolini that was the one the girls at the Academy spoke of. You are rapidly replacing Marco on the gossip charts."

"You realized that Marco is a member of my gang?"

Patel nodded, "Yes, and Flora and I are also members of the gang. Just because we spend more time studying doesn't mean we are not devoted to Yuri and you and the others. I am telling you to just be careful. Consider my advice as one Gorski Gang member warning another. Tell you what I will do for you. If you think you are going to hook up, come by and I will give you one of the pills. You can slip it in a drink and it will dissolve quickly. It is colorless, tasteless and emits no aroma at all. You will be able to have the woman and not have to worry about her coming after you nine months down the road."

"You would do that for me?"

"What are fellow gang members for? I got your back, Rolf. Just do me a big favor?"

"Anything for you Supreet."

"Your mantra of keeping things quiet. Please tell no one about this night. Michel would be really pissed if he found out you boned his sister and my family would flip out if they found out I had my legs in the air for a white guy. My father and my five mothers are very nationalistic and believe in racial purity. They plan on marrying me off one day to a man from India."

Rolf stroked his hands through her hair, "Is that

what you want?"

"No, I do not. But my parents might find a stud like you for me and then I would gladly marry him. Unfortunately, I have met the families that my father interacts with. All of their sons are nothing like you. And now that I know how good it feels to have your cock inside of me, I doubt that any man my father tries to force on me would ever measure up."

"You could tell him no."

"My father is not a man that accepts the word no from one of his daughters. But that bridge will be crossed another day. Right now, you need to get dressed and sneak back to your dorm room before too many other girls start roaming the hallways. They see you leave our room and they will start gossiping. Remember the words of Professor Warren? Loose lips destroy ships."

"Got it," Rolf kissed her lips and rolled out of the bed to collect his clothes. "You can bet your last dollar that I will be back."

"I hope so," Patel smiled. "So does your family force you into arranged marriages like mine?"

Rolf laughed, "No. Never. I have two twin sisters back on old Earth and they are both single. Klaus has two twin sisters and an identical twin brother. We have some younger siblings as well. But no, my parents told us to live out our lives as we see fit. So, no marriage for me."

"Never?"

"Never."

Gorski and Staszko woke up early to go visit Michel Evart and Elektra Papanikolaou in the recovery ward at the main hospital. They met Evart first and found that he was in a neck brace, sitting in a wheel chair with a very handsome doctor pushing him down the hallway. Gorski and Staszko stopped them and hugged Evart.

"You look great," Staszko told him.

"And you, my dear," Evart took her left hand and

kissed it, "still tempt me to become heterosexual. You are a lovely sight." He then smiled to Gorski. "Yuri my friend, I am sorry that I let you down. We would have been amazing together at the tournament."

"Don't worry, Michel." Gorski said sadly. He hated that Evart would not be able to go to the tournament with him. "After the way you helped out against those assassins on the Blitzkrieg, you are one of the most popular heroes on campus. We are going to win this for you."

Evart smiled, "Oh, my manners. This is Doctor Juan Flores."

Gorski and Staszko shook his hand.

"He is my personal doctor," Evart said laughing.

Staszko looked the doctor over, and found that he was very handsome and athletic. She could tell immediately that Doctor Flores and Evart had already become lovers simply by the manner that the two men looked into each other's eyes.

"When do they release you?" Gorski asked as they walked down the hallway.

"Tomorrow. But I will be staying with Doctor Flores for a week or so, until I am feeling better."

"Which may be never?" Staszko laughed as she observed the body language between the doctor and his patient. Flores and Evart laughed as well.

Gorski seemed to not catch the joke. He saw Zhao, Evart's shadow, walking behind them. It was as if seeing the military intelligence undercover operative brought Gorski back to reality. There was still a possibility of danger out there.

"Let's go visit Elektra," Gorski suggested.

"Splendid idea," Evart pointed to the elevator lifts. "She is one floor below. By the way, there were several injured cadets here that received limb replacements. Expensive items. Elektra got one of the best arms money can buy. You two wouldn't know how that happened?"

"No idea," Gorski said.

"I tried to get Juan here to tell me but he won't say. It is supposedly confidential." Evart leaned forward and whispered to Staszko. "I even gave him my best oral performance and he won't talk. I must be losing my touch."

"You should try torture instead girl-friend." Staszko was laughing. "Might be more effective."

After a few minutes walking through the hospital, they arrived at Elektra Papanikolaou's room. Sitting in a chair next to her bed was a sleeping Arch Frazier. He had stayed there every night to be with Elektra.

There was a second bed in the room and Sara Stewart was sitting on top of the bed with her laser pistol aimed at them as they walked in. When she recognized Gorski and Staszko, Stewart lowered her weapon.

Papanikolaou's face lit up with joy when she saw her friends. "Yuri! Jen! Michel! It is so good to see you."

Papanikolaou sat up in her bed and received hugs from them all. Gorski was elated to see that her right arm looked natural. The surgeons even matched her skin tone to the new synthetic skin that covered the mechanical right arm.

Gorski felt her right arm, "It feels like real flesh." He was amazed that the medical technology could accomplish such a miracle.

"Yes, I have feeling in the entire arm, just like before." Papanikolaou told them. "The only difference is that, let me see..." She was looking around the room. "Ah, hand me that metal bed pan over there."

Staszko saw the item Papanikolaou was referring to. She handed it to the younger girl. Everyone watched as Papanikolaou grasped the metallic pan in her right hand and crushed it with little effort. The others heard the sound of the metal pan being crushed under her mechanical hand. Gorski raised his eyebrows at Staszko as they watched the feat.

"That is the difference," Papanikolaou dropped the crushed pan on her bed. "Nobody can mess with me now, except for Hera and her furies."

"That is very impressive," Evart remarked, ignoring the woman's statement paying homage to her patron Goddess. Evart never questioned the beliefs of others. Conversations regarding religion generally went over as well as a fart in church. "Glad you are still with us, Elektra."

"Yuri," Papanikolaou said softly. "Who paid for my arm? My family says they didn't do it, although they would have gladly paid. Arch is the only one that has been sweet on me and he doesn't have that kind of money. My aunt has some military connections as a naval officer, but she is not here on New Edinburgh. Any idea who did this for me?"

Gorski shrugged. He had also wondered who the generous benefactor had been. "I have no clue. It was an anonymous donor. They clearly wanted to remain private. Perhaps we should respect that. The important thing is that you are alive and well and even better than before. Be grateful for that."

Dirk Fenster had been able to bring Theodora home after one day at the veterinarian hospital. His timber wolf had recovered quickly from her wounds and she had no negative reaction to her medication. Theodora sat up in Arch Frazier's bed as Fenster woke up. Ann Harcourt was asleep next to him. Fenster jumped in the shower, getting ready for the day's events. He heard his alert buzzer go off, which meant someone was at his door. Fenster jumped out of the shower and wrapped a white towel around his waist. Harcourt was stirring, having been disturbed by the buzzing noise. Theodora was at the door, sniffing.

"Identify yourselves," Fenster demanded.

"It's me, Daniella." Fenster recognized the voice of Daniella Day.

"Open the door," Fenster instructed the computer.

Daniella Day walked in and saw Theodora. She knelt down and petted her behind her ears. She turned and noticed that Ann Harcourt was lying in the bed with the covers pulled up over her. Harcourt was glaring at Day. Harcourt was aware that Day and Fenster had been involved some time ago.

"I will be brief," Day told them, more for Harcourt's benefit than anything else. "My family and I wanted to thank you for what you did for Dorothy. You did probably the most kind and generous thing I have ever heard of. Thank you Dirk Fenster."

Day pet Theodora some more and whispered to her, "I miss you little Dora." She then looked back at Fenster. "You all have a great day." With that being said, she left his room.

"What was that about?" Ann Harcourt was curious. She rarely pried into Fenster's business as he was a very private man. Her relationship with him was one of sexual convenience. As a Child of Athena, Ann Harcourt could read minds. She would sometimes read Fenster's mind when they were in the throes of passion. She did not do so purposely, it was instinctive. From those few times she was in his mind, she learned that although Fenster enjoyed having sex with her, he did not love her. Harcourt had determined that she was fine with that as she enjoyed his company just the same.

Fenster always felt that he could trust Ann. She had proven to him that she knew how to keep a secret. "Ann, I saw a lot of good people get hurt the other day. I could not just stand by and do nothing. I paid the hospital a lot of money to treat Dorothy Day's injuries. I did it anonymously. Only Sophia DuBravac knows about it. Daniella must have figured it out; she was always a smart one. I would like to keep it quiet, if you know what I mean."

Ann nodded slowly. Her gifts as a Child of Athena were many. She was capable of making Fenster fall in love with her. Now, more than ever, she understood that this was a man of generosity and caring for others. She resisted the urge to use her skills to cause this man to love her. Ann could not do that to Fenster, or anyone else for that matter. She sometimes wished she could be more scheming and vicious like Melissa Harcourt was. Ann wondered how she turned out so differently from Melissa, given they both had the similar genetics.

Ann Harcourt stood and hugged Fenster close to her. "I will tell no one. You are a wonderful man, Dirk."

After enjoying the singing of the Irish citizens of Clovis City, Lila Zapata and Jurgen Doernitz spent a night of passion together. They acknowledged their love for each other. Zapata was so excited she could not sleep. She sent letters via the computer satellite service to her parents and siblings. She was so happy that she wanted the world to know. She was in love.

She could not wait to see DuBravac and let her know the good news.

Colonel Nikolai Gorski and Major Sigebert Evart had assembled three battalions of Marines at four a.m. Armed with arrest warrants for the entire Rosenburg family, Gorski boarded a military Raumschiff, leaving Major Evart behind in command of the United Nations military forces on New Edinburgh.

The four hundred Marine and Army Raumschiffs lifted off, escorted by a thousand small fighter ships. The reign of the Rosenburg's was about to end. Gorski said a silent prayer to his deceased wife, Melita. He asked her to be proud of him, and to be proud of their two sons, Yuri and Piotr. In his mind he thought she answered him he heard her voice telling him to be careful and that she loved him. Gorski had arranged with General Leta Tan of Military Intelligence to join forces for the mass arrests. Tan had dispatched fifty Raumschiffs with several companies of her best trained MI staff. Tan had assigned two of her MI Captains and ten Lieutenants to lead her forces onto the Rosenburg Ranch.

Attorney Sean Collins watched from his office window as the force lifted off at the United Nations Administration Building military ship landing strip. Collins knew that there most likely would be blood shed at Rosenburg's Ranch. The Rosenburg's would not surrender easily, nor would the Ragnarsson widows and their children. Collins was thankful that Gorski took more troops than necessary.

Rebecca Rosenburg did not take her arrest lightly. She spewed out venomous and threatening phrases at everyone. Collins' favorite threat was that they would all be skinned alive with dull knives and dipped in lemon juice. For a young girl to say such horrible things was not lady like at all, Collins thought to himself.

Collins drank his coffee and ordered his computer system to keep him apprised of the battle over the Rosenburg Ranch. Collins had endured a verbal lashing from New Edinburg Secretary General Alexander Lyss. Arresting his personal assistant did not go over well with the planetary chief executive. Lyss demanded to see the evidence that would be used against Rebecca. Collins had to refuse Lyss' request as his prosecutions and investigations were confidential until trial began. Lyss went into a rage, screaming and threatening to have Collins fired. The tirade ended after about ten minutes. Lyss finally stormed out of Collins office when the Secretary General realized the lawyer would not budge.

Collins sighed. The prosecution of the entire Rosenburg family, or at least the majority of the family, would be one of his most difficult cases ever. The decision to file the charges was easy for Collins to make. Killing a judge, a prosecutor, attacking a space station, covering up a murder, committing numerous murders and attempting murders were all some of the most serious infractions known to Collins. He had to make sure he did the right thing and protect the public. The rule of law must be respected.

Collins checked with his computer for the news updates around the Empire. He noticed the shadow of a man against his far wall. Collins stood up, startled, as he had thought he was alone.

"Please, I am not here to harm you," the shadow said. It was a man's voice. "I was sent by Penelope Rosenburg. She wanted me to deliver this computer diskette to you. She also said you could give me my life back."

Collins looked suspiciously at the shadowy figure. He was wearing grey sweats with a hood over his head. His face was obscured by a hood over his head. He was holding a black leather bound brief case in his right hand. Collins judged the man to be close to six feet tall. He had been expecting the mystery man since the woman named Penelope had informed him that such a person would be seeking him out.

"Reveal yourself," Collins instructed the man.

Collins watched the figure move closer and set the briefcase on the floor. He pulled the hood away from his face. Collins recognized the man before him.

It was Drayton Love-Easter.

"How in the name of the Stars....." Collins began to blurt out dozens of questions. It was impossible. Collins had seen the body of the young man when the coroner did the autopsy. He personally observed the slash on the throat, the knife wounds on the back and chest. The man before him had been as dead as could be. "Impossible."

"No, it is very possible," Drayton Love-Easter #2 said to Collins. "The Rosenburg woman, Penelope, she took some of my blood when I was murdered. Her sisters used some alien race technology to download all of my brain patterns to a specially created computer disk. All of my thoughts, experiences, feelings, dreams, hopes, education and values, everything that was me, was imprinted on that computer microchip. The Doctor, Nicolette, she transferred everything on the microchip into the brain of this DNA replica of the original Drayton Love-Easter. I am me, but yet I am not me."

Collins slumped into his chair as he was trying to process the information in his mind. "This cannot be. I have never heard of such advances in medical science. Are you flesh and blood? Are you a robot or some form of synthetic being?"

"I am a human in every sense of the word," Love-Easter said. "I had the same questions and confusion when they woke me up, or activated me as the doctor explained it. She said that her duplication machinery could make a copy of any carbon based life form in a few weeks. I was created in a tube and it was my location as I grew into the form you see before you. I know that I died. I do not remember dying, as I was out cold from a laser stun blast. So I suppose that I am here to seek out a second chance in life, to try and get it right this time."

"It is a miracle," Collins walked around him, inspecting the face and saw that it was a perfect duplication of the original man.

"In this briefcase I have information that you will need to bring down the Rosenburg family. Miss Penelope was very generous in the information she has provided. Everything you need to know to bring them to justice is here."

"Thank you," Collins said slowly. His mind was still reeling from the sight before him. "How? How did they re-make you?"

"There was an ancient alien race that had come to this planet centuries ago," Love-Easter said. He moved toward one of the chairs. "May I sit?"

Collins nodded and motioned to the chair, "Would you care for some coffee?"

"Yes, please." Love-Easter sat down and waited as Collins poured him a cup of coffee. Love-Easter waited for Collins to sit down before continuing. "The alien race came to remake this planet. They wanted to co-exist with the indigenous population of New Edinburgh. They built a large cross section of underground tunnels complete with intricate rail systems. Their space ship was massive and full of amazing technological advances. But they made a serious error. They decided to test a life form here, a small entity; most of them were only an inch in radius high and wide. These small creatures were like leeches, but more deadly. They secrete an acidic liquid that can burn through metal, clothing and flesh. And they hungered for flesh.

"These small leech-like creatures got loose on the alien ship. They began eating the members of the advanced race. In an attempt to escape the horrible death that awaited them, the aliens sent many of their scientists away, in much smaller space crafts, to warn the other members of their species. Some of those smaller craft were infected by the leeches, which fed on them all." Love-Easter drank the coffee. "Here on New Edinburgh, the few survivors found a method to eliminate the leeches, by using a form of solar power and radiation. They used this weapon and killed them all. That is why we have never encountered those things on New Edinburgh."

"And the alien scientists?" Collins wondered where they were.

"They were still here when we began colonizing New Edinburgh. At least those that had survived were here. There were not many of them left. The Rosenburg family made contact with them. Alfred Rosenburg used his assassins, the Ragnarsson's, to murder or capture all of the alien scientists. In an effort to steal all of the alien technology Rosenburg had the aliens beaten, electrocuted, whipped and forced their heads under water and had them fighting for air. Some of the Rosenburg children were involved in the tortures. The aliens began cooperating with the Rosenburg's and taught them everything they needed to know regarding their advanced sciences and engineering. The Rosenburg's stole the alien technology and they made the aliens teach them how to use it. Then the Ragnarsson's killed the remaining alien survivors."

Love-Easter drank from his coffee cup. He looked out of Collins window. "My friends, Les, Yuri, Michel, Drew, Marco and Dominic? Are they safe? The others in the gang? Penelope told me bits and pieces of the current events. I am worried about all of them."

Collins nodded, "Yes. Elektra was almost killed. Michel has some pulled muscles in his neck and back. Yuri and Jen really took it to the Ragnarsson's. Yuri killed one of them. Jen and Elektra killed another and Jen put Ella in the ER. Now that we are rounding up all of them, I think that your friends are safe."

Love-Easter was silent for a moment, "I miss Les. I miss Yesenia so much. I miss them all." His voice sounded tortured. "Penelope told me you would help me get my life back. She suggested a cover story that would be plausible."

"What do you need me to do?" Collins was willing to help. As insane as it might be, if this was a perfect replica of the original Love-Easter, his living again would bring a happy ending to many, just as Penelope Rosenburg had said.

"I need for your coroner to purge the results of my autopsy and for my medical records to be altered from death, to coma." Love-Easter explained "I need for me to come out of that coma soon. Miss Penelope said that my son was going to be sent to an orphanage now that Yesenia is widowed. I need to get to her, marry her, so we can keep and raise our son. I cannot bear knowing the pain Yesenia will feel if she has her son taken from her. Our government is so unfair and the orphanage laws are far too draconian. I must get to her. Please."

Collins sat his coffee cup down and smiled, "I will do what needs to be done to help you. The coroner is my uncle. He will have no problem changing the records."

The duplicated Love-Easter put his head in his hands and began to weep.

Cadet Klaus Rhinehard showered and brushed his teeth. He was at April Mejia's dormitory room, as he had been every night since they first made love. She was standing next to him, brushing her teeth. She smiled at him, her mouth full of tooth paste foam. Klaus laughed. She knew how to bring out his humorous side. After they both rinsed their mouths out, they proceeded to dress into their Class-C uniforms for the day of class lectures.

"Klaus," Mejia said softly. "Remember when I said I would be honored to give birth to your child?"

"Yes, I remember." Klaus responded as he was zipping up the front of his uniform. "I will never forget that."

"Well, you are going to be a father," Mejia said smiling.

"What?"

"You have some potent sperm, lover. I am pregnant."   Klaus pulled her into his broken, but healing arms and kissed her. "I am so happy. I love you girl!"

Mejia buried her head in his chest, "I love you too."

"Let's get married. Today." Klaus suggested quickly.

"Today?" Mejia looked surprised. "Are you sure about that? I am not the kind of woman that will allow second or third wives. You marry me, then I am it. You understand?"

"Hey, I love you. I am not like the other men that want multiple wives. I want you and nobody else." Klaus was stroking her chin affectionately. "So, you going to marry me or what?"

Mejia nodded her head, "Oh yes. I will be the best wife ever."

They sealed their offer and acceptance of marriage with a kiss.

CHAPTER ELEVEN

The tournament team training continued throughout the week. On Friday evening, all ten team members were assembled in one of the Engineering lecture halls. The hall was rectangular in shape, with a stage and huge screen at the front. There were two hundred chairs in the pews, facing the stage. The stage had a glass lectern and a four foot long desk.

Yuri Gorski was sitting next to Drew Harrison in the row to the far left of the room. Both of them were still in their gymnasium clothing and had lifted weights for about an hour and completed thirty minutes of aerobics. Harrison had been keeping sober, which was a relief for Gorski. Harrison did not react negatively when they ran into some of the Yutong sisters at the gym. When they had been new to the Academy, Harrison had slept with one of the Yutong sisters. After a few months, the girl was pregnant and fingered Harrison as the father. Based on advice from Marco and Dominic, Harrison asked for a paternity test. The Yutong family was livid that Harrison would dare suggest that the girl had more than one sex partner. The test was refused and the Yutong's hated the Gorski Gang members ever since. Some of the Yutong brothers were some of the fiercest fighters of the original Bragg Gang and their confrontations had been many. When Gorski and Harrison saw the Yutong women, the meeting was cordial and not a cross word was uttered. It was quite the change from the past explosive run ins between Harrison and the family.

Les Gillis and Julia Steiner were sitting behind Gorski and Harrison. Steiner was in her medical training uniform and Gillis in his cadet Class-C uniform.

In the center of the room were Eamon O'Grady, Porfirio Cardenas, Jurgen Doernitz and Pierre Zerbe. All of the men were in gymnasium garb as they had also finished a bout of kick boxing. Cardenas had a bottle of juice he was drinking.

Marco Andolini and Mary Lincoln were sitting to the far right of the room. They were both in their Class-C flight suits.

Admiral Seward and Dean Harvard walked in and the ten cadets promptly stood to attention.

"Be seated," Seward instructed. "Before we begin, I wanted to let you know that I was able to get the Raumschiff you requested for your flight to the Moon."

O'Grady frowned at that comment, "We didn't request any ship."

"I did," Doernitz spoke up. "The Fenster Corporation designed and have been building a series of new and improved models of the Raumschiff. It is their fourth version. It is sturdier, faster, has better maneuverability. I wanted us to have the absolute best."

O'Grady took in a deep breath of frustration. He had hoped that Doernitz would be different from the others. Clearly all the time the youngest cadet on the team spent with Marco was having an influence on him. The kid did not respect the chain of command. O'Grady pointed his index finger at Doernitz. "I am the cadet in charge. You shouldn't be going over my head on decisions like that."

"Sounds like the kid made a pretty good call on that, Eamon," Marco defended Doernitz. "Cut him some slack."

Seward walked to the left edge of the stage and

crossed his arms. There was no time for this constant bickering among the group as there was much more work to be done. He cleared his throat to get the cadets focused back on the mission. "Computer, download my power point presentation on the opposing Teams."

The front wall of the lecture hall lit up with ten photographs. The pictures were in two rows, five photographs to a row.

"Who are these ten people?" Harrison asked.

"These are the members of one of your opposing teams," Harvard answered. "The other Academy's announced their rosters today. You need to study their profiles."

"Which Academy are they from?" Lincoln inquired.

"These are the cadets from Newton Academy," Seward told them. He pointed to the first photograph on the top left. It was a white male, short blonde hair, blue eyes, strong cheek bone structure. "Their team leader is Cadet Admiral Alan Anderson."

"Anderson?" Gorski raised his eye brows. "I know him. Dray and I met him at Spetsnaz training. He's one determined cadet."

Seward nodded, "Correct. Alan Anderson is a graduate of the Spetsnaz training and is working on his search and rescue doctorate at Newton Academy. He received his pilot credentials as an undergraduate. He has good scores from his marksmanship classes and survival courses. He is going to graduate with his doctorate in Deep Space Search and Rescue. He is from old Earth, Western Australia Province. Do not under estimate this man. He will be a worthy opponent."

"The second picture is Cadet Captain Nicolas Curtis. He is the declared second in command of the Newton Academy Team." Harvard was pointing to the second picture. Curtis was black, with short dark hair, light brown eyes and very handsome features. "Curtis is a military intelligence student. His grades are perfect. He can rival Gillis and Gorski in hand to hand combat. He is certain to have a bright future in the Space Command. If you get the opportunity, stun him. Go toe to toe with him at your own risk. His family is from the Georgia Territory in what used to be the United States. His father is a martial arts instructor and his mother a black belt. They taught him self-defense at an early age."

Seward pointed to the picture of the dark skinned woman depicted in the second row, far left. She had long dark hair, dark eyes, and an attractive smile. "This is Cadet Captain Ellen Benson. She is the leading pilot for the Newton Academy cadets. She also has perfect marks in her grades. Her profile suggests she is very heroic and takes risks at times. Her family descended from one of the few families in Africa that survived the Wars. Her father and mother were pilots and they began teaching her how to fly at a young age. So you need to be ready for her. She will have far more experience than the average cadet.

"Next to her are her pilots, Palmer, Woods and Carter," Seward continued. "They are all top notch cadets. Palmer is their one under class man in the group. He is some kind of wunderkind, like Doernitz, so watch yourselves if you end up in an aerial battle with Benson and her team. They will be formidable."

O'Grady raised his hand. Seward pointed to him. "Admiral, will we get dossiers on all of the opposing cadets?"

"Yes," Seward assured him. "And they will receive yours. You will need to study them all. Your opponents will know all about each of you. I have down loaded these ten profiles to each of your personal web pages. Study them. I will send you the profiles of the other teams tomorrow and Sunday. I expect each of you to have everything memorized about them by Monday morning."

Seward paused and walked in front of the

photographs. He pointed at one of the top row pictures. It was a white male, dark hair, light colored eyes. "This one here is of particular interest. His name is Laurence Thompson. He is a computer genius. He could hack you in his sleep. Because he is on the other team, you had best devise a failsafe encryption program to communicate with. This Thompson kid, well, anything you say on your communication devices or holo-coms he will most likely hear it. He will hack your system. That is why you must know your adversaries. They all have talents and they, like you, want to win.

"In less than ten days you will board your Raumschiff and fly to the Moon of Semiramis. You will be graded by how quickly you arrive. You will be graded by how quickly you set up your headquarters." Seward was pacing, his hands behind his back. "The eight Judges on the moon will be giving out scores for everything you do. They will also give you demerits for mistakes and the rest of the planets of the Eight Solar Systems will be watching your performance. If you win, you become stars, heroes. If you lose, well, then no one will remember you."

Seward stopped in front of O'Grady for dramatic effect. "Eamon, if any of these other nine get out of line, I want you to kick their ass all the way back to New Edinburgh."

O'Grady looked over at Gorski and Harrison and back to Seward. "Yes sir."

Gorski clenched his right fist. O'Grady looked his way as a slight against him. When this is over, Gorski thought to himself, O'Grady and I are going to settle our differences hand to hand.

Porfirio Cardenas had requested that his pilots gather at the Simulator Room after the meeting with Harvard and Seward. Doernitz, Zerbe, Lincoln and Marco complied with that request as they had every evening since being on the tournament team.

The Simulator Room had thousands of chairs with flight controls to make a cadet in training feel as if they were actually flying an actual space craft. The entire facility would go dark and broadcast a three hundred sixty degree replication of any terrain that was ordered of the computer.

Cardenas had them work on aerial tactics for two hours. Cardenas assigned Zerbe to serve as the Raumschiff pilot while Lincoln and Andolini would be each other's wing man. Doernitz was to be Cardenas wing man. Using the advanced computer graphics of the Simulator Room, Cardenas had the pilots fly formations over the realistic images Moon of Semiramis. Cardenas wanted his team to know the lunar surface like their own dormitory rooms. He worked them and worked them, day after day, night after night.

None of the cadet pilots complained about the extra work hours. They were all becoming a cohesive unit, learning each other's habits and their strengths and weaknesses. Cardenas was impressed with the dedication exhibited by all of his team.

After each training session, they would all five go to dinner together. Most of the time they would be joined by their significant others. Cardenas had become fond of Zapata and Perez-Guerrero. Freya Cardenas had also grown to like the two women. Perez-Guerrero seemed to have strong maternal instincts in the way she would interact with the two Cardenas children.

Cardenas observed that Zerbe was generally the quiet one with not much to say. Marco was the most expressive of the group and seemed to interact quite well with Lincoln.

The pilot team, their significant others all met at one of the local Seafood Restaurants once each week. The party of ten had a grand time together, sharing a five course meal and several bottles of wine. They dined on blackened

Janniffe, a white fish that was indigenous to New Edinburgh's oceans. The Janniffe was a large fish that was known to grow as long as twenty feet long and were predators. The meat of the Janniffe was considered to be among the better tasting aquatic cuisine on the planet.

Porfirio Cardenas had suggested the dinners as a part of team building. He felt it was important for the team to be friends and enjoy the company of one another. His plan had worked. The dinners were always full of fun and laughter.

The Cardenas children liked being a part of the nightly meals.

Little Alejandro Cardenas was already referring to Lila Zapata as "Tia Lila." That, of course, made Zapata feel accepted by the family. She also loved the ring of it.

Maria Cardenas enjoyed being cradled by Mary Lincoln and Cara Perez-Guerrero. Sometimes the two women would argue about who would get to hold and feed Maria.

Freya enjoyed the time she had with her husband and two children, growing fond of their new found friends, Marco especially. The Italian was a good influence on her brother, Jurgen. It was as if Marco had taken Jurgen under his tutelage as a little brother. Jurgen seemed to admire the Italian for the courage he had displayed when they had rescued Tina Martinson and for his ability as a pilot.

Yuri Gorski would also attend team meetings in the evenings at the Collins Mansion. Les Gillis, Drew Harrison, Julia Steiner and Eamon O'Grady would discuss the different strategies for the tournament. They would argue, raise voices, and sometimes agree. But mostly they would argue. On some occasions Ginger Collins O'Grady would come down the stairs and tell them all to be quiet. She had an uncanny ability to calm down her husband, Eamon.

Although Gorski did not like O'Grady, he did

admire him for one quality. O'Grady was deeply in love with Ginger. Gorski could see it in the way O'Grady would look at her, the way he treated her with gentle kindness. There was a strong bond there.

The other Collins siblings lived in the mansion as well. Occasionally Cormac Collins would come downstairs to give Steiner a kiss. Harrison would struggle to not let his jealousy show, sometimes he would have his hands underneath the table tops, rubbing them together each time Cormac and Steiner showed each other any affection.

The youngest Collins cadet, Liam, would sometimes sit in an empty chair to listen to the team members debate strategies and plans of attack. Liam was an inquisitive young man that was a beginning student at the Academy. He had dreams of one day competing in the tournament so the strategy sessions were interesting to him.

The other sister, Siobhan Collins, would only say hello and good night. She had always been friendly with Steiner and Gillis.

Although the relationship with Siobhan and Gorski ended a few years earlier, Gorski could remember how much he had enjoyed making love to her on the family couch, or in her bed room. Gorski observed that Siobhan was still as beautiful as ever. Gorski reminded himself he had Staszko waiting for him. Thinking of the past might be a way to make a person stronger by growing from the experience of the events. But to dwell on what might have been was never healthy.

Gorski remembered that the older Collins siblings had a step-mother that had died tragically. Through their deceased step-mother there were several other children born to Sean Collins. Gorski never saw the other children at the team meetings. He often wondered where those other children were. If they were in the Collins mansion they were certainly quiet.

The days passed quickly. Soon, the cadets would be

off on their adventure to represent their Academy on the Blood Moon.

CHAPTER TWELVE

The joint military incursion onto the Rosenburg Ranch went without incident for the Marines and Army forces under Colonel Gorski's command. The Raumschiffs landed and Marine forces jumped from their transports and began securing the major town where the majority of the Rosenburg family was thought to live. They went house to house, waking occupants and arresting the individuals with warrants.

Colonel Nikolai Gorski led his men on the ground. He was not a commander that believed in sending his troops in harm's way without sharing in the risk. He had his laser rifle slung over his shoulder and a laser pistol in his right hand. Gorski led three squads of Marines to the main Rosenburg mansion. They began to surround the large dwelling, aiming lasers at the windows and the roof top. A Raumschiff was flying above the structure with lasers ready to pick off any would-be snipers.

Nikolai Gorski accepted a small microphone given to him by a Lance Corporal. He spoke into it, "This is the Marines. We are here to execute warrants for arrest for about thirty more individuals. The rest of the occupants may leave in peace. The arrest warrants were duly signed by the Judge. We wish to serve these documents as peacefully as possible."

The area was silent for about thirty minutes. Gorski had to repeat his message twice. He began to believe that he would be forced to lead his Marines into the mansion and take the structure by force of arms. He had hoped to avoid that course of action due to the intelligence reports that indicated that there were children and innocent slaves living in the building.

As Gorski was pondering how long he would wait to order military action, the front sliding metal doors to the large home slid open. A single woman, dressed as if she were going to a dance party, walked out. She was beautiful and walked with grace. She stopped when she was a few feet from the Marines. The male soldiers were certainly enamored with her beauty. Gorski recognized her as one of the Rosenburg children that had been named in the arrest warrants. Her name was Carla.

"I am alone and unarmed," Carla Rosenburg stated loudly. Her father had given her the speech she was about to deliver before he had left. Carla had memorized every word her father had written. "Please send me a list of all that are wanted and we will surrender without a fight. We are peaceful people and we want to cooperate with the Courts!"

Gorski looked to Lieutenant Simms, "Give the woman the list of names."

Simms slung his laser rifle over his shoulder and walked quickly to the woman. He handed Carla the list and waited as she read the names. She saw her name in the middle of the page. For the first time in her life, she was hit with the reality of the actions of her family involvement. She was going to be arrested and locked up. She controlled her breathing as best she could and swallowed. Her father had promised that if she was arrested, he would get her out of jail quickly. Carla had believed in her father, who was also her lover. Simms found that he could not take his eyes off of the lovely woman.

"Lieutenant," Carla announced with a smile, "I will have the ones present surrender to you. Several of the names on this list are not here. I am on the list so you will have to take me into custody as well. May I have one of my sisters take the list and wake up the ones you are searching for?"

"That would be fine," Simms told her. As attractive as she was, Simms was ready to agree to just about any reasonable request she made of him.

Carla turned her head back to the mansion. "Juliana! Please come out. They mean us no harm."

Juliana Rosenburg slowly walked out of the mansion. She was wearing a red sweater with black jeans and red boots. She walked with ease across the manicured lawn and the paved street that circled the mansion. She silently joined her sister and took the list from her. Juliana read the names on the list without comment. She took in a deep breath when she noticed that her name was also printed on the paper. She hesitated for a moment as she wondered what it was that she did to deserve to be arrested. She had never been a leader in her family. She had been a follower that never really did anything. Juliana hoped that she could escape prosecution since all she did was stand back and do nothing.

"I will return with everyone that we have here," Juliana finally promised.

"Just a minute!" Nikolai Gorski called out as he began walking toward them. "We scanned the mansion and found that there are over eighty human life forms inside. Send them all out here so we can determine who is here."

Juliana and Carla looked at each other with surprise as neither woman had expected such a demand from the Marines. The prospect of each and every person being subject to inspection had not been considered and their father had not prepared them for that contingency. Carla had deduced that her family was out-gunned in this situation. They were surrounded on the ground by well-armed Marines. There was a battle ready Raumschiff hovering above the mansion and the rest of the property was crawling with Marines. Any resistance would be hopeless. Even if the Rosenburg's were successful in repelling the Marines, Carla knew that there were other forces on the southernmost portion of the Rosenburg Ranch searching for the Ragnarsson family members. Those forces were from the infamous General Leta Tan's Military Intelligence branch. Carla preferred surrendering to Gorski and his Marines so they could avoid the unpredictable wrath of General Tan.

Carla shrugged as she made the decision that it would be best to fully cooperate, "Everyone in the mansion, please step outside!"

It took some time, but each and every person in the mansion walked outside. Some of the Marines conducted DNA and finger print scans on the large group and many were identified as those wanted by Collins for prosecution and were shackled and led away. Carla and Juliana Rosenburg were also placed in restraints and searched. One of the Marines, a Lance Corporal, ran his hands slowly over Carla's body. She made note of his name and face. The man lusted for her. She would remember him, just in case. She watched as her full blood siblings, Thomas, Peter and Victoria were each placed in shackles and led away.

Two of the wives of Alfred Rosenburg, II, were also arrested. Petra and Alana Rosenburg allowed themselves to be searched and shackled. They were both questioned regarding their children and neither woman would reveal any information as to the whereabouts of their offspring.

There were three fifteen year olds standing next to one another on the far left of the group. One was a boy and he had two girls on either side of him. They were shaking with fear and holding each other's arms. The Marines could not identify the three on their computer DNA scanners. Nikolai Gorski saw the confusion on the faces of his men and walked over.

"What is the problem?"

"Sir, these three have no identity," a female Army Lieutenant named Shen answered.

Gorski turned his attention to the three teens, "What are your names?"

The boy looked at Gorski, "Sir, my name is Steven McAdams. These are my sisters, Delisa and Natalie."

"Are you slaves here?" Gorski asked.

"No sir," Steven McAdams answered. "We are Rosenburg's. We just have a different mother than the rest of them."

Gorski noted that there seemed to be some divisions in the eighty plus individuals that had walked out of the mansion. It was an odd dynamic to observe.

"Where is your mother?" Gorski asked the young teen.

"We never met her," Delisa McAdams spoke up.

"We think she is dead," Natalie McAdams added.

Gorski sighed. What to do, he wondered. He could not leave minors alone without adult supervision and he could not allow any adult wanted for arrest to stay behind to watch over the children. He turned his attention to Lieutenant Shen. "How many of the eighty that are not being arrested are adults?"

"There are about sixty, sir." Shen answered and led a woman toward Gorski. "This is Francesca Rosenburg. She claims to be a wife of the fugitive Alfred Rosenburg, II. She is not on the list for arrest."

Gorski looked over the lovely woman. Francesca Rosenburg looked to be no older than twenty years old. "How many children do you have, madam?"

Francesca Rosenburg looked to the dark sky, tears forming in her eyes. "Alive or dead?"

"In total," Gorski said softly.

"I have had eleven children, Colonel," Francesca said with her voice quivering with emotion. "Two are dead, one is missing, she left and did not tell me where she was going. Thank God you are here, sir. Please, spare me my children. I cannot lose any more."

Gorski could see in the man-made light that the woman was crying. He motioned with his thumb to the three McAdams children behind him. "Do you know these kids?"

"Yes Colonel," she was wiping the tears from her face.

"Can you tell me where their mother is?"

Francesca looked down to the paved ground and to the three fifteen year olds. "She died a long time ago. My husband, Alfred, had her killed. She was a traitor to the family. She tried to escape from here and they killed her for it. They made an example of her."

"Can you care for these three?"

"Of course I will, they are wonderful children." Francesca walked over to the McAdams triplets and embraced them. "They are not criminals, Colonel. I will protect them."

"Good enough for me," Gorski told her as he walked over to Simms.

"How many did we get?" Gorski whispered to Simms.

"Over half of the warrants were served, Colonel."

"Okay, let's move out!" Gorski ordered. He turned to Francesca. "Best wishes to you madam."

Francesca and the McAdams children watched the armed forces board their ships and fly off into the red-orange sky line. The majority of the Rosenburg children were arrested. Francesca began to realize she was now the default matriarch of the family. Magdalena was missing, the other two wives, Petra and Alana were now incarcerated and her husband was on the run. The Ragnarsson assassins were either gone or dead.

Francesca noted that only a handful of the children

of her husband were still there. She smiled when she saw her own children, Beyonce, Aimee, Tammie and Kelli standing by her side. Her daughter Nicolette had been gone for several months. Her sons Cush and Darryl were dead. Her other sons Jacob, Joseph and Joshua were hiding in the belly of that underground alien space ship. She looked to the remaining children around her.

"Tomorrow is a new day. We begin to run this place free of fear and death," Francesca announced to them all. "Now, return to your rooms and get some rest. We have much work ahead of us."

"What about us?" Natalie McAdams asked.

"Come with me and let me tell you about your mother," Francesca said.

"You knew our mother?" Steven McAdams asked with a hint of excitement in his voice.

"She was the bravest of us all," Francesca told the three teens. "I regret that the rest of us just sat in silence when she stood up to the Rosenburg family."

Delisa McAdams stood watching the large space craft depart. She was in awe of their size and he sheer number of them. She decided that one day she would learn to fly one of those ships. She wanted to find out how she could one day wear the uniforms that the Colonel and the other soldiers had on.

While the arrests led by Gorski seemingly went smoothly and lacked violence, the arrests led by General Tan's soldiers were filled with death. Tan's Raumschiffs met with stiff resistance on the southernmost point of the Rosenburg Ranch Territory. Her squadron of Raumschiffs flew low over the walls surrounding the territory and began firing automatic lasers on the Rosenburg snipers that had foolishly fired on Tan's forces first. The bodies of the snipers were obliterated by the laser bursts, leaving burned shadows on the concrete and metal walls as the only evidence that they had ever lived in the first place.

The preliminary intelligence on that area indicated that there were rows of mansions, some as high as thirty floors up, occupying large lots of land with manicured lawns and gardens around them. The rooftops of the mansions had been armed with laser canons and slave soldiers to operate them. Whether the slaves had been told to stand down or not was never learned. All that mattered was that they opened fire on the approaching military space craft.

The light red, round energy balls that shot from the canons were powerful enough to breach the thick hulls of the ships and several suffered direct hits. Tan had stayed behind at her palace headquarters located in Lynott's Land and watched the melee from her tactical monitors in her personal quarters. She cursed at the sight of some of her ships exploding in the night sky and barked orders for her pilots to return fire.

The pilots did as instructed and launched R-5 rockets at some of the offending mansions, causing massive explosions that split the buildings metal and brick foundations as balls of fire rose into the air. The occupants of the buildings and the laser canon operatives on the rooftops were killed by the explosive and incendiary devices. Chunks of the mansions were thrown into the air and the screams of the dying were drowned out by the louder sounds created by the rockets eruptions.

Matthew Rosenburg had lived in one of the mansions that had been attacked. He had sent his wives and children to hide out in another portion of the territory in preparation for the raid. He had hid out in the basement of his mansion and tried with futility to contact the military ships to call off the attack. His mansion was hit by a direct hit on the third floor of his twenty-seven floor mansion. Matthew felt the temperature rise all around him as the mansion shook from the blast created by the rocket. He ran for the underground tunnels that were connected to his basement and cursed as the floors above collapsed and brick and metal crashed down all around him, blocking off his route of escape. Matthew turned around so that he could make his way to a secondary tunnel just before several slabs of wood crashed down on top of his head. Matthew slumped down to the floor and landed face first as more rubble fell on top of him. Everything around him went dark as he lost consciousness.

Some of the ships landed near the properties that the intelligence reports had indicated held some of the Ragnarsson assassin families. Those troops also met with tragedy due to the traps that had been set by the occupants.

Lieutenant May Ling led two squads of Military Intelligence enlisted women and two non-commissioned officers toward a large seven floor mansion that had been identified as the home of Junior Ragnarsson. Ling had ordered that they land their black colored Raumschiff to the south of the building. There were no gates or walls surrounding the structure, which was curious to Ling. Surely a master assassin would have better protection for himself and his family than what was observed. Ling noticed only green grass and multiple rows of flowers of different sizes and color. Ling stopped for a second and activated her holo-com device to communicate with her commander. She waited as a life size holographic image of General Tan appeared before her.

"General, we are at the mansion of Junior Ragnarsson," Ling reported.

"Good. Take it by force," Tan instructed. "Kill the men and the boys. Spare all of the women and bring them back to us for integration. Make certain that none of the technology inside is damaged. I want to learn everything that these people have been hiding from me all this time."

"Yes General," Ling answered and waited as Tan's image faded away before she repeated the orders to her crew.

Her two squads were waiting in silence, holding laser rifles in their hands. Ling looked over at the mansion and pointed at it as she faced her troops. Ling pulled her laser rifle off her shoulder and held it in both hands.

"You heard General Tan. We kill the men and spare the women. Move out!"

Ling led the two squads of Military Intelligence women onto the grounds surrounding the mansion. The unfortunate MI soldiers did not get past thirty feet. A pink laser pulse suddenly appeared before the women and enveloped them in seconds. Ling and her fellow soldiers screamed in agony as their flesh was dissolved from their bodies. Their uniforms erupted in flames. Ling and the others were dead in seconds. Nothing remained of them.

Inside the mansion, the widows of Junior Ragnarsson had been prepared for such an attempted home invasion. The Ragnarssons had spared no expense in obtaining the best and most advanced in security technology. One of the women outside stepped on one of the underground weight sensors that activated the mansion lasers and internal alarms. The widows began rounding up their children and took them to the underground tunnels to escape the next wave of attack.

CHAPTER THIRTEEN

Avery "Big Bad" Jackson enjoyed practicing his martial arts at the gymnasium. Now more than ever, he needed to be prepared. Jackson relished the fact that soon he would have Yuri Gorski face to face. Gorski was a worthy opponent and could not be taken lightly. Jackson had learned that Gorski had killed one of the best assassins in the several solar systems between New Edinburgh and Sikorsky's Planet. Jackson had been training daily ever since Caine Rosenburg gave him the news they would be alone on the Moon of Semiramis for about a week. Jackson had been practicing with spears, long swords, short swords, knives, lasers and hand to hand.

Jackson entered the floor of his Academy gymnasium where twenty freshman level cadets were training. Their martial arts instructor saw Jackson enter the training room and smiled at the sight of him. The new cadets seemed unmotivated and took their martial arts training as a leisurely event. They needed to be taught a lesson which prompted the teacher to turn to Cadet Jackson.

"Cadets, this is Cadet Jackson. He is one of my most celebrated students. Today, each of you must learn humility. You must experience defeat. How you handle being beaten, what you take from the experience of being bested is just as important as how to win." The instructor bowed to Jackson and stepped aside.

Jackson moved into the middle of the training room. A gymnastic mat was under his feet. He stood ready.

The instructor clapped his hands together, "Everyone, stand up. All twenty of you. I now command you to fight Cadet Jackson. If any of you can take him down, I will personally raise your grade in this class by one point."

The twenty stood and were looking over Jackson. He was big, muscular, confident and had a scary look in his eyes. But one against twenty was not even a fair fight. The twenty cadets began to charge in. Some were laughing and other were making comments that Jackson was in for an ass kicking.

Jackson waited until the first waive was close enough. He leaped into the air and kicked two cadets in the face. Jackson landed on the back of a third cadet and wrapped his hands around his head and chin. Jackson snapped the young cadet's neck like a twig. Jackson leaped into the air, kicked another cadet in the midriff and then landed on his feet, standing on the body of the dead cadet. He began punching and kicking in every direction as the cadets surrounded him. The other cadets were stunned that one of their fellow students was just killed in front of their eyes. Many tried fighting back, only to receive painful kicks and punches. Jackson flipped many and broke their wrists. Jackson snapped the leg of another cadet with a well-placed kick.

The melee continued until only one cadet was left standing to face Jackson. Jackson noted that the last cadet had not rushed in. He stood back, watching the others and how Jackson dispatched them all. Jackson looked the last opponent over and noted that he was wearing a black belt.

Jackson charged at him and the cadet stepped aside. They began sparing. The kid was good. He was able to deflect each of Jackson's kicks and punches. The fight went on for ten minutes. It ended when a whistle blew from the instructor.

"Time is up, Jackson."

The final cadet bowed to Jackson. Jackson kicked his opponent in the groin while his guard was down. The cadet with the black belt fell to his knees, groaning in pain.

Jackson walked out of the gymnasium leaving one dead cadet and several injured. He was confident that the Rosenburg family would cover up the death for him, just as they did on many other incidents before.

Jackson felt prepared for Gorski. Jackson would not kill Gorski easily. He was going to torture him. When Jackson and Gorski met on that Moon, the Russian cadet was a dead man.

The morning for the tournament had arrived. Yuri Gorski had not been able to sleep at all. Although he was prepared, insomnia had claimed Gorski and he tossed and turned all night long. Lying soundly asleep beside him was Jen Staszko. Gorski had memorized the three competing teams' rosters and had studied the opposing cadets' files. Gorski had gone over the profiles of the Achilles Academy cadets one last time. What Gorski and his team did not know was that the Dean of Achilles Academy had not submitted the profiles of the real team. Gorski and Gillis would have certainly recognized pictures of Avery Jackson, Kai Chin, Cleon Alexander or Caine Rosenburg, due to the past confrontation on Space Station Cy-7. But they were not included. The profiles of Achilles Academy were fraudulent. The profiles from Tyr Academy were impressive as well. The Tyr tournament team had a Harcourt woman participating. Gorski and O'Grady had determined that Tyr had to be the first target, mostly because of the Harcourt and her Child of Athena abilities. But the other reason was that the Team leader of Tyr Academy was Cadet Admiral Edmund Ross Koch. Koch was the leader of the winning team in the last tournament. He was smart and savvy. When O'Grady and Gorski interviewed Lieutenant Junior Grade Frank Glenn, a graduate of Clovis Academy and a member of last year's tournament team, they were warned about Koch. In that previous tournament, Koch and his team executed an ambush that Glenn and his team mates could not overcome.

Gorski was confident in his team mates. He saw that Drew Harrison and LaShondra Lewis were asleep in the other bed, their arms wrapped around one another. Gorski slipped out of his bed and crept silently to Harrison. Gorski nudged his friend until he saw Harrison's eyes flutter open.

"Shhhhh," Gorski told him. "The girls are still asleep. We have to shower and get to the launch pad. We leave in two hours."

Harrison sat up in his bed. He had experienced a passionate night with Lewis and she was still asleep. Each of the team members had attended the going away ceremony the previous night that had been sponsored by the Academy cadets. Harrison had forced himself to avoid any liquor or ales so that he would be clean and sober for the ceremonial lift off. Harrison stood up and moved toward the showers. The day had come for them to travel through one solar system to another. Their destination was the dreaded Moon orbiting planet Semiramis. Harrison was excited. He had already contacted his family and let them know of the event. His highly decorated father had told him that he was proud.

Porfirio Cardenas had also been unable to sleep. He had made love to his wife, Freya, and she fell asleep afterward. They had shared a last dinner with the pilot's team the night before and went home. Cardenas remembered that Lila Zapata had spent the night at their home, sleeping with Jurgen Doernitz in the spare bedroom. Cardenas rose to shower, dress and then say good bye to his wife and children.

Jurgen Doernitz was asleep when he felt someone

shoving his arm. He opened his left eye and saw little Alejandro Cardenas pushing him. "Tio, wake up," the child was urging him. Zapata was naked next to Doernitz. He quickly covered her with a bed sheet. Not good for the young boy to be seeing such things so young, Doernitz thought to himself.

"I'm awake," Doernitz sat up. He ran his fingers through Alejandro's hair. "Go find your father and mother. They have to wake up, too."

The child ran off and closed the bedroom door behind him. Doernitz reminded himself that he needed to make sure the doors were locked. He looked at the beauty lying next to him. She was brilliant, sweet, giving, loving, beautiful and excitable at times. Doernitz knew he was in love with Zapata. Before the last pilot team dinner, he had taken her fishing at his favorite stocked river that was located on the southernmost point of Clovis City. He taught her how to cast a line and spent a few hours enjoying the sound of the flowing water and the peaceful feeling of being so close to nature.

Doernitz took some time to relax in the shower, the water cascading over his head and body helped him to think clearly and clear his mind. He was not apprehensive regarding the pending trip to the Blood Moon. On the contrary, he was looking forward to flying as a wing man with his brother-in-law, Porfirio, and competing alongside his new friends Pierre, Marco, Mary and Les. Due to the extra time they spent preparing, Doernitz was confident that they would win.

Pierre Zerbe had made love to Cara Perez-Guerrero two times that night. When he woke up he showered quickly. While he was in the shower his lover joined him. Perez Guerrero pushed her body against his and kissed him passionately. Zerbe could smell her hair and wrapped his arms around her.

"I think I know why I love sex so much," she said

between kisses.

"Why is that?" Zerbe began washing her back with soap.

"Well, getting to know Freya's children. I realized it was the animal instinct to breed that made me so sexualized. I have a strong desire to have children." She began applying shampoo to Zerbe's hair. "All those times I was stalking guys so I could get them to bed me, I was trying to get myself pregnant."

Zerbe was now washing her hair with her favorite shampoo. "You really think that is the reason? You want a baby?"

She nodded as he lathered her hair. She let the rushing water clean the shampoo off her face. "I do. And I wanted you to know you succeeded. Or, we did."

Zerbe looked into her eyes, "So, we are going to have a baby?"

She smiled and nodded, "Oh yes. You seem surprised."

"I am a little," Zerbe admitted. "I guess I should not be, as often as we have been having sex together." He smiled and began lathering the rest of her body. "We are going to have a child. I like that. You do realize we have to get married? The social workers will take our child away from us if you are still single."

"You want that? You certain? We are both crazy for each other." She laughed at herself. "I suppose that makes us very compatible. You are a rare man. Most men hold it against me, I mean my past." She stood under the water a bit longer. "Okay, I will marry you if you promise that you will keep up your stamina in the bed."

Zerbe started laughing, "With you as my wife, that will be easy. You turn me on like there is no tomorrow."

She kissed him and they made love again in the shower. This time, Zerbe was more gentle with her. She was pregnant with his child and he did not want to do anything to hurt their chances of going full term. As he made love to her, Zerbe realized this woman had changed him. He no longer needed to have multiple women or get involved in deviant acts. .

Marco Andolini and Mary Lincoln had packed their duffle bags the night before. They spent the night in his dormitory room, cuddled together in his bed. When the computer chimes began alerting them that the time had come, they both got out of bed and began to get ready. The normal chatter-box Marco Andolini was silent. He had little to say and seemed deep in thought as he walked hand in hand with Mary Lincoln to the launch area. He had been equally distant with the Andolini clan the last time they attended a family gathering.

Dominic was expressive and full of conversation as was their father. But Marco seemed withdrawn as if his thoughts had control of him. Marco only reacted when several of his siblings informed him that they had been accepted by Clovis Academy as cadets for the next year's class.

Eamon O'Grady had been the first to wake up. As team leader, he felt it his obligation to arrive at the launching pad first. He had to set the example. His wife, Ginger, woke up with him and ran downstairs to start making breakfast. O'Grady showered and dressed in his Class-C uniform. He picked up his pre-packed duffle bag and carried it down the stairs. He received a warm round of applause from the Collins family.

Everyone in the house was awake.

Sean Collins hugged O'Grady. "I was very proud when you married my daughter. You are a born leader and you will do a great job out there."

"Thank you, sir," O'Grady said with a smile.

He was hugged by the sons, Cormac and Liam. Siobhan was also awake and gave him a hug. He saw Julia Steiner there waiting at the kitchen table. She had stayed the night with Cormac. O'Grady noticed that she was packed up and ready to go, her light blue duffle bags were stacked in the corner of the hallway that led to the front door. Ginger ordered everyone to sit as she began serving scrambled eggs, poggie bacon and juices. They ate with gusto and soon it was time for O'Grady and Steiner to make their way to the launch pad.

O'Grady kissed his wife good bye, "I will be back soon."

Steiner also shared a kiss with her boyfriend, Cormac. She was excited to get to the Blood Moon. Seeing new worlds was the reason she decided to go to the Academy. She was prepared for the new adventure.

Les Gillis rolled over in his bed and found that Cosmos the cat was lying between him and Sophia DuBravac, which seemed to be his preferred location. Gillis pet the friendly cat behind his ears for a few moments and he began purring and digging his claws into the bed sheets.

DuBravac stretched her arms over her head and smiled at them. She pet Cosmos and kissed Gillis. "I love waking up next to my two favorite men."

"We love having you here," Gillis ran his fingers through her hair. He was looking into her enchanting eyes, doing his best to burn the image of her lovely face into his mind. "I am going to miss you."

"Me or Cosmos?"

"Both. But mostly you." Gillis sat up in the bed. "It all happened so fast, this whole year. When I get back, I will graduate a month later."

"I know," DuBravac said softly. The issue of what they would do following his graduation had been the reason she had ended her relationship with him before. She had learned that she needed to be more.

"And then we will be separated for a year. I don't want to think about that."

"I understand things will be difficult while we are

apart," Gillis said as he took her hands in his. "I love you, more than anything. I would fight like hell to get back to you. I feel sorry for anyone that stands in my way of seeing you again."

She smiled, "Just come back to me and remember that I love you too."

They kissed for several minutes. Cosmos meowed at them as if to warn that the time had come for Gillis to leave.

"Before I go, I have something to give to you."

"What is it? You know I love gifts." DuBravac stood up and threw on a purple bathrobe to cover herself.

Gillis walked over to his desk of drawers and found a small black velvet box that was hidden under some of his Clovis Academy sweat shirts. He turned around and faced her. He smiled nervously.

"I love you, Sophia."

"And I love you. What are you holding in your hands?"

Gillis knelt down in front of her and held the box out to her. "It belonged to my great grandmother and has been passed down to me from generation to generation. I am now asking you, begging you and hoping that you will accept it and agree to spend your life with me."

DuBravac gasped as Gillis opened the leather box to reveal an engagement ring. She covered her mouth with her right hand as a single tear drop rolled down her left cheek. For once in her life, she was momentarily speechless. "Are you asking me to marry you?"

"Yes, I am Sophia DuBravac. I want to be your husband and love you forever. I want to be there to meet our children as they are born and I never want to go through life without knowing that you will always be my best friend. Please marry me, Sophia."

"Yes, Les. Yes."

She knelt down on the floor with him and allowed

him to slip the diamond ring on her finger. They kissed softly and held each other close, as Cosmos meowed at them from the bed.

O'Grady and Steiner were the first to arrive at their Raumschiff. There were banners at the docking bay saying all kinds of things such as "Good luck!" "Win it for Clovis Academy!" and other slogans. O'Grady looked over the Fenster Corporation Raumschiff Model Four. The outside did look different than the last Model. Perhaps the Doernitz kid made a good call by requesting this specific version of the vessel.

They walked up the entry way plank to board the ship. They sat down their duffle bags in the cargo area. O'Grady began checking the weapons section. Ten hand lasers, several dozen restraints, flares, digging supplies, ropes, and other various useful items. The ship had been inspected by the Tournament Judges to ensure no illegal weapons were on board.

Steiner checked the medical station and quickly inventoried her supplies. She had everything she needed in case she needed to treat an injured crew member. She then went to begin the last check on the life support section of the ship.

Gorski and Harrison arrived soon after, followed by Admiral Seward.

The retired Admiral greeted them, "Are you ready?"

"Yes sir," Gorski responded as salutes were exchanged. "We will give the other teams the fight of their lives."

Seward shook their hands, "Of that, I have no doubt."

Cardenas and Doernitz were next to walk up the landing plank. They plopped down their duffle bags and began conversing with O'Grady. Zerbe showed up soon after. Gillis, Marco and Lincoln were the last three to arrive.

The Team was all present and accounted for. Zerbe and Cardenas climbed the ladder up to the pilot section and began firing up the engines. When the precise second came they wanted to be airborne. Cardenas was determined to arrive in record time and earn the extra points from the Judges.

As the team was preparing for launch, the rest of the Gorski gang showed up to watch. The Rhinehard brothers and April Mejia were the first to make it. Papanikolaou, who had been released from the hospital, was present alongside Fenster and Frazier. Dominic Andolini and Harumi Shigeta were holding hands, waiving at the ship with their free hands. There were over a dozen of the Andolini younger siblings present as well; waving flags of the local soccer team that Marco and Dominic had been on. Two of the sisters, Giola and Venus Andolini, had on the futbol jerseys of Marco and Dominic, respectively.

Yesenia Guevara was there as well, clapping for her friends. Staszko, Lewis, Perez Guerrero, DuBravac, Zapata, Blossom Li, Supreet Patel, Flora Evart and Freya Cardenas were present and waiving. Ann Harcourt woke up early to see them off. Jack Harcourt was pushing the wheel chair bound Michel Evart to give their friends a good send off.

More cadets arrived as the time for lift off got closer and closer. Dirk Fenster found himself surrounded by Lupita Calderon and her brothers and sisters. He glanced at each of them and noted that he was in the middle of Reynita, Karlita, Estrellita, Jose, Pepito, Juanito, Manuel and Xavier. Most of the Calderon children were Academy students, and they all had heard rumors that Dirk Fenster paid the hospital bills for their sister because he was sleeping with her. Of course, Fenster and Lupita both denied those rumors. But her brothers were now following Fenster around and demanding answers to questions. To make matters worse, all of the Calderon brothers were prominent Bragg gang members.

Marco, as if struck by panic, darted out the back of the Raumschiff and began waving at the crowd. The cadets and professors in attendance cheered him. He saw his brother in the dense crowd and ran to him. Dominic let go of Shigeta's hand and the twins embraced.

"You be careful out there!" Dominic told Marco.

"I will!" Marco promised him. He turned and hugged Shigeta. "I will be back soon to see you marry my brother."

Shigeta smiled, "Give Mary, Drew, Yuri and Les our best."

Marco then embraced his younger brothers and sisters before he ran back to the Raumschiff, with the same speed in which he had left. He leaped onto the docking plank and turned and waived at the cheering crowd one last time. He ran inside to join Lincoln and the others. O'Grady would most likely give him the evil eye for leaving the ship like that without permission.

After another ten minutes passed, the loading ramp began to close shut. Doernitz, Lincoln and Marco began the last second safety and engine checks. Everything was clear for lift off.

Porfirio Cardenas had taken the chief pilot seat on the three seat cockpit of the Raumschiff. He looked over to his co-pilot, Zerbe. "Ready?"

Zerbe gave him a thumbs up. The counter on their pilot computer display hit "zero." Cardenas began moving the controls to lift the Raumschiff up into the sky. The cadets and professors on the ground cheered as the purple ship with the white words on each side reading "Clovis Academy" began to rise.

Inside the Raumschiff, the other eight cadets were sitting in chairs, their safety harnesses over their shoulders. The ship was traveling upward and winning the battle against the planetary gravity pull. Soon, they would begin to hit speeds over four hundred thousand kilometers an hour. The flight to the moon over Semiramis would take a week. They relaxed and began to tell jokes over the roar of the engines.

After the ship left the view of the cadets on the ground, the crowd began to disperse. There were hugs shared by many as the majority of the present students had decided to get in line at the main cafeteria for breakfast. Others were ready to go back to bed due to their exhaustion and hangovers from the party the night before.

DuBravac, knowing Perez Guerrero's propensity for multiple lovers, looked at her and asked. "So, Cara, what are you going to do with yourself for the next month?"

The other female cadets were listening for the answer. They all wanted to ask the question, but only DuBravac had the courage. They had speculated that Perez-Guerrero would go back to her "Resident Nympho" behavior once Zerbe was gone.

Perez Guerrero began massaging her stomach with her left hand. She knew that the other women probably had been gossiping about her and Zerbe. "People can change, right? I mean, I think I have changed."

"How so?" Blossom Li noticed that Perez Guerrero was holding her abdomen.

"Are you pregnant?" Freya Cardenas asked. She had seen some women that were expecting hold their stomachs, in a way of showing their joy.

Perez Guerrero smiled at them, her face seemed to beam with pride. "Yes. I am so happy."

The other women began to congratulate and hug her. Perez Guerrero was surprised by the reaction. Most of the other women did not normally associate with her due to her well-deserved reputation as a nymphomaniac and avoided being a part of the group offering her their best. Many of the female cadets had been jealous of her since she had been successful in bedding some of the men that they had privately longed for. She hugged the ones that pronounced their joy for her pregnancy, elated that the other women seemed to genuinely care for her. "All I needed to do was find a man that could take care of my urges. Pierre does that, and so much more."

"So, no more catting around?" DuBravac was skeptical.

"Those days are over, Sophia. I am a one man woman now." Perez Guerrero promised.

Freya gave her a tight hug and whispered into her ear, "Cara, you come see me at the hospital tomorrow. We need to get you on a proper diet and get you on a vitamin regimen. We will make sure your baby is nice and healthy."

"Thank you. I will be there first thing in the morning." She promised.

Guevara never cared for Perez Guerrero and stayed away from the group offering her congratulations. She began her long walk to her cadet housing, alone. She had the unsettling feeling that someone was following her. She began to walk faster and could see several high rise office buildings in the distance. Given the early hour of the day, they would most likely be closed and locked up. But she determined that she would attempt to sneak into one of the buildings and see if she was indeed being tracked. She began to walk even faster. She could hear footsteps behind her on the transparent concrete streets.

As Guevara rounded the corner of the first building, a hand grabbed her left arm and spun her around. It was Bret Bragg.

"Let go of me!" She struggled as Bragg grabbed her other arm. "I'll scream!"

"And no one will hear you," Bragg laughed. "Time for you to pay for my brother, bitch."

Guevara looked around her and saw that James Cobb and two other Bragg gang members were surrounding her. She tried to wriggle free. Cobb grabbed her right arm with both of his hands. Another member of the gang,

Johann LeSkaysner, grabbed her other arm.

"Let me go!" Guevara demanded. She was kicking at Bragg, but he would step away from her legs.

Bragg laughed and reached out with both of his hands and ripped open Guevara's blouse. "My brother always said you had a hot body. I think you need to let us all take turns on you."

Guevara spat in Bragg's face.

His face contorted with rage and he raised his right fist to hit her. But before he could swing at the defenseless woman, someone intervened. Guevara watched as a man in grey sweats and a hood systematically beat each and every one of the Bragg Gang present. The stranger in the hood was a skilled martial artist and was systematically sending each of the Bragg gang crashing to the paved ground. Bret Bragg went down with a broken nose, Cobb was crawling to escape after being kicked and punched. LeSkaysner and the other Bragg member began running after sustaining injuries.

The stranger gently lifted Guevara up, holding her arms. She was sobbing.

"Hey, you are safe now," The familiar voice told her. Guevara looked into the face of Drayton Love-Easter. Her eyes widened in disbelief and she fainted in his arms.

CHAPTER FOURTEEN

The olive green gas on the surface of the moon was a bit unsettling at first sight. Boris Ilyasova, former officer in the United Nations Space Command and former assistant chief pilot on board the Science Cruiser the U.N.S.C. *Colorado*, landed his Super Raumschiff on the surface. He watched the gas move like a thick fog around his ship from his transparent metal windows. Ilyasova had heard of the horrors caused by the moon and wanted to depart quicker than he had arrived. His superstitious nature was getting the better of him as he barked orders to his co-pilot, Heinrich Hahn, also a former officer in the service. Hahn sighed when the landing gear touched the lunar surface, growing weary of Ilyasova's rants about all of the past tragedies on the moon below them. Although there was plenty of oxygen on the Moon orbiting planet Semiramis, the presence of the four to six foot high chlorine gas on the surface convinced Hahn to keep his protective enviro-suit on.

Ilyasova and Hahn had been ordered by the Rosenburg family to accompany other Super Raumschiff's to the Blood Moon for the purpose of delivering four cargo containers, numerous one pilot fighter space craft, deposit extra soldiers at one of the cadet buildings and leave reinforced metal sheets at that location and then leave. Easy mission, in and out. Ilyasova and Hahn had two of the four containers magnetically attached to the sides of their space craft. The cargo containers were red, sixty feet long, fourteen feet wide and high. Ilyasova had been told that the contents of the cargo containers were illegal weapons.

After successfully landing on the moon, Ilyasova released the magnetic tow on the containers. Hahn watched on the computer view screen as both of the large containers fell to the lunar rock. The green chlorine gas billowed as the contact occurred.

In the distance about two hundred yards away, Ilyasova could see the second Super Raumschiff had discarded its' cargo containers as well. The second ship was piloted by Barry Flynn, a long time Rosenburg employee and Jericho Griffin, a former officer in the space command that had lost his rank along with Ilyasova and Hahn.

Ilyasova then opened the rear cargo plank to his Super Raumschiff. The second portion of the mission was to deposit six Allen Corporation Fighter Type CC76A3 space ships on the lunar grounds. The six ships were all painted with the colors of the Clovis Academy, purple, and had the logo of that Academy painted on the side of the ships in white. Each of the ships had a full arsenal of four armor piercing rockets on the bottom of the craft, and fully charged combat laser batteries from either side. All six were resting on a huge metallic conveyer belt that had been specifically constructed to handle the several tons of weight that the ships carried. Ilyasova and Hahn watched as each of the smaller Allen Corporation space ships were slowly rolled out onto the moon by the conveyer belt. The whole process took over half an hour to complete.

The other ships were conducting the same action, depositing the smaller fighter ships, one by one. Soon, all twenty-four of the Allen Corporation Fighter Type CC76A3 space ships were lying on the moon, ready for use.

"Mission accomplished," Ilyasova and Hahn heard Flynn's voice over their space craft communication system.

"We need to make best time back to planet New Edinburgh. I just received a holo-com report that there are problems at the Rosenburg Ranch. The soldiers from General Tan's Brigades attacked and there are many of our people missing. They need our immediate attention."

"Roger that," Ilyasova responded. He was looking forward to returning to New Edinburgh where there was plenty of women and liquor to be had. Ilyasova especially wanted a little revenge. A young lady from Chile and Mexico City, Mejia, had caused him to be kicked out of the Space Command. Ilyasova wanted to pay her a special surprise visit. The Super Raumschiff's blasted off at full speed leaving behind the moon and their deadly cargo. Ilyasova never questioned why they had been ordered to transport the items to that moon as they had done. He had only cared for the money that he would receive from his generous employers. Morality was a weakness that Ilyasova was glad he never obtained.

Dell Ragnarsson was on the lunar surface at the same time. His presence there was for a different purpose, but it was tied into the overall goal which was to kill Yuri Gorski and his fellow cadets once and for all. There were twelve thirty foot tall communication beacon towers on the Blood Moon. The beacon towers were all a bright red and had a warning light that flashes on and off at three second intervals to warn approaching space craft of their presence. The purpose of the towers was to send and receive messages, live broadcasts to the satellite system and support face to face communication and all other forms of interaction with persons or technology not on the moon. Dell had been requested by Alfred Rosenburg, II, to prepare each of the beacon towers to be shut down remotely via a wireless transmitter. Dell complied with that order by placing on each of the twelve computer-communication beacons a foot long and foot wide, computerized, green metallic jamming instrument. Each of the Jammer's, as they were called, were magnetized at the base and extremely effective. Once activated by a long distance communication device, the Jammer would block all broadcasts out from the communication beacon. There would be no broadcasts to the waiting satellites orbiting the moon.

He was not wearing an enviro-suit as was recommended by the experts. Dell stepped onto the lunar surface time and time again, placing the Jammers onto the towers and humming music to himself as he did so. The chlorine exposure did not concern him. He stood taller that the gas clouds and his head and shoulders were easily high enough to take in the man-made oxygen above the chlorine. Dell smiled as he placed his last Jammer onto the twelfth tower. The entire exercise took the assassin over four hours to complete. Now, the Clovis cadets were doomed. The world would see the Gorski crew commit several atrocities and then the rest of the events would be blocked. No one would see the Clovis cadets die. But the broadcast would continue after their deaths with the heroic cadets from Achilles Academy as the only survivors. Dell was satisfied with the plan. He would have revenge for the death of his son and Yuri Gorski would be remembered only as the cadet that went insane and murdered innocent people.

Dell stepped onto his Raumschiff. He had one last task to complete. There was a surprise gift he had to deliver to the Clovis Academy Headquarters. The Rosenburg's had given him a dozen Saharakaree slaves to be used for a deadly purpose. Dell had been ordered to leave them in the Clovis Academy Headquarters. The twelve aliens were sitting calmly in the bottom level of his Raumschiff, the microchips in their brains kept them under control although they would have gladly stormed the assassin and stabbed him to death with their poisonous tails had they not been under the mind control. Del walked by them without fear. They watched him with their black eyes as he passed by them. Each of the scaly red-orange skinned aliens had computer chips in their brains to control them. He glanced at the twelve deadly creatures and noted their tails, with their razor sharp tips and poison venom dripping from them which made the aliens perfect assassins. Once impaled, a victim must receive an injection of anti-venom within ten minutes. Otherwise, the victim would suffer extreme hallucination, intense fever, back spasms and a painful death.

When Gorski and his friends arrived at their headquarters, they would be treated to a lethal welcoming.

The boredom many faced during extended space flights could be overcome by engaging in many various activities. Some people read books, others watched movies, some delved into some hobby such as painting. The majority of humans chose the option of going into cryo-sleep, with the idea that the crew would wake them when we they arrived at their destination. The Clovis Academy tournament team chose to work on their way to the moon. Yuri Gorski, Drew Harrison, Les Gillis and Eamon O'Grady had spread out their strategic plans on the walls of the spacious break room. They had further spread out the photos of the thirty opposing cadets and taped them to the tables.

Gorski kept looking over the Achilles Academy cadets. None of the listed cadets were outstanding by any means. No special training or extra-curricular activities to speak of. None of them were first in their class in any of the University. Compared to the cadets from Tyr, Newton and Clovis Academies, the Achilles cadets were substandard. And that statement was being too kind.

Gorski voiced his thoughts on the Achilles cadets. Gillis agreed that he also felt the University seemed to be intentionally throwing the competition.

"So just what are you alluding to?" O'Grady wanted to know.

"It is just odd," Gorski said. "Look at you Eamon, high grade marks, doctoral candidate, you won cadet of the year two years ago and you are one of the most intelligent people I ever met. Then Les and Julia? They are the top two in our graduating class in their grade point average. Compare just you three with all of these Achilles Academy cadets. They sent the bottom level students, cadets that would end up serving at the worst duty stations after graduation. Some of them are on academic probation!"

"I am with Yuri," Gillis agreed. "I think that Achilles Academy is up to something."

"Perhaps the Dean of the University bet money against his own team?" Harrison speculated.

Everyone laughed.

O'Grady ran his hands through his hair, "I agree with your observation, Gorski. Something is amiss." He looked over the entire team from Achilles Academy. "They must want to throw the tournament. It's as if they want to lose on purpose. This is really out of the ordinary. Every tournament team over the eight solar systems sends their best and most promising, but not this school. I am going to call it in to Admiral Seward."

"I am going to the pilot section," Gillis announced. "I hear the star scenery in this part of the solar system is spectacular."

"Enjoy," Gorski told him and then turned his attention toward O'Grady. "Cardenas and Doernitz wanted to talk to you and Julia about something."

"What now?"

"Doernitz said it was a sling shot maneuver," Gorski shrugged.

O'Grady rose to locate the two pilots and see what it was he wanted to speak about.

Harrison was staring at the pictures of the Newton Academy cadets. "Yuri, these Newton cadets, they seem top notch. You really think we can take them?"

"No doubt about it," Gorski said boldly. Gorski shared Harrison's concern that the Newton cadets could be a formidable adversary. "We are also the best of our school, Drew. Don't ever forget that. Victory against that team would be potentially difficult given the skills of their team members. Did you and Julia install the security lock downs on our internal and external communications? I don't want that expert hacker of theirs hearing anything unless we want him to."

"It's done. Julia, Les and I wrote a really good protection program for the on board computer. No one will hack us." Harrison sounded confident.

"Good," Gorski stood up. "I am going to the computer room to do a live chat with Jen. I really miss her."

"We've only been in space for one day!" Harrison laughed and slapped his friend on his back.

Gillis was bored and wanted someone to talk to. He climbed up the ladder from the command section to the pilot control portion of the Raumschiff and found Pierre Zerbe sitting in the pilot's seat, monitoring the star charts and speed of the ship. The co-pilot and tactical seats were empty.

"Care for some company?" Gillis asked.

"I would love some," Zerbe answered, relieved that he would have someone to talk to. Zerbe had been alone for about an hour and longed for some company. "It sure gets lonely up here in the pilot section. I wonder why they engineered these Raumschiffs to have only three seats in the flight control section?"

Gillis shrugged, "No clue, my friend. That question is above my pay grade. Ask Doernitz, he would know." He looked out the large observation window of the ship and stared at the distant stars and the darkness of space. "It is more beautiful than I could have imagined."

"You didn't see all this when you left old Earth to live on New Edinburgh?" Zerbe asked.

"No, I was in cryo-sleep the whole trip," Gillis told him. "It was a several month long flight between the solar systems. I elected the sleep part on my questionnaire before liftoff. I regret doing that now. I wish I had spent the whole flight just watching the stars and planets."

Zerbe smiled at him, "That's why I wanted to become a pilot. It is so peaceful out there. Just the hum of the engines and your personal thoughts to keep you company. My older brother always said I was nuts to become a pilot. He said that statistically pilots go into battle first and suffer the most casualties."

"But you guys also get laid more than the rest of us," Gillis laughed at himself. "The ladies love the fly boys. Your brother, what does he do?"

Zerbe took a metallic container from a wall mount and drank from it. It was a liquid high in minerals and vitamins to keep one sharp and on their toes for long flights. Porfirio Cardenas had divided the flight shifts up for eight hours rotation between the five cadets.

"My brother is in the Space Command as a Lieutenant in Marine Corps Security. He is serving on a Science Cruiser called the Wisconsin. He said he hates it and has requested a transfer. He told me all of the women on the ship are not that pretty."

Laughing, Gillis recalled his freshman year. There had been a senior weapons major cadet named Francois Zerbe. "Didn't your brother graduate from Clovis?"

"Yes, he did."

"He used to run a gang! He was the one that got William Bragg and taught him the art of intimidation," Gillis remembered and was still laughing.

"Yeah! I remember him. Bragg was a freshman and he was a senior. He used to be into a lot of the hazing on campus."

"Did he and his friends ever get you?" Zerbe felt badly about his older brother's actions. He had done some pretty awful things to other young cadets such as hanging cadets on flagpoles by their underwear and other mean acts. Zerbe had heard many of the stories that had grown into urban legend around the Academy. The action of his older brother was one of the reasons Zerbe kept a low profile at Clovis City. He did so to avoid any retribution from his brother's past victims or their families.

"No, not me. I ran too fast. One of our classmates, when you and I first started as freshmen, what was his name? Short kid, wanted to study computers. Andrews? I think that was his last name."

Zerbe laughed as he recalled the cadet Gillis was referring to. "Henry Blackstone Jameson-Andrews! I remember him well. He was living in the dorms in the same hall I was. He transferred out to another college to get away from my brother and Bill Bragg! My brother forced Andrews to eat poggie dung!"

"That was a shitty thing to do," Gillis laughed. "Poor kid. We all thought it was funny, but I felt so bad for him."

"He wasn't the only victim," Zerbe told him, still laughing about the memory of his older sibling. "My brother was a real jerk. He hurt a lot of cadets and broke a lot of hearts."

"So, are you going to join your brother after we graduate?" Gillis stared out at the stars.

"I don't know. Cara is pregnant now and that changes things for me in a dramatic way. I hoped to get assigned to one if the Battle Cruiser's that will get assigned to search for the lost fleet or the missing Bismark. Now that I have Cara, I am hoping I don't draw one of those assignments. I just never thought about being a father or a husband. I'm excited, but scared, all at the same time."

Gillis put his hand on Zerbe's shoulder, "You will be a wonderful father and a great husband. You were the only man on campus that could tame Cara. All of the men on campus respect you for that."

"According to her, I was the only one that cared enough to try and tame her. I don't know. The first night with her, man, I was hooked. She is so beautiful, so wild in bed. I had no choice but to try and convince her that I was the right one for her. She had me under her spell from the first kiss. The crazy thing is that I used to love having sex with the Kotek women, you know, the half human and half feline hybrids? I would look at my body in the mirror after sleeping with a Kotek and see the scars on my chest and back from their claws. That was a badge of honor for me because I knew I gave it to them good. Then along comes Cara and she rocks my world in way I never dreamed possible. I was in love after our first night together, I just didn't tell her because I was afraid of scaring her off. Eventually I got the courage to tell her how I felt. I love her more than anything."

Gillis nodded as he understood where Zerbe was coming from. "It was the same for me with Sophia. Look, you were not the first to try and tame Cara. But you were the better man than all the rest. I think she saw that in you. Thank the Stars for women."

"I second that sentiment. And you? What are your plans after you graduate?"

"I am already registered to attend the Academy at Sikorsky's Planet to work on my doctorate. Sophia and I will get married before I go."

"You know, I was never in your gang but we are connected in a morbid way," Zerbe told him.

"How so?"

"Well, that transport ship that was blown up, you remember? The one you and your friends were supposed to be on?"

"I remember," Gillis nodded.

"I had a girlfriend and she was the pilot of that ship. I really liked her, Les. She was so nice and sweet and a great lover. She died in the explosion. I was really broken up over losing her, you know? It was tough."

"I can't even imagine."

"So, based on that, I feel as if I am connected to you and the Gorski Gang in a way. I don't know, maybe I am thinking crazy thoughts."

Gillis shook his head, "Losing someone close to you is never easy, my friend. By the way, why did you not join the Bragg Gang?"

Zerbe was quiet for a few seconds before responding, "I was a member when I was in my first year at the Academy. One day, I got sick of it and told my brother to go to hell. I quit."

"That takes guts. I heard no one ever walked away from the Bragg Gang."

"Hey!" Zerbe said, changing the subject. "You want to see something that will really take your breath away?"

"Sure."

Zerbe ordered the computer to display the planet Osiris on the screen. Osiris was a giant gas planet in the same solar system as New Edinburgh. Osiris was approximately thirty times the size of New Edinburgh. The planet appeared on the left view screen. Zerbe instructed the computer to magnify the image of the planet.

Osiris was full of colors, different shades of purples, reds, yellows, blues, orange, white and black streaks across her surface. Gillis marveled at the view of the distant planet. Words could not describe the beauty of the gas giant.

"How far away is she?" Gillis asked.

"We are about a hundred thousand kilometers from her. Perhaps on the way back we can convince O'Grady to let us swing by for a closer look. I always thought that Osiris is the most eye catching planet in the universe."

"She is a beauty," Gillis agreed.

"I once told my brother that if I died, I wanted to be

buried on Osiris. I know it is impossible because no human could withstand the conditions on the surface. It could never be done."

Gillis watched the colors of the spectacular gas planet swirl with no apparent rhyme or reason. "I would join you in that. What a resting place she would be."

O'Grady had requested that Doernitz, Cardenas, Andolini, Lincoln and Steiner meet with him on the ships' command section. The command area had been divided into four parts, one area for meetings, another for the computer section officer and staff, a third section for up to three engineers to work and the fourth section for scientists. Up above the command section was the two seat pilots section where Zerbe and Gillis were. To reach the pilots section from the command station, one had to ascend a twenty foot ladder. O'Grady focused on Doernitz at this meeting. "I hear you wanted to talk to me about a sling shot move?"

"Yes, sir. I wanted us to break the time set by the previous teams so we could earn the extra points," Doernitz began. He pulled out his hand held computer from his breast pocket of his flight uniform. He punched a few buttons on his electronic item and a large, three dimensional holographic display of the solar system was before the group. "So, I felt we could use this planet we are going to pass, Osiris, as a way to increase our speed."

"You mean by flying in close and using the intense gravity to shoot us out faster than when we started?" Lincoln had heard of the theory in her physics class. "Interesting plan."

"Have you done the mathematics to ensure that this specific ship could handle the strain of the gravitational forces, the increase in motion and the long sustained speeds?" Steiner jumped into the conversation.

"Yes I did," Doernitz ordered his small computer to display his mathematical equations. A three dimensional view of his calculations appeared before them in green letters, numbers and symbols. Steiner was walking around the large view of the conclusions Doernitz had calculated and was studying them intently. At one point she glanced over at Doernitz, a look of new found respect in her eyes for the younger cadet.

"So, by this schematic you mean to use the gravity of the giant gas planet to make us go faster than the ship was designed for?" O'Grady walked around the mathematical equations. He had been one of the better math students and also began to believe there was more to Doernitz than he first thought. O'Grady was impressed, but not sold. "Wouldn't the ship break apart? She was not built to go double the speed she can go on her own."

"Triple," Doernitz pointed to one of the lines on his multi-level mathematic formula and conclusions. "Triple the speed. I asked for this specific Raumschiff because I believe the Fenster Corporation designed this vessel to withstand speeds over ten times the level our technology will obtain for us. The ship will be fine. She can handle this."

"And can this ship maneuver around Osiris quick enough to avoid being sucked into her gravitational pull." Marco told them.

"The ship on auto pilot, no." Doernitz added to Marco's point. "But I can do it manually. Any one of us could do it." Doernitz motioned to the other cadet pilots.

"How can you be so sure of that?" O'Grady was raising his voice.

"I tested my theory in the simulator at the Academy three days before we left," Doernitz said softly, a bit startled by the way O'Grady raised his voice at him. "I did the test five times. Each time I was able to fly the ship at the center of the gas giant, go hard right at the last possible second and whip around the planet."

Doernitz was demonstrating, using his fist as the

planet and his other hand as the ship. "We swing around her and break out of the gravity hold and we would be propelled back on our original route, at three times the current speed."

"If this is possible, why hasn't anyone ever done it before?" O'Grady demanded as he crossed his arms over his muscular chest. "I think you are going to get us all killed. First you go over my head and request a different Raumschiff and now you wait to spring this on me? This is not a game we are playing here, Doernitz. We are on a mission and we can't be your personal science project to try untested or unproven theories."

"It will work," Doernitz said with confidence. "I took into account the net force, the acceleration, the mass of our ship; I have the total weight of her in my calculations. I left nothing to chance."

Cardenas stepped up to O'Grady, "If my son in law says it will work, I believe him. He is the most talented pilot I have ever seen. I vote we try."

"Vote?" O'Grady bellowed. "This is no democracy! I am in command here." O'Grady was getting angry. He did not like being challenged.

He spun around and faced Steiner. "Julia, is something like this even possible?"

"I need to inspect the calculations some more. But yes. In theory, I think it could work." Steiner pulled out her own hand held computer. "Jurgen, send me your work. I am going to the medical lab to look it over. Eamon, come with me. We can judge this together."

O'Grady nodded and followed Steiner down the ladder to the level below. When they arrived at the entrance to the medical section, Steiner stopped in the hallway and pointed her finger into O'Grady's chest. "How the hell does Ginger put up with you? You are an ass. The kid is correct. His math is fine. We can do this. You need to stop being such a dictator with the others. You are losing the team."

"I am in charge," O'Grady defended himself. "Admiral Seward picked me to lead."

"Then lead with a little more patience. Stop yelling at everyone. That kid is brilliant. This will work. Let the Doernitz kid do it."

Steiner turned her back on O'Grady and sighed. "Eamon, they don't know you like I do. While I know that you are worried about the safety of everyone on board and you take that responsibility to the extremes, the others do not understand that about you. Your temper will split this team apart. Please tone it down for the sake of the others."

O'Grady was silent for a few seconds. He admired and respected Steiner for her friendship, intellect and honesty. "You always are the conscience of the group. You were able to verify his equations in the few minutes we were up there?"

"Yes, because I did a paper on this subject two years ago in my Newton's Law of Force class," Steiner explained. "Doernitz has the exact same calculations I came up with in my research paper. There are many other scholars, professors, engineers, physicists, theorists and pilots that agree with Jurgen and me."

"And, if it works? Can this Raumschiff take the extra speed?"

Steiner nodded and faced him, "The Fenster Corporation only design and build the best. I did some checking on my own before we left New Edinburgh. This ship could take on gravitational forces double the amount Osiris will throw at us."

"I am still not sold."

"Give the kid a chance. What is the worst that can happen? His theory is wrong and we lose about thirty minutes of flight time. The ship will be able to pull out of Osiris gravity with no problem. No harm, no foul."

O'Grady nodded slowly, "Okay, let's go join the

others.”

He led Steiner back up the ladder to find the others waiting. O'Grady could tell by the way they looked at him that some of the team did not like him. Steiner was correct, he had to change his leadership tactics or he would lose the team.

“Jurgen,” O'Grady put his hand on his shoulder. “Julia says your math is flawless. She agrees with you that this can work. As commander of the team, I am still uneasy. This is an untested theory, so, I think we need to decide this by a majority vote.”

“And you will abide by it?” Marco seemed surprised by O'Grady's softened approach.

“Absolutely,” O'Grady told him. “If Doernitz pulls this off, we all make history. Not something to take lightly. There is the risk of crashing on the gas planet. So, I think this goes way above my authority. We should all have a say in whether we do it or not.”

O'Grady yelled up to Gillis and Zerbe, “You two been listening in?”

Gillis and Zerbe both climbed down the ladder.

“We heard every word,” Zerbe answered.

O'Grady looked to Doernitz, “Get Gorski and Harrison up here. They have equal votes in this.”

“Yes sir!” Doernitz smiled and asked the ship's computer to summon the two missing cadets to the command section.

Within seconds, all ten of the teams were assembled. Doernitz repeated his theory to Gorski and Harrison. Steiner explained to the two that she supported it. O'Grady instructed everyone to raise their hands if they were in favor of taking the risk. The votes came in nine for the attempt and one abstaining. O'Grady was the only hold out.

“Okay, let's do this,” Marco said with excitement in his voice. Like Steiner, he had also studied the theoretical papers on the subject. Marco wanted to see if the theories had any merit.

"I need a co-pilot with fast reflexes," Doernitz said. "Everything has to be done manually."

Marco stepped toward the ladder leading to the pilot section. "Let's go, Jurgen. I was the best goal keeper in the New Edinburgh soccer league. I think it would be fair to say that I have the best hands on this ship. I am with you."

Noone spoke up to challenge Marco in his assertion. Doernitz followed the Italian up the ladder.

Cardenas turned to Zerbe and Lincoln, "Let's set up in the engineering section and monitor the stress levels on the engine and the structure of the vessel."

Gillis nodded to O'Grady and Harrison, "We should take the computer duties."

Steiner looked to Gorski, "That leaves us in the science area. We'll monitor everything and record it. This may earn us all an Honorary Doctorate somewhere."

The cadets all moved to their positions and quickly strapped themselves into their safety harnesses. It was sure to be a rough ride.

CHAPTER FIFTEEN

With confusion on her face, Yesenia Guevara woke up in her housing unit. She was in a black and gold kimono that had been a birthday gift, given to her by Harumi Shigeta. She still lived in the married students homes due to her status as a single parent. She thought of her child and sat upright in the bed, looking all around her. She was in her bed covered with satin sheets and a thick red blanket. She did not recall how she arrived home or how she ended up in the bed. Realizing that her son had to be picked up from day care, she stood and found her torn blouse on the floor. She had believed that the attack on her and the heroic rescue had just been a dream since her dead lover could not have been there. It was not possible.

"It had to be a dream?" She asked herself.

"No, it was not a dream," Guevara heard a voice respond to her question. She turned to see Drayton Love-Easter standing before her in her bedroom doorway. He had a glass of orange-cranberry juice, her favorite drink, in his right hand. He handed her the glass. "Sit down, drink your juice. I have much to tell you."

"The day care..." Guevara began to tell the man of her son, still in a state of disbelief.

"I already picked up our son while you were sleeping. Sit down and relax. I know you have a million questions and I will answer them all for you."

He had been named by Doctor Nicolette Rosenburg

as Drayton Love-Easter #2 and had been charged with the mission of living the life that should have been the life of the original man. While all of the clones of Love-Easter desired revenge on Caine Rosenburg, they listened to the pleas of the three Rosenburg women to assist in a mission with a much bigger scope. The other duplicates of the original Love-Easter would voyage to the ends of the eight solar systems to start a civil war, while Number Two would take the place of the man that had died; live his life as the original would have and protect his son.

Guevara slowly sat down on her bed and took several deep breaths with her heart fluttering and her mind racing. Was she really getting a second chance with the love of her life? She composed herself and began asking question after question. He answered them all.

He told her that he had been in a coma while the authorities told everyone he had died so the killers would not finish the deed. The official reports of his demise had been a ruse to protect him. He woke up last week and had been going through some physical therapy, to get his muscles used to functioning normally again. The lawyer, Sean Collins, had Love-Easter wait until he was ready to reveal himself to anyone. He chose Guevara to be the first.

"Why not Les? He was your best friend." Guevara asked between sips from her glass.

"True. But had I gone to him first, he would not have gone on the tournament team. The other cadets needed Les with them and he could really use the team experience as a feather in his cap for his resume. I did not want to jeopardize that for him. So I waited until they were gone before I came to you." Love-Easter explained.

"But, Les and Jen, they told me your throat had been cut. They said you bled out." Guevara inspected his neck. "There is no scar. How can that be?"

"Medical technology is very advanced in skin grafting."   Love-Easter answered and hoped that she bought the explanation. "Or so they tell me. Any other questions?"

"No, I can't think of any now."

"Good. I have a few for you. First, can you re-integrate me with the gang? It would be best if you take me to Jen, Michel, Klaus, Elektra, Arch and the others."

"Of course I will, you don't even have to ask." Guevara drank her juice. It was ice cold, just the way she liked it.

"And will you go with me today to the Wedding Chapel? I want us to be married before those vulture social workers come and steal our son."

"You want me to marry you so we can keep our son?" Guevara frowned.

"Yes and no," he moved over to the bed and sat down next to her. He held her free hand in his. "Yes, I want to protect our son. But the main reason I wish to marry you is because I love you. I always have and always will. I think the only reason I am still alive is because I had to see you again. I had to make amends for my wrong actions in the past. I want us to always be together."

Guevara swallowed and squeezed his hand. She was silent for a few moments and then nodded, "I feel the same for you. Yes, yes. Let's go today. I never stopped loving you. The biggest mistake I made was leaving you for Bill. You were always so kind and loving while he was cruel and demeaning. I learned that a man like you is so hard to find. I swear to love you forever."

They stood and embraced. She felt blessed to receive the miracle of a second chance to get it right with the father of her child.

"I will never leave your side," Love-Easter promised her.

True to her word, Guevara began the process of reintegrating Love-Easter back into the Gorski Gang and the Academy. She first took him to the Dean and Admiral

Seward and restored his place in the classes he had been enrolled in. The next morning, the remaining Gorski Gang members were at the Cadet Cafeteria, enjoying breakfast. There were others there that had never been made "official" members, but they felt at home with the group. Seated around the rectangular table on the left were Klaus Rhinehard, April Mejia, Rolf Rhinehard, Flora Evart, Michel Evart, Supreet Patel, Cara Perez Guerrero and Mia Nguyen. On the right were Jen Staszko, Sophia DuBravac, Lila Zapata, Elektra Papanikolaou, Arch Frazier, Dirk Fenster, Dominic Andolini and Harumi Shigeta. Seated at the head of the table was Jack Harcourt. There were several other empty seats around them. They were eating the normal cafeteria spread, several conversations going on at the same time between the groups.

Admiral Seward approached their table and all of the cadets immediately stood at attention when they saw him.

"At ease!" Seward bellowed and the cadets all sat down in unison.

"I just wanted you all to know that the news media is here," Seward told the Gorski Gang members. "They are going to want to interview you regarding your friends in the tournament."

"When did they start doing that, sir?" Dominic asked. "The media rarely cares about the tournament."

"They do when one of the teams just tested an old scientific theory and proved it correct," Seward responded. "Your friends just used the gravity pull of the gas planet Osiris and the force propelled them at three times the speed of any Raumschiff. Ever. Your friends are going to be written up in science journals and probably wanted on the lecture circuits."

Zapata began clapping, "Wow! I told you they would do it!"

She had been the one to put the idea in Doernitz'

mind to use Osiris as a test on the old theory. Zapata had worked out the mathematical equations with Doernitz. She was beyond ecstatic that the theory had worked.

DuBravac put one of her arms on Zapata's hands, "Lila, please calm down." She then looked at Seward, "It was confirmed? The fastest a Raumschiff has ever reached was five hundred thousand kilometers an hour."

Seward smiled, "Try the new record that was just set by your friends. Take the fastest speed ever and quadrupled it."

Staszko dropped her fork in disbelief, "Say again?"

Several of the others were in stunned silence. The ramifications of such an event was not lost on any of them. No Raumschiff ship had ever reached such speeds. Klaus and Rolf Rhinehard were left speechless by the news. Jack Harcourt leaned back in his chair and began to consider the implications in his head. It would not be as important as the ability to harness dunkle material, also known as dark matter, that was in abundant amounts in space. Humanity had stolen the technology necessary to use the hidden energy sources in space from the conquered Akarzdamedians.

"And it was in a Fenster Corporation Ship!" Dirk Fenster announced proudly as he broke the momentary silence. "I knew our newest models were the best."

"O'Grady reported that Doernitz was apologizing to everyone for promising three times the best speed. His calculations were a little off." Seward laughed as he began to walk away. "There is someone else here to visit with your group. Enjoy the rest of your day."

"They really did it?" Klaus asked aloud. "Do you know what this means?"

"It means astral navigation will be changing for the better." The old familiar voice said from behind Jack Harcourt. The group looked over Harcourt's shoulder and saw Yesenia Guevara and Drayton Love-Easter standing there, holding hands and smiling back at the table.

There were several gasps and then a long silence.

DuBravac slowly stood and ran to Love-Easter. She touched his face and looked into his eyes. She had wept many times for the loss of Love-Easter. She had comforted Gillis on several occasions when he would break down in tears because of the memories of his dear friend. "Is it, is it really you?"

"In the flesh," Love-Easter smiled at her.

DuBravac hugged him and began to weep in his arms. Of all the group members, DuBravac and Gillis had been the closest to Love-Easter. Dominic was up next and wrapped his arms around Love-Easter and DuBravac both. Most of the other cadets were speechless.

The one that showed the most emotion was Papanikolaou. She had been living with the guilt that Love-Easter had been killed defending her. She had been having consistent nightmares about that night when those men stabbed him and cut his throat. She began crying tears of joy at seeing him alive. Frazier put his arms around her and she buried her face in his chest.

The shifts for sleep and duty stations had been outlined by Eamon O'Grady the week before the tournament team left planet New Edinburgh. Porfirio Cardenas, Jurgen Doernitz, Pierre Zerbe, Les Gillis, Yuri Gorski and Drew Harrison were asleep in the bunk beds of the Raumschiff when the news regarding Love-Easter came in. There were seventeen triple bunk beds in all. The cadets had let loose with some shots of tequila after breaking the speed record and Doernitz was the one that defiled himself the most since the move had been done at his urging. Even the dictatorial style of O'Grady changed enough for him to join in for a toast to the team.

O'Grady had split the cadets up into twelve hours shifts and the pilots to eight hour flight shifts. He was awake working in the computer section, while Steiner was in the science section. Both of them were collecting data for the history they had now become a part of. Marco was in the engineering section, checking the dark matter converters, while Lincoln was piloting the Raumschiff.

A priority message came in for O'Grady from Admiral Seward which the cadet promptly responded to. "O'Grady here, sir."

O'Grady saw Seward's three dimensional image on the screen before him. The Admiral had a rare smile on his face which indicated something good.

"Son, the Academy is very proud of you and the team. I wanted to let you know the news that was released today and I think you will need to tell Gorski and Gillis right away. Their friend, Drayton Love-Easter, is alive."

O'Grady was speechless, "Say again?"

"You heard me. He had slipped into a coma and the doctors saved his life. The news that Love-Easter had died was a cover story so that those Ragnarsson killers would not make an attempt on his life. He came out of the coma about a week ago. He is trying to catch up on his classes so he can graduate on time with the rest of the senior class. As team leader, you need to tell all of his friends."

O'Grady nodded as he took in the information, "Yes sir. I will take care of it now. O'Grady out."

He stood and took a drink from his cup on the table next to the rows of computer panels that surrounded him. He walked into the engineering room and saw Marco Andolini typing into a holographic computer key pad. Marco heard the footsteps on the metal floor and looked up at O'Grady.

"You look like you just saw a ghost," Marco remarked when he saw O'Grady's face.

"It would seem the Clovis Academy has a ghost. Your friend, Drayton Love-Easter? He is alive," O'Grady reported.

Marco stopped what he was doing and stood up,

"Are you sure? How?"

"Admiral Seward's word on it. He had been in a coma and just now came out of it."

"Damn," the Italian ran to the ladder to the pilots section and told Lincoln the news.

O'Grady walked to the science section and found Julia Steiner on a swivel chair, gliding across the floor on its' wheels as she was running about six programs at once. She was fantastic at multi-tasking. She had on a set of headphones, listening to her favorite musical group from old Earth named Abba. She noticed that O'Grady standing before her. She stopped her chair and pulled off her headphones.

"What is it?"

"Drayton Love-Easter is alive."

Steiner frowned and then smiled. During her time with Harrison and the Gorski Gang, she had been fond of Love-Easter. Like all of the other members, she had mourned his loss. She had cried at his funeral. She wanted to cry again for the good news that the man was alive. She maintained her composure. "I guess today is the day for the impossible. I should tell Les. They were best friends."

"Please. I think it would be most appropriate if this news came from you." O'Grady nodded as Steiner ran to the ladder and descended to the lower level.

She woke up Gillis, Gorski and Harrison and took them outside. As she told them the news, the three men were showing signs of disbelief, shock and joy.

Gillis excused himself so that he could be alone. He walked down the winding corridor toward the food storage area. When he was certain he was by himself he leaned against the wall and covered his face. The loss of his dear friend left an open wound in his heart. The news that he had actually survived the inflicted knife wounds although impossible, was the best thing Les Gillis had been told in some time.

CHAPTER SIXTEEN

The large Super Raumschiff entered orbit around the moon over Semiramis and began to glide toward her surface to land. David Rosenburg had been a skilled pilot since the age of eight and was one of the best fathers Alfred had ever seen. David landed their space craft on the lunar surface. Next to their ship was the familiar Raumschiff that belonged to Dell Ragnarsson. After the engines shut down, David stretched his legs and walked to the back of the ship. He visited the weapons section of the Raumschiff and secured a laser pistol, attached the pistol to his weapons belt that was around his black flight pants and then contacted Dell for permission to join him for coffee and lunch.

The assassin agreed and allowed the father and son aboard his large craft.

"Is everything prepared?" Alfred Rosenburg, II, demanded.

"All is ready," Dell reported, a tone of joy in his voice to hide the fact that he despised Rosenburg. The least the man could have done was ask Ragnarsson how he was doing or offer some form of welcome.

"The Jammers are placed on the satellite towers. The Akarzdamedian's are on board their fighter ships, which we have loaded with armor piercing rockets and combat laser batteries. The Saharakaree are in the Clovis Academy headquarters and ready to ambush the Gorski team."

"Good," Alfred shook his hand for a job well done. "My information is that the eight Judges will arrive tomorrow and take their places in the observation towers. We kill them first but not until my son arrives. We need to make certain the other cadets are already present on the moon when we strike so that they will not be able to turn around and avoid their worthy deaths. As we blow the judges to hell my son and his team will take out the Tyr Academy cadets."

"Why them first?" Dell asked as he handed the two men cups and began to pour coffee for them.

"They have a Harcourt, a woman. She could use her special powers against us so she has to be killed quickly." Alfred said waiving his hand in the air as if he were insulted by Dell for daring to question his plans. "They can make you fall in love with them, make us turn on each other and they supposedly can read your mind. She has to be killed quickly."

"Understood," Dell agreed. "I read up on the Newton Academy cadets. Their commander, Anderson, is a Spetsnaz graduate. He could be formidable. Once the violence begins, he and his team might be difficult to deal with."

Alfred laughed at the thought and slammed his fist on top of the table where the coffee cups rested. "We have superior fire power. We have weapons and they do not. In a few days, all of the cadets will be dead and my son Caine will be a universal hero."

Dell hoped that Alfred was not being over confident.

David drank his coffee in silence as he listened to his father and the assassin banter about.

Les Gillis kept his agreed upon time for live face to face computer chat with Sophia DuBravac. They spoke at length of Drayton's coma and coming back to them. Gillis had held his emotions in check as best he could until he spoke to her. They both cried given their mutual happiness for the return of their friend. DuBravac told Gillis that Love-Easter had come over to see Cosmos. The cat had reacted favorably, rubbing his head against Love-Easter and purring as if there were no tomorrow. Cosmos had remembered him well.

Yuri Gorski had also kept his assigned time with Jen Staszko. Their conversation had been similar to the one between Gillis and DuBravac. Staszko informed Gorski that the rest of the cadets were very proud of their breaking the speed record. The event had brought with it an overwhelming tide of Clovis Academy pride. Cadets were celebrating in the streets and alumni were donating money to scholarship funds for future students.

The news media was there in full, interviewing everyone; no story was too small for them to cover. It was like a circus all over the campus. Dean Harvard was even honored by the Glorious Leader during his weekly state of the eight solar systems speech for producing students that had the knowledge and courage to attempt the feat. Gorski and Staszko spoke of their love for each other before ending the communication.

Similarly, Marco Andolini would spend an hour each day with his family, mostly with Dominic. But he would also spend extra time with his parents and his huge group of siblings. One of his sisters, Venus, seemed to have become a darling of the news media, riding the coattails of his newfound fame. Marco laughed at that news as Venus had always been the one that liked to have her picture taken and volunteered at all of her high school thespian events. She had even considered a modeling career if she failed to gain acceptance into the Academy.

Porfirio Cardenas would spend his spare time chatting with his wife, Freya. His son Alejandro, would sometimes interrupt their conversations and tell him he loved him. Cardenas also would receive calls from his father, Rear Admiral Alejandro Cardenas, the commander of a fleet of five Battle Cruisers and held considerable power within the Space Command. His father was proud that his son had been a part of the historic event by breaking the Raumschiff speed records.

Jurgen Doernitz spent his time split between his sister Freya, Lila Zapata and his adopted parents, the Yamamoto's. After breaking the Raumschiff speed records, Doernitz heart filled with pride when Admiral Yamamoto had told him, "You bring honor to our family."

Mary Lincoln enjoyed speaking with her father, Marine Corps Colonel Jamal Lincoln, the commander of the United Nations Space Command Battle Cruiser called the *Cortez*. Her father would express his undying love for her and his pride in her accomplishments.

Pierre Zerbe spent all of his allotted time with Cara Perez-Guerrero. With Zerbe's encouragement, she would strip in front of the camera for him and perform erotic acts for his enjoyment. They would talk sexually to one another and of the things they would do together when reunited.

O'Grady was missing his wife and each day he made time to speak with her so he could see her lovely face. He could not wait to get home to her.

Thanks to Doernitz and his maneuver, they were only two days away from the Blood Moon.

The team of Judges arrived at the Moon orbiting Semiramis. They came in a Raumschiff, painted white so that it would not conflict with the similar vessels of the competing cadets. The chief of the officials was retired Captain Galvan of the United Nations Military Intelligence. He was a highly decorated soldier with thirty years in the service and had just celebrated his sixty-third birthday. He enjoyed helping out in events such as this and volunteered his time. Galvan was one that would never turn down the opportunity to lend a hand to his fellow man.

The assistant chief official was retired Commander Sammon of the United Nations Space Command. Sammon had served as a First Officer on the Battle Cruiser *Pegasus* for many years. She had always hoped for a command of her own, but it never came. After being passed over for promotion to Captain on several occasions, Sammon elected to retire. She normally would officiate sporting events on his home planet, but her true love was to watch the young cadets compete against one another.

There were four towers for the officiating crew. Two judges would be assigned to each tower. Sammon and Galvan took the north tower and the remaining six judges went to the south, west and east. Their assigned task was to grade the performances, award and deduct points according to the tournament rules and make certain that the cadets received proper medical treatment in the event that they were injured.

Galvan was excited about this tournament since the Clovis Academy cadets had caused much uproar by not just breaking the old Raumschiff speed record, but they blew it off the face of the map. Galvan was looking forward to shaking each of their hands.

CHAPTER SEVENTEEN

Caine Rosenburg felt that the day of reckoning had finally arrived. He could feel it in his bones. All of the traps were in place; the soon to be deceased were unaware that death was waiting for them. He was so certain that victory would be his that he had made reservations at Café de Ole in downtown Clovis City one week after the tournament would be over. He imagined how he would arrive home as a hero, vanquishing the cowards from Clovis Academy and avenging the murdered innocents on the Blood Moon. Caine nodded to the man to his left, Avery Jackson. Although Caine desired revenge on Gorski, Jackson lived and breathed it. Jackson had not said more than ten words to any of their team mates during the week-long trip through a fold in space and past all the planets in their solar system. Jackson had spent his days and nights sharpening knives and ensuring that all of the laser weapons were fully charged.

The Achilles Academy team landed their Raumschiff at their headquarters before the other cadet teams. Peter Lomax and Keith Austin had been the main pilots for the Achilles team and skillfully landed their Raumschiff fifty feet north from the entrance to the two floor building. Green was the official color for the Achilles team. Lomax would not have missed the opportunity to go along in the trip for anything else in the world. He was happy to accept the pay Caine's father had offered, but the truth be known, Lomaz would have gone along without any money. Austin, on the other hand, was there for the money. The fact that he was going to have an opportunity to kill strangers was just icing on the cake.

Lomax observed that the outer shell of their headquarters was a mix of metal, one way glass and wood columns. The building looked sturdy enough from the sky.

Austin commented that to the east were twenty small fighter ships, painted purple and fully loaded for war. The smaller craft had been covered by a thin metallic tarp that blended in with the olive green color of the chlorine gas to avoid detection by the judges and other cadets. Sitting in each of the small fighter ships were the slave Akarzdamedians pilots, each controlled by a small micro-chip in the base of their brain. Soon they would do as they were forced to by their oppressors, the Rosenburg's, and begin killing innocent cadets.

On the south of the building were the four authorized smaller fighters for the Achilles Academy. Those were painted green and had the logo of the Academy on each side. Dell Ragnarsson, David Rosenburg and Alfred Rosenburg, II, had loaded the four authorized fighter ships with real weaponry as well, just in case.

On the east side of the headquarters was the Raumschiff of Dell Ragnarsson. It was also covered with a tarp, to avoid detection from the other parties on the moon. The attacks needed to be by surprise. Ragnarsson wanted to ensure that the judges and cadets had no opportunity to fight back.

Caine Rosenburg was the first to jump from the landing plank of the Raumschiff onto the lunar surface. He was wearing his enviro-suit to avoid any negative effects from the cloud of chlorine gas around him. He was followed by Cadet Kai Chin and they both walked with an air of invincibility to the entrance to their headquarters. The computer inside the headquarters building sensed their movements and the front doors slid open. There was a powerful generator inside the structure that kept the heavier chlorine gas from entering the facility. Caine and Chin removed their helmets and sat them on the closest table to the entrance. They began to inspect the interior of their temporary home away from home.

The lower level consisted of many medical items and there were several beds in case of emergencies. There were numerous medical cabinets and surgical instruments in the metallic cabinets. The kitchen was also in the lower level and it was wide and spacious. There was more than enough room for ten cadets to share fellowship and dine together. Chin noticed that Cleon Alexander and Burton Stapler had joined them in the main hallway. They all four ran up the stairs to the upper level, where there were bunk beds for them to sleep in. In the center of the upstairs floor were ten laser rifles, ten hand lasers, numerous knives, stun darts, flame darts and machetes.

"Load up," Caine told them as he took hold of a laser pistol. He turned and saw that Avery Jackson was there by his side. "The Tyr Academy cadets are on their way."

Avery Jackson began grabbing weapons and inserted them into holsters and sheaths that were attached to his web belt. He had a look in his eyes that even made Caine a little nervous. Jackson meant business.

The Newton Academy cadets arrived next and landed at their facility. Their Academy colors were red with white trim. Cadet pilot Ellen Benson skillfully landed the Raumschiff onto the moon. Her co-pilot, Cadet Jeff Carter, gave her a smile.

"Great landing, Ellen," Carter complimented her.

"Did you expect anything less of me? We are clear," Benson broadcast to the remainder of the crew.

The team leader, Cadet Alan Anderson, had the other cadets assembled with him at the exit ramp.

"All right team Newton! I want the facility up and

running in fifteen minutes. Secure your stations. I want the outer defenses to be up in two hours! Captain Benson, I want you and your flight team in the air within the hour!"

"Yes sir!" The rest of the cadets yelled.

"Move out!" Anderson ordered as the ramp lowered.

All of the Newton Academy cadets ran out onto the lunar surface. Their enviro-suits were protecting them from the chlorine gas that came up to their chest level. They moved with precision and purpose. Anderson had spent a month training his team. He was a great leader and he intended to win the trophy for his Academy.

The purple Raumschiff of Clovis Academy approached the moon from the east. All of the ten cadets were at the side observation window, save Mary Lincoln who was in the pilot seat. The moon was glowing a light green.

"So that is the infamous Blood Moon," Porfirio Cardenas said. "Doesn't look like much to be afraid of. Kind of wonder how such a small satellite could cause so much death."

"The universe is not a safe place," Gorski grunted and walked to the other side and grabbed his enviro-suit. "Remember that the majority of the surface is covered in chlorine gas. Time to suit up."

"You heard the man," O'Grady told the others. "No one on the surface without your suits. Let's move. We should be landing at our headquarters within the hour."

Drew Harrison began putting on his uniform as he glanced over at Julia Steiner's direction. She was wearing a skin tight half shirt and panties. His eyes wandered over her firm legs, flat stomach and the rest of her body. For a moment, he remembered how wonderful it was to hold her in his arms and to be the man that had the pleasure of making love to her. He turned his back to her since watching her, when he knew that she was now involved with another man, was akin to emotional torture.

Gillis was dressing into his uniform quickly. He was standing next to Gorski. "So, Yuri. When this is over and we win, what choice of duty station would you want?"

Gorski was silent in thought as he pondered the question. "If I had my choice, some station in military intelligence. If not, I would be just as happy being a pilot in the space command. You?"

"I don't care," Gillis laughed. "Now that we know Drayton is alive, nothing really matters any longer. You remember all those times I locked myself in one of the computer library cubicles to study while the rest of you went off to party? Looking back on it, I wish I had gone out with the gang more often. I just want to have Sophia with me. I want to spend time with Dray and Yesenia like we used to. I know when I graduate I will miss you and the others terribly. Other than that, I don't care."

Gorski smiled, "Glad you are on my side, Les. Sounds like you have figured out the secret to life. Some things just don't really matter. What are those?"

Gillis realized Gorski saw his pouch with his thin magnesium strips. "Oh, I was going to set up magnesium trip wires around our HQ. Anyone gets close, they trip the wire which I will have rigged up to ignite the strip. It will be a bright flash of light. Just a precaution."

"How many did you make?"

"Several dozen. I'm a cautious guy." Gillis handed Gorski a few. "Just pull the attached string on the side and it will ignite. Just in case."

"Glad you are on our side," Gorski repeated.

"Just don't look at them if you ignite them. It could blind you," Gillis warned.

Gorski was now feeling the anticipation of stepping out onto the moon. Other than old Earth and New Edinburgh, Gorski had not been to any other worlds. Even his training for Spetsnaz had been on old Earth. The Blood

Moon would soon be the third world that Gorski would experience and he could not wait for O'Grady to give the order to lower the receiving ramp and take the headquarters.

CHAPTER EIGHTEEN

The light blue Raumschiff of Tyr Academy began to land near her headquarters on the Moon of Semiramis. The cadet commander, Edmund Ross Koch, ordered his cadets to get ready for securing their building. Koch had commanded last year's Tournament Team victor. Sara Barnes stood next to Koch and held his hand. They had been lovers at the Academy for years. He had lobbied for her to be part of the team for the competition as he wanted her by his side for the week long flight through space and the time they would spend on the moon. The Dean allowed her to participate even though there were some reservations given the relationship between Koch and Barnes.

"We are going to win, right?" Sara Barnes kissed Koch on the cheek.

"No public displays of affection in front of the others," Koch whispered with a wry smile. They had been sleeping together the entire flight and the rest of the team knew that Koch and Barnes were an item.

Lionel Barnes, the second in command and Sara's older brother, approached them. "ETA to landing ten minutes."

Koch nodded and shook his hand. Since his Academy had the highest entrance standards, the most renowned faculty and training facilities, his team was the best of the best. They would win easily, just as they had the previous year. He looked over his crew. His secret weapon was Jayla Harcourt, a Child of Athena. She could use her special powers to influence the men on the other teams to surrender. It was too easy, but the tournament rules allowed participation by any registered cadet, regardless of their abilities. With her powers and Koch's superior knowledge, they would win within three days' time.

Captain Galvan and Commander Sammon had turned on the power to all of the broadcast towers so that the signal of the Tournament could be sent out to the entire planetary reach of the Earth Empire. The top floor of the judges towers were filled with row after row after row of computer monitoring screens. The multiple screens enabled the judges to see all of the events on the moon. The judges would decide, by watching the screens, whether to reward points to a team or deduct them through demerits.

Galvan and Sammon waited until the large two hundred inch by four hundred inch wide monitor screens on the walls before them came to life with images of other planets. Galvan began to confirm that the Dean of each of the four competing Academies were watching. Galvan noted that the Glorious Leader was on one of the screens, eating grapes and watching intently.

"This is Chief Judge Galvan. All of the judges are in place on their towers. The last two cadet teams are arriving as we speak. I hope that all citizens of the Earth Empire enjoy this Tournament. The four teams come from different academies and different planets. They are well trained and motivated and are the best from their respective schools."

The Glorious Leader, Vladimir Sikorsky was watching the broadcast from the comfort of his great tower. Several of his wives were massaging his legs and feet as he drank red wine. He laughed at what he knew was about to happen. Ten feet to Sikorsky's right was metal bed with a naked eighteen year old woman struggling to free herself from her restraints. Her hands and legs were strapped down on the bed by metal straps. She was cursing, trembling with fear and begging to be freed. Sikorsky motioned to two of his wives and he turned his head to watch. His wives slowly walked toward the young woman and they began to pull out sharp cutting knives from sheaths hidden under their clothing. The young woman saw the knives and screamed out loud for someone to help her. Vladimir Sikorsky laughed and applauded as he watched his wives begin to skin the woman alive.

At the student activity centers of the four Academies, cadets were watching to cheer on their teams. At Clovis City, New Edinburgh, the O'Malley family opened their bar up for twenty-four hour service so the cadets could watch all of the event without interruption. All of the Gorski Gang and their friends were there clapping their hands and ordering appetizers and drinks. DuBravac was holding Zapata's hand. They watched retired Captain Galvan give his speech about the rules. No lethal weapons, no killing. Only capturing cadets on the opposing teams was allowed. He began to go over the point system. The time had come.

The tournament was about to begin.

In the middle of Galvan's speech, Sammon interrupted him. "Sir, the other three towers report that a small fighter ship has arrived and they are training their weapons on them. My monitors confirm what they are reporting. Those cadet ships have locked R-5 Rockets on the other three towers."

"Excuse me?" Galvan asked with a confused expression on his face. He had never known Sammon to be a practical joker or a prankster, which led him to quickly conclude that something was going wrong.

"She said your towers on the south, east and west sides of the moon have one of my fighter ships there." Alfred Rosenburg, II, said through a voice muffler. He was wearing a purple enviro-suit, which were the colors of Clovis Academy and his name tag read "Gorski." His helmet was on to hide his true identity from the vast viewing audience. Rosenburg had a laser pistol in each hand aimed them at the two retired officers.

Next to him in a purple enviro-suit was Dell Ragnarsson. His name tag read "Gillis." He also had kept on his helmet to protect his identity. Dell had a laser rifle in his hands, aimed at the two stunned referees.

Dell Ragnarsson and Alfred Rosenburg had been hiding in the North Judge's Tower for several hours while waiting for the moment to strike. The attacks had been orchestrated to occur quickly and on a tight time schedule. Rosenburg and Ragnarsson wanted to leave no margin for error. The judges had to die first and the citizens of the eight solar systems had to believe that Yuri Gorski had them all killed. The computers in the Judge's Towers were operating and the citizens of the United Nations of Earth were witnesses to the events as they occurred.

"What the hell is going on here?" Galvan demanded. "You are not allowed in the judges towers! You will be assessed demerits for this! Or worse, suspended!"

Rosenburg laughed and pointed his left index finger at Galvan. "To hell with your rules. We are going to make up our own rules. Watch the screens."

Galvan and Sammons looked at the three small purple fighter ships were hovering over the other three judge towers. Each of the space craft had the logo of Clovis Academy painted on the sides.

"Fire!" Alfred Rosenburg ordered into his wrist band communicator.

Cadets Rutger Stenerud, Keith Austin and Clive Doornink were the pilots of those craft and awaited the order while thay sat comfortably in their individual Allen Corporation Fighter Type CC76A3 ships. They had been directed by the Rosenburg's to fly the small fighter ships and arrive at the Judge's towers and await the order to fire their rockets. The three cadet pilots did as instructed and had been hovering over their targets for only a few minutes before the order to fire was received. When the command was given, Stenerud, Austin and Doornink fired all of their armor piercing rockets at the towers.

The entire viewing population over eight solar systems watched as the Clovis Academy ships fired upon the three judge's towers. Each one erupted in brilliant explosions of metal, concrete and tile. The men and women inside them had no chance and died instantly, their bodies ripped apart and incinerated in the blasts. The three towers collapsed as the explosions continued. Brick, glass, wood, plastics and metal scattered across the lunar surface.

Galvan quickly realized his life was in danger. If Galvan attempted to flee, they would just gun him down. Galvan was an experienced soldier and knew that in an ambush your chances of survival were better if the target charged the attackers. He hoped that these two cadets would not be expecting such a bold move. Galvan ran at the two purple clad men before him. Having contemplated that the judges might attempt such a heroic stunt, Dell Ragnarsson was prepared. He fired his laser rifle and blew a hole into Galvan's chest. Galvan's body flew backwards from the impact and slammed into the wall. His body slid to the floor, leaving a trail of his blood on the wall.

Seeing her friend murdered before her eyes, Sammon panicked and began running for the emergency exit. Alfred fired both of his hand lasers into the back of Sammon's head. Her brains and skull were splattered against the walls as Sammon's headless body hit the smooth floor and tumbled for several feet before coming to a complete stop.

Dell walked over to Galvan's body and kicked it. The judge did not move.

"Let's go," Rosenburg said through the voice muffler.

The two men ran out of the tower and walked

toward a camera. Dell pulled out a detonator device in front of one of the cameras so that all of the people could see him do it. The assassin had placed explosives around the base of the tower before confronting the two judges. He pressed the button for all of humanity to see. The North tower exploded and then collapsed as the charges they had planted in the basement did their work.

The judges were all dead and now all that remained was the cadets. To the dismay of many in the world, the last thing anyone expected was that the Clovis Academy Cadets would arrive on the Blood Moon and then commit the murderers.

The government controlled news media was all over the Clovis Academy campus conducting interviews with students, parents of the participants, siblings and teachers. The main dormitories had several large three dimensional screens set up in the student unions so that the cadets could watch the entire tournament. The general reaction to the cold blooded murders of the tournament judges was one of stunned disbelief. Only some of the Bragg Gang cadets were vocal in telling the reporters that they always knew that Yuri Gorski was a killer.

Dean Golden Harvard was welcoming an alumni group at the Academy Auditorium West when one of his many wives interrupted to inform him of the tragic events. She whispered into his ear and the alumni attendees noticed the change in Harvard's expression as the woman continued to speak to him. Harvard politely excused himself as he walked out of the auditorium to seek out more information as to the events on the Blood Moon.

Admiral Seward was relaxing in the hangar area with several of his pilot instructors, sharing coffee with his fellow teachers when he heard someone calling their collective attention to the large three dimensional screen at the south part of the hangar. Seward and the others watched the gruesome murders as the media replayed the events, over and over again. Seward spilled his coffee when he saw the tragedies as they appeared on the screen. He sat up and turned to his staff, "Raise O'Grady! What the hell is going on! Someone get O'Grady on the screen now!"

At O'Malley's, the Clovis Academy cadets were standing in silence. They just watched as their friends commit cold blooded murder for the world to see. Several cadets covered their mouths with their hands, their eyes wide. The O'Malley family stopped working and were watching in stunned silence as the large towers fell.

Jen Staszko was shaking her head in disbelief, "That could not have been Yuri. He would never do such a thing!"

DuBravac was backing away from the broadcast screen. "No. No, no, no, no! That could not have been Les! No!"

Cara Perez Guerrero had a similar reaction and covered her face and began to cry. Even though her relationship with Pierre Zerbe had been short, Perez Guerrero knew he would never commit such a cowardly act. He would never be a part of such a thing. The man she grew to know and love had a caring and compassion nature in him for others.

Lila Zapata was holding her hands over her gaping mouth. She was too shocked to speak.

Harumi Shigeta dropped her plastic cup filled with iced tea on the floor, spilling the drink and cubes of ice all over the floor. She had come to O'Malley's without Dominic Andolini and her first thoughts were to wonder if he knew what had just transpired on the Blood Moon. Shigeta knew that Marco and the rest of their friends would never be a willing participant in such an atrocity.

The news media that were present were filming the reactions of the students. The reporters felt that the responses to the killings would make great theater and boost their viewer ratings and the fact that they were the first to film the lovers of the killers would net them fame and fortune. Several of the reporters began uploading the video feeds to their respective stations and news agencies. The entire matter was about to spread like a wildfire across the citizenry of the eight solar systems.

"This cannot be," Shigeta said softly to her friends at the table, looking over her shoulders to make certain that none of the vulture news media were filming or recording her.

Staszko wrapped her arms around Shigeta at her left and Perez Guerrero on her right and whispered to them both as the crowd at O'Malley's were screaming at the three dimensional view screens. "We all know that the people that attacked us on Cy-7 and during the dust storm are behind this. We need to get the few people here that we can trust and come up with a plan to help out our friends over there. You girls with me?"

"Damn right I am," Perez Guerrero growled.

"Just tell us what to do," Shigeta nodded.

CHAPTER NINETEEN

The cadets from Tyr Academy did not see the towers destroyed as they were concentrating on other matters. Cadet Edmund Ross Koch was barking orders to his team as they were beginning to leave their Raumschiff. After each of the ten cadets confirmed that their internal enviro-suit temperature gauges, oxygen generation and communication functions were operational, Koch yelled out his final orders on how he wanted the perimeter secured. They were ready to begin what they had hoped to be a historic competition. They had no idea they were about to be slaughtered.

The bay doors on the back of the Raumschiff opened and the landing ramp lowered to the lunar surface. Edmund Ross Koch and Sara Barnes were first to run down the landing ramp. They moved quickly toward their headquarters to begin preparations for the games. Jayla Harcourt was next to Lionel Barnes, both walking slowly to the building. The Tournament was a dream for them and now they were finally on the Blood Moon as a part of the competition.

Peter Lomax had been the one chosen by Caine Rosenburg to take out the team led by Koch. Lomax waited over the horizon until the Raumschiff landed. Lomax was ready, piloting one of the small one man Allen Corporation Fighter Type CC76A3 ships that had been painted purple and had the Clovis Academy logo on each side. He flew the ship toward the Tyr Academy Headquarters at a rapid speed. Caine had instructed Lomax to kill as many of the Tyr cadets as possible. Lomax was happy to oblige, not because he enjoyed killing, but because he simply loved money and Caine had promised to pay him well for his services.

From the cockpit of his fighter ship, Lomax watched as the Tyr Academy cadets were leaving the safety of the Raumschiff. Lomax laughed and fired two armor piercing rockets at the Tyr Academy Raumschiff. This was too easy, Lomax thought to himself. He felt bad for the cadets. But a hundred thousand Empire Dollars was an amount the Lomax could not refuse.

The Tyr Academy Raumschiff erupted in a fireball, sending metal, moon rock, debris and supplies flying in every direction. One of the Tyr Academy cadets was sliced in half by the flying metal caused by the destruction of the Raumschiff. The remaining nine Tyr Academy students had been thrown to the surface by the force of the explosion. Some were covering their heads out of reflex, concerned that the flying debris might hit them.

As the metal pieces of the Raumschiff came to rest on the Blood Moon, Koch ordered his team to their feet. They had been attacked without reason. As the team commander, the responsibility of the survival of the other cadets fell on his shoulders.

Koch and the others turned to see the Clovis Academy ship swinging around for another pass.

"Get to the individual ships!" Koch bellowed. He was dumbfounded as to the purpose of the sneak attack. He turned to Sara Barnes. "Get to the HQ! Go!"

Barnes heard his order over her communication system that was inside her enviro-suit helmet. She began running toward the safety of their building as large and small pieces of metal from the Raumschiff landed around her. Some of the metal pieces were several feet long and wide. Others were small fragments.

Lomax watched the Raumschiff split into pieces in the explosion on his targeting screens on the inside of his small fighter ship. Lomax flew his ship in a left arc and came back around for another pass at the panicking cadets. His voice was also intentionally muffled to throw off the audiences all over humanity that were viewing the slaughter from the live satellite feed. "This is Andolini. I should be finishing off these other little shits in a second."

Lomax began firing lasers at the four Tyr Academy CC76A3 ships that were still on the ground. Lomax saw that four cadets were attempting to get the ships airborne. Lomax fired his last four rockets at them. Lionel Barnes was one of the four cadets that had hoped to get their ship off the ground and mount some form of defense. Lionel Barnes' body was shredded when one of the armor piercing missiles hit his small fighter ship. The explosion shook the lunar surface. Rock and dust flew in all directions, along with the metal from the demolished space craft. The olive-green chlorine gas was swirling around the devastation.

The other three cadet pilots fared no better. Their ships erupted in an explosion of fire and metal due to Lomax and his pinpoint accuracy. The small vessel's lifted into the air and split apart violently. The cadets had either been climbing on board or were too close to the doomed craft when the missiles slammed into their individual space ships. They all died, their bodies obliterated.

Koch heard the screams of the dying over his enviro-suit's internal communication system. He had been thrown to the ground by the concussion of the explosions. He pushed himself back up to his feet and was yelling for any survivors of his team to run for the headquarters building. He knew that even the shelter of the metal structure would not be enough to protect them from an armor piercing rocket. Without weapons to fight back, Koch and his remaining team members were as good as dead.

Lomax swung his ship around again and asked his targeting display to locate the remaining life forms. Time to wipe out the others.

Koch had followed Sara Barnes into the headquarters. His team was practically wiped out. Koch watched helplessly as the purple ship began firing lasers at the remaining cadets. Lomax laughed as two of the remaining cadets tried to fire at him with hand lasers. Lomax knew that the cadets only had stun capability and could not harm his ship. Lomax unleashed a fatal volley of laser fire and one by one, the bodies of the cadets exploded. The majority of the corpses were obliterated. Jayla Harcourt did not have time to scream when the top of her body was vaporized. Only her scattered legs remained on the surface of the Blood Moon.

Lomax flew his ship around the headquarters building twice and saw no other cadets moving below, so he pulled his half-moon steering column upwards which caused his small craft to rise higher into the sky. He pushed the controls to full throttle and sped away. He used his on board communication system to report his success. "This is Andolini! Mission accomplished!"

Hearing that Lomax has done his job, David Rosenburg pulled out his hand held computer-communication device. He had been sitting in the safety of the Achilles Academy building as he waited for the moment to finalize their plan.

"Activate the Jammers," David Rosenburg ordered his hand held computer.

The magnetized Jammers on the base of each of the twelve lunar surface satellites activated. The live broadcast ended. On every planet, moon, space craft, space station, satellite and outpost, the Tournament reception was blocked at the source. That is save everywhere except for the reception received by the Glorious Leader, Vladimir

Sikorsky. He continued to receive all of the action occurring on the Moon around Semiramis.

The events that occurred next on the Blood Moon were blacked out.

David Rosenburg was pleased with himself as everything had gone as planned. It was perfection. Gorski and his friends were framed for murders they did not commit. History would record the team from Clovis Academy went crazy and suffered from a blood lust sickness. Soon, little brother Caine and his friends would be worshiped as new heroes to humanity by vanquishing the coldhearted Clovis cadets.

At O'Malley's, Dominic Andolini arrived after receiving several frantic messages from Harumi Shigeta. He had rushed over to join the entire Gorski Gang that were left speechless by the events on the Blood Moon. They were staring at the black screens that hung on every wall at O'Malley's after just witnessing Dominic's twin brother murder a t least eight cadets in cold blood. Dominic's mother, father and his large group of siblings were also in attendance. Some of the younger Andolini children were crying, others sat in silence. Dominic was embraced by Shigeta as he slowly walked toward the others. He could hear the news reporters implicating his twin, Marco, in the murders of several innocent cadets. Two of his younger sisters, Giola and Venus, ran to him and hugged him.

"This can't be!" Elektra broke the cacophony of news reporters accusing Gorski and the others from Clovis of murder. "Those are our friends! They would never do something like that! This is wrong!"

Colonel Jamal Lincoln watched the events unfold while resting in his quarters on board the U.N.S.C. *Cortez*. He immediately decided he had to take action. His daughter, Mary, was on that moon. Mary would never be a willing part of cold blooded murder. The Tyr Academy cadets suffered an extremely wicked ambush. The poor kids had no chance to defend themselves. The attack had no honor to it. The ambush on the eight judges was a similarly cruel act. Colonel Lincoln had not raised his daughter to be one that showed no mercy. He had raised her to have compassion for others, to respect the rule of law and to never kick another while they were down.

Lincoln contacted his command staff through the *Cortez* internal communication system. He ordered them to prepare to leave the orbit of their current assignment. Their ship had been ordered to investigate a mass grave found on a moon orbiting planet New Berlin. He had previously dispatched Lieutenant Laura Murdock to lead the initial investigation at the sight of the mass grave and collect physical evidence to the on board crime lab to evaluate for clues. Lincoln contacted Murdock and her Military Intelligence crew that were on the lunar surface to abort the mission and return immediately to the *Cortez*. He ordered Lieutenant Junior Grade Frank Glenn to set a direct course of the Moon over Semiramis. He ordered the junior officer to wait until Murdock and her team returned and them to begin the trip at full speed. Colonel Lincoln knew it would take the *Cortez* a minimum of one week to arrive at the destination. He prayed that his daughter Mary Lincoln could hold out that long.

Cadet Sara Barnes had made it to the inside of her headquarters. She thought herself safe from the carnage outside. She felt guilty for not staying with her teammates to try and fight off the unprovoked attack. She could still hear their screams ringing in her ears. She ran to the center of the kitchen area. She was stopped in her tracks by a man that was almost seven feet tall. He was a black man that she had never seen before. His chest and arms were solid muscle. She tried to run from him, but he held her in his massive arms.

Sara Barnes screamed.

Caine Rosenburg, Avery Jackson, Kai Chin and

Cleon Alexander had been hiding inside the Tyr Academy Headquarters, waiting to pick off any survivors. To their joy, one of the cadets that had survived the ambush orchestrated by Lomax was a lovely woman.

Edmund Ross Koch rushed in and saw Sara Barnes in the arms of a large man. He quickly noticed that there were three other men, all aiming laser pistols at him. Koch stopped running and looked to his right and left for any kind of weapon he might be able to use to defend himself with. He saw nothing that would assist him against three men with lasers.

"Computer, shut the doors!" Caine Rosenburg commanded. The headquarter doors slid shut. "Both of you, get out of your enviro-suits. Now!"

"What is the meaning of this?" Koch demanded. "Why did you murder our friends?"

Jackson snarled and ripped off the helmet of Sara Barnes enviro-suit. Jackson pulled out a twelve inch blade knife from his belt and held it to her throat. "Out of the suit or I cut her throat!"

"Okay," Koch said as he removed his helmet. He was trembling with fear and rage. He had no choice but to do everything the saboteurs demanded of him. He slowly removed his protective space suit. After he finished all he was wearing was a pair of thermal shorts and a white t-shirt. "Can you please tell us why you attacked?"

Caine began laughing like a maniac. "We did not attack you, good sir. No. Not us. It was those rebellious cadets from Clovis Academy. They killed your friends."

He slowly turned his attention to Sara Barnes. "Now you. Out of the enviro-suit."

Barnes was shaking from fear. She could feel the strange men watch her as she removed the suit. She was stripped down to her panties and a loose fitting, short sleeved shirt.

"What is this all about?" Koch asked again, his

voice less demanding.

Caine approached the highly decorated cadet. He put his arm around Koch, "You see, several months ago, one of my brothers was killed. He died horribly. He was stabbed in the chest and he bled to death. Then when we attempted to have justice against the murderers of my departed brother and more of my close associates died. Yuri Gorski, one of the Clovis Academy cadets, did much personal injury to us. Many of my family and friends suffered greatly at the hands of the cadets at Clovis Academy. Gorski and his allies must answer for what they have done. We are here for revenge."

"But how does that concern us? I do not know Gorski! We have nothing to do with his school! Please, you must understand that. If you seek revenge against the Clovis Academy cadets, then why attack us?" Koch was confused and began to try and wriggle free of Caine's arm. Caine pulled a Stun Dart from his breast pocket and injected it into Koch's neck. Koch felt himself lose all control of his muscles. He would have fallen to the ground had he not been in the arms of Caine.

Sara Barnes screamed as she realizing that something horrible had been done to her boyfriend by these strange men.

"Please do not scream," Caine said calmly. "He's not dead. He is only stunned, but he will be able to move by tomorrow." He was still holding Koch upright and Caine whispered into his ear. "Horrible, is it not? You want to move, but you have no control. You will want to protect the girl, but you will be unable to no matter how hard you struggle. You will have to watch what we do to her. You will hear her screams. She will beg us to stop as all women do. But you see, I know that they all want me. I am desired by all women and I know it, even if they refuse to admit it. That is why I kill so many of them. They lie and hide their true nature with words with no meaning. I have read up on all of your team and I know that you love this woman. By raping and killing her, I will be doing you a favor. The sad thing is that when I read your files, I thought that you and I could be friends in another life. Unfortunately, we have to kill all of you today. This really has nothing to do with you, Cadet Koch. You are just collateral damage in the game we have been playing against our true prey. But do not despair; all of the other cadets will join you in death soon. You can die a happy man in that we freed you from a life time of misery with this bitch and the other cadets will meet deaths far worse than the death that awaits you."

Caine gently laid Koch onto the floor and moved his head so he could see Barnes. Caine nodded to Jackson. Barnes saw the men walking toward her and she began breathing heavily out of fear. She saw in their eyes that she was in danger. Jackson grabbed her arms and spun her around, facing Chin and Alexander. She began to sob when Alexander grabbed her shirt and ripped it open. She felt his hands on her breasts and heard some of them making crude comments about her body. The other man, Caine, ordered the others to throw her on the ground.

She cried in vain as each man raped her, save Kai Chin. Chin wanted nothing to do with the act of violating a woman. He stood aside as his friends committed the despicable act.

Koch struggled against the poison of the stun dart, desperately wanting to help her. His only desire was to save her. But he could not move. It took all of his strength to simply breathe. All Koch could do was listen to her cries of agony as each of the four men beat her and raped her again and again.

When it was over Koch saw that Barnes was unconscious from the multiple assaults. Her attackers left her laying there, her clothing in shreds.

"We are finished here," Caine said. "By now the Clovis cadets should have been ambushed by our trap. We need to return to the others and make plans for our attack on Newton Academy."

"What about him? "Alexander pointed at Koch as he dressed.

"Throw him out on the surface," Caine shrugged as if it meant nothing to him. "Let the chlorine gas take him."

Koch felt the big man, Jackson, and the Asian man, Chin, lift him up. They carried him out of the headquarters and threw him onto the lunar surface. The deadly chlorine gas swirled around Koch. He tried not to breathe it in. He held his breath as long as he could but eventually he had to inhale. Koch knew he would be dead in an hour.

Koch watched helplessly as a Raumschiff landed about fifty feet from him. The four assailants boarded the new ship and departed, leaving Koch to face a slow and agonizing death of pulmonary edema from the chlorine gas. His eyes began to water and he was coughing. Koch wanted to tell Barnes he was sorry for not saving her. But he was unable to speak to her.

"What about the rest of the solar systems? "Alexander asked quickly. "If we leave won't they see our faces on the satellite feed?"

"No, they are watching screens filled with distortion and static. By now David has cut the broadcast. The world believes that Gorski, Gillis and his bastard friends killed the judges and Koch's team. We will soon be heroes of the human race!" Caine's voice kept rising in decibel level as he spoke. He put his arm around Chin and smiled at him. "Each of you will be rich men by the end of the week and you will be famous beyond your wildest dreams!"

Chin said nothing as he helped Jackson toss Koch out onto the deadly lunar surface.

On the other side of the moon, Mary Lincoln guided the Clovis Academy Raumschiff to a safe landing several hundred feet from their assigned headquarters. None of their team were aware that they had each been framed for murder and that their fight for survival was about to begin.

END OF BOOK FIVE

TO BE CONTINUED IN BOOK SIX

BURDENED WITH MORALITY

www.ingramcontent.com/pod-product-compliance
Lightning Source LLC
Chambersburg PA
CBHW070618170726
48291CB00003B/789